ALSO BY RACHEL INGALLS

THE

PEARLKILLERS

Four Novellas

RACHEL INGALLS

SIMON AND SCHUSTER

NEW YORK

These stories are works of fiction. Names, characters, places and incidents are either the product of the author's imagination or are used fictitiously. Any resemblance to actual events or locales or persons, living or dead, is entirely coincidental.

COPYRIGHT © 1986 BY RACHEL INGALLS
ALL RIGHTS RESERVED
INCLUDING THE RIGHT OF REPRODUCTION
IN WHOLE OR IN PART IN ANY FORM
PUBLISHED BY SIMON AND SCHUSTER
A DIVISION OF SIMON & SCHUSTER, INC.
SIMON & SCHUSTER BUILDING
ROCKEFELLER CENTER
1230 AVENUE OF THE AMERICAS
NEW YORK, NEW YORK 10020
ORIGINALLY PUBLISHED IN GREAT BRITAIN
IN 1986 BY FABER & FABER LTD.
SIMON AND SCHUSTER AND COLOPHON
ARE REGISTERED TRADEMARKS OF SIMON & SCHUSTER, INC.

DESIGNED BY EVE METZ

MANUFACTURED IN THE UNITED STATES OF AMERICA

1 3 5 7 9 10 8 6 4 2

LIBRARY OF CONGRESS CATALOGING IN PUBLICATION DATA

Ingalls, Rachel.
  The pearlkillers.
  Contents: Third time lucky—People to people—
Inheritance—Captain Hendrik's story.
  I. Title.
PS3559.N38P4   1986   813'.5'4   86-31468

ISBN: 0-671-63340-6

CONTENTS

THIRD TIME LUCKY

Lily had married first when she was eighteen. He'd been killed in Vietnam. She'd married again when she was twenty-one. He too had died in Vietnam. She'd had proposals after that, but she'd refused without even considering the possibility of accepting. She was sure that if she said yes, he'd be killed just as the first two had been. It was like having a curse on you: she could feel it. Perhaps when she'd agreed to go to the Egyptian exhibition she'd been attracted by the knowledge that there was something called the Curse of The Pharaohs.

She'd forgotten all about that. She didn't remember it again until long after she'd heard the radio interview with the old woman who lived in Cairo.

Lily listened to the radio a lot. As a child she'd been introduced to literature through the soap operas; even at the age of seven, she'd realized that the stories were preposterous, but she loved them. She'd also liked the way they gave you only a little piece of each story every day, so that if you were lucky enough to get sick, or if school had been canceled because of snow, you could hear the complete collection from morning to late afternoon—like eating a whole meal of Lifesavers, all in different flavors.

In her teens she'd watched television, mainly the late-night movies. And then later, when the most popular family show had been the war, she'd stopped. She'd gone back to the radio. Her favorite station broadcast its programs from the other side of the ocean in British voices that sounded just like the people in the movies. She was charmed by their accents.

The woman who lived in Egypt had spoken in one of a number of interviews compiled by an English woman reporter. The programs set out to make a study of British people who had lived in Egypt for a long time. All the broadcasters were women: that, apparently, was the point of the series.

1

One of the speakers was a girl who'd married an Egyptian; she talked about what it was like to become part of the family, how it was different from life at home, and so on: she seemed to have a very happy marriage. She could also throw in foreign phrases as easily as she spoke her own language, her voice full of enthusiasm. She praised her mother-in-law. Lily was drawn across the room as she listened; she went and sat right next to the radio to make sure she didn't miss anything or that she could retune if the speech broke up in static—a thing that often happened during the international programs.

She was fascinated by accounts of other people's marriages. She couldn't hear enough. It was like being told fairytales, and yet it was the real thing—real people her own age. Once she'd grown up, she'd started to prefer fact to fiction. That was what she thought, anyway.

Immediately after the young married woman came an archaeologist. And after her, the reporter introduced the old woman.

Her name was Sadie. She'd been born and brought up in London. When she was six years old her father had taken her to the British Museum to look at the exhibits. There she had seen a room full of Egyptian mummies and had been so impressed by them that she couldn't sleep. She'd said to her parents that her home was in the place where those people had lived, and that was where she wanted to go, because that was where she belonged. Her parents had told her not to be silly. When she persisted, they called in a friend who wasn't exactly a doctor, but who knew a lot. The friend succeeded in restoring Sadie's sleep by assuring her that strange as her story sounded to everyone else, there might be something to it. She would be free to test the truth of it as soon as she grew up. But to insist on instant transportation to a distant country wouldn't be fair to her parents while they were still trying to give her a good home and make sure she was well-fed and healthy.

Sensible man, Lily thought. That was the kind of doctor people should have—not like the ones who'd tried to deal with her and who'd probably primed her mother with a load of nonsense until the whole family was driving her crazy. It

2

had been as if twice in her life she'd become a freak—like a woman who'd been struck by lightning and survived. It was almost like going through the sort of thing she'd read about in magazine stories: accounts of women who'd had to keep on living in a community when everyone there knew they'd been the victims of some shameful act of violence or humiliation.

Of course people felt sorry for you and they hoped to make you well again. They believed that you ought to recover. They tried to cheer you up and yet they wanted you to be suffering the correct amount for the occasion, otherwise they got nervous: there might be some extra grief around that wasn't being taken care of. She herself had sometimes thought: *Am I feeling the right things? Am I even feeling enough?* She didn't know. She thought she didn't know much of anything any more.

She started hanging around the museum in order to fill up her days. She'd gone back to work, but there were lunch hours when she didn't want to be eating her sandwiches with the rest of the girls, and the museum wasn't far from the job she'd had at the time.

She began by just walking around. That first day she saw Greek statues and Roman coins. The second time she went, she looked at Chinese jade and Japanese scroll paintings. On her third visit she got lost trying to find the Etruscans, and came upon ancient Egypt instead. It hadn't produced an instant, revelatory obsession like the one experienced by the six-year-old Sadie, but it had certainly done something extraordinary to her. She had felt magnetized by the appearance of everything: the colors, the style of drawing, the mysterious hieroglyphics—the whole look. The museum had several items that were rare and important; a black wooden panther surmounted by a golden god in a high hat; a painted mummy case that was covered in pictures of birds, animals and pictograph writing; a gray stone hawk that stood about four feet high; and a granite statue of a seated Pharaoh who had a face framed by a headdress that merged with the shoulders, so that he too had the silhouette of a hawk.

She knew then, at her first sight of the sculpture and painting, that she wanted to find out more about the people who

3

had made them. She picked up a leaflet at the main desk. It turned out that there were museum lectures you could attend in the mornings or afternoons. There were even some that took place during the lunch hour. She signed up in a hurry.

Her real conversion to the art of Egypt happened in semi-darkness, to the accompaniment of a low hum given off by the museum's slide projector. She studied temples, frescoes, jewelry, furniture, corpses thousands of years old. She felt that all these sights and objects were familiar to her in a way that her own life was not.

The Englishwoman named Sadie hadn't needed lectures. After the family friend had made her see reason, she'd struck a bargain with her parents: that she'd be good and do what they told her, as long as they realized that her one ambition was to go to Egypt, and that she actually did plan to go there as soon as she was grown up. It took several more years, and undoubtedly a certain amount of research, before she narrowed down the rather vague passion for Egyptology to a specific dedication: she found out through a dream that in a former life she'd been a priestess of Isis and many centuries ago she had lived in a particular house, where she'd had a wonderful garden full of flowers and herbs, and plants that possessed healing properties. It became her mission to return to the house, live there and replant her garden.

It had taken Sadie twelve years of work in London to raise the money for her fare. On her arrival in Egypt she attached herself to British archaeological societies, which allowed her to earn a little by helping them, although—because she'd had so little formal schooling—they discounted anything she had to say on their subject. It came as a surprise to the official bodies when she discovered the ruins of what she insisted was her house, and which, as it was excavated, proved to have contained at one time a plentifully stocked courtyard garden. It was surprising, but not in anyone else's opinion a matter of supernatural or preternatural knowledge, as Sadie claimed. In spite of the skepticism of the experts, she managed to present the urgency of her desire so convincingly that she was given permission to camp out in the ruins and eventually to try to reconstruct the house and garden.

like the one worn by the sphinx. And the whole thing, according to the description underneath, was part of a canopic jar. She'd forgotten what canopic meant.

She stepped aside, to let other people see. In front of the cases of jewelry, a young man had come to a standstill; he'd apparently been in the same place for a long while, because an official was trying to get him to move. The young man responded immediately, saying—in a very audible voice—that he'd paid his money and he had a right to look for as long as he wanted to. The official backed away, murmuring about being fair to the other people: he didn't want to start a fight in the middle of the crowd or to disrupt the discreet, artistic and historic hush brought about by the presence of so many tons of gold and lapis lazuli.

She took a good look herself at the young king in his blue-and-gold headcloth, which fell in stripes to his shoulders. And as she walked on, she realized that she'd worked her way around to the exit. The others were nearby. Sometimes people went through exhibits at such different rates that it made more sense to split up for a set period; but they'd all finished at about the same time.

They moved out into the shopping area where people were selling books and postcards. Lily opened her bag and got out her wallet. She unsnapped the coin compartment and began to rummage inside it. She couldn't feel her lucky-piece. She couldn't see it. She shook the bag from side to side. Sue asked what was wrong. Charlie said, "If you're looking for your wallet, you're already holding it in your hand."

The next thing she knew, she was screaming. Everyone tried to calm her down but she let go completely, shrieking hysterically, "I've lost it, oh God. It isn't anywhere."

"Something important?" a voice said.

"The most important thing I've got," she spluttered. "It's my lucky-piece." She wanted to go back into the exhibition rooms, to make the museum authorities turn up the lights and hold the crowds back, so that she could go over the whole floor.

They couldn't do that, everyone told her. They'd report the

loss and hope the staff would pick up the coin at closing-time.

That wasn't good enough, she yelled.

Shock, embarrassment, distaste, were on people's faces. She didn't care. She could barely see them but she could hear the change in the sounds around her, and especially the difference in their voices as they let her know that everything she wanted was impossible and unreasonable. They thought her lucky-piece was insignificant; she was in the presence of Art and of the past, and of an entire civilization that had been lost. She even heard one of their own crowd whispering about her—though later on she wasn't sure if she might not have imagined it—saying, "Don't know why she wants it back—it didn't do her much good, did it?" All she knew was that losing the coin seemed to her the final blow. She'd lost everything else: she couldn't lose that, too.

The lucky-piece had had little worth as silver and no real value to anyone but her. Nevertheless, despite the efforts of the museum authorities and their cleaning crew, the coin never turned up. And she finally learned to accept its loss, as well as to understand that she'd had some sort of collapse, and that maybe she had needed to express her grief in that way, in public. She also realized—many months after the event—what she must have forgotten at the time: that all those wonderful objects they'd been admiring had been the contents of a grave.

And, eventually, it seemed to her that the loss of the lucky-piece had been a sign; it had been intended to happen, so that she would have no doubt about the fact that there was a curse on her. She had married two men and both of them had died. She was certain that if she tried to find happiness again, the same thing would happen a third time.

She didn't say anything about the curse to the men who took her out, courted her, and wanted to marry her or just to sleep with her. She merely said no. When Don Parker asked her to be his wife, she said no for four months, said maybe for two, and in the end told him she would if he'd take her to Egypt for the honeymoon.

"You don't know how lucky you are," her mother said to

her one evening. "The chances you've had. They aren't going to keep asking forever, you know."

From across the room Lily gave her newspaper a shake. Her mother sewed a button on the wristband of a blouse. They were waiting for channel two to show the play. That week it was a repeat of an old one—Ingrid Bergman and Trevor Howard in *Hedda Gabler*. Lily read in her paper about an African bird called a hoopoe that had been closed up inside a packing crate by mistake and been found at a German airport; the authorities had trapped it in an airline hangar and were just about to catch it with a net—in order to send it back to its own country—when it flew into one of the wire-strengthened glass panes up near the ceiling and broke its neck.

She turned the page. The paper crinkled noisily. She held it high, the way her father did at the breakfast table. She read about floods, fires, insurrections, massacres and robberies. She read about a chemist in Florida who believed that the building blocks of ancient Egypt's pyramids could have been poured into molds rather than quarried.

Everything she saw now reminded her of Egypt. It was like following the clues in a detective story. It was like being in love. Once you were aware of a thing, a name, or a word, you began to notice it everywhere. And once you had seen the truth of one cause of pain, you could recognize others. It was only after her breakdown in the museum that she understood how little her mother liked her—in fact, that her mother had never loved her. Perhaps she'd never loved Lily's sister, Ida, either. Ida was married and had two children; her husband had divorced her. And now Ida and her mother and the two children—both girls—were locked in an insatiable battle of wills that everyone except Lily would probably have called familial love. To Lily it seemed to be an unending struggle invented by her mother because otherwise life would have no meaning. Lily's father hadn't been enough of a challenge. And Lily herself had escaped into the protection of the two tragic events that had isolated her from other people.

"There's a man down in Florida," Lily said, "who thinks the pyramids were poured."

9

"Oh?" her mother answered. She wasn't interested. She probably thought it meant they'd been poured through a funnel.

"It could be true, I guess. There's been a lot about Egypt recently. There was the woman who believed she was the priestess of Isis. I told you about her. She went to live there."

"Just another nut. She's like that woman who says she's receiving spirit messages from Mozart and Beethoven, and then she plays those cheap little things."

"That isn't a very good example. She's such a nut, she's made millions—on TV and everything. But in her case, you really wonder if she's a fraud."

"Are you kidding? Of course she is. You think Bee-thoven—"

"You wonder if she's tricking people deliberately, instead of just deceiving herself. Now, this other woman—well, what you wonder about that, is: could there actually be some deep, biological, hereditary impulse directing her? Something we don't know about yet. See what I mean? I read an article a few years ago that talked all about people's sense of direction; it said they've found out that we've all got this magnetic center in the brain."

"Oh, boy."

"Well, that's what it said."

"What does Don say when you come out with these things?"

"He said yes. I told him I'd marry him if he took me to Egypt for the honeymoon, so he said he would. He's getting the tickets this week."

Her mother's face came up from the buttons and thread. "What are you talking about?"

"We're getting married after New Year's," Lily announced. "I just said so." Her mother looked astounded. "I told you," Lily repeated. "When I said we were going to Egypt."

"I didn't take it in," her mother said. She stared.

"Well, that's the end of the news."

"That means . . . the wedding, the invitations, the catering. Why does it have to be so soon?"

"That's the best time to go."

"Go? Where?"

"To Egypt," Lily snapped. "Are you feeling all right? We're planning a quiet wedding, in a registry office. His mother's going to take care of the reception at that house they've got down in the country."

"You don't know how lucky you are," her mother said again.

And you resent that, Lily thought.

"To have a boy like that."

It doesn't matter how nice people are, if you don't love them. You love him more than I do. To me, he's unexciting. I've been at parties where girls were flirting with him, and I've said to myself: well, they just don't know how dull he is. I've even been in a shop where the tie salesman obviously thought he was the nearest thing to a classical statue he'd ever come across. But not for me.

"So good-looking."

So boring, and actually sometimes irritating. I couldn't last out a lifetime of it. I should never have gotten myself into this mess. But it's nice to be admired like that; it's flattering. And I can't go on living this way.

Her mother said, "I guess that extrasensory, reincarnation stuff started back in the twenties, when they found the tomb."

"No. It began before that. It was part of the Victorian interest in psychic phenomena. It all had to do with the disintegration of Christianity."

"Is that right?"

"That's what they told us in school."

Her mother went back to her sewing. They didn't talk again. They hardly ever talked, anyway. Ida had always taken the brunt of her mother's blame, inquisitiveness, disapproval, worry and desire to interfere. Lily used to think that that showed a difference in the quality of her mother's love, though recently it had occurrd to her that maybe it was simply a matter of positioning: that she had been in the wrong place at the wrong time, so that the only mother-love she could remember had come from her father, her grandfather, one aunt, and a cousin who was of her grandmother's generation. She knew how lucky she was about that: some people didn't have anyone at all.

She and Don had the vaccinations they needed, got the

passports ready, and rushed out invitations. Lily had no time to go to the museum any more, but she began to have the same dream at night, often several times in the week: she found herself standing in sunlight, under a blue sky, and looking up at a huge, almost endlessly high sandstone wall above her; it was a golden-tan color and carved all over with strange writings like hieroglyphics. In the dream she stood and looked at the picture-writing and couldn't figure out what it said. She guessed that the lines on her lucky-piece had been the same—they'd meant something, but no one knew what. She liked the dream. Very few dreams in her life had ever repeated; the ones that did were all landscape-dreams: just special places she remembered, that were good spots for nice dreams to start from. She'd never had a repeating dream that was a puzzle, but it pleased her to be standing in the sun, under the hot sky that was so blue and far away, and examining the foreign shapes of an unknown language. In real life, outside the dream and outside her apartment, the air was bitter, there was deep snow on the ground and more blizzards had been forecast. She hoped that the airlines wouldn't have to ground their planes for long. She was impatient to leave.

.   .   .

Two days before they were due to fly, they read and heard about a sandstorm that had closed all the airports in Egypt. The storm was actually a giant cloud. The papers and television said it stretched from Cairo to Israel. Lily became agitated. She thought they might not be able to take off. Don patted her arm and smiled at her. Ever since she'd accepted his proposal he'd been smiling inanely; it made her so guilty and annoyed that she almost wanted to hurt him in some way. She could feel herself burning up, unable to get where she was going, or do what she wanted to do. She meant to reach Cairo even if she had to walk.

"These things usually blow themselves out within twenty-four hours," he told her. "We'll be OK."

"I hope so," she said. "We wouldn't get any refunds. This is one of those things in the Act-of-God clause, isn't it?"

He sat up. "Of course they'd refund us. They'd have to."

"I bet they wouldn't. It isn't their fault there's a sandstorm."

"Well, it isn't mine, either."

"Tough," she said.

He got on the phone about it and tried to force a response out of the travel company. No one would give him a straight answer because so far nothing had gone wrong; but they seemed to be saying that if things did go wrong, then it wouldn't be up to them to indemnify anybody. In a case of delay the agency might—as a gesture of goodwill—be able to offer a day in a different country, but not an extra day in Egypt once the plane got there. He hung up.

"Told you," she said.

"I guess they could send us to the Riviera. That might be nice."

"It's freezing there. This is the coldest January they've had in Europe since 1948 or something like that."

He put his arm around her and said he didn't care where he was, as long as he was with her.

She smiled back, feeling mean, unable to join him except by pretense. She knew already that she could never stay faithful to him. She'd been faithful to her first and second husbands, both when they were alive and after they'd died. But she could tell this was going to be different.

She honestly didn't love him, that was the trouble. And all at once she couldn't believe that she'd said yes, that she had the ring on her finger and was on her honeymoon. Why hadn't she just gone to bed with him and left it at that?

.   .   .

When they arrived, the air smelled hot and scorched, the sky was still laden with the aftermath of the storm: tiny particles that were invisible, but made it impossible to see clearly for very far. Lily didn't mind. She didn't mind anything, now that they were there.

Their hotel windows looked out on to two nineteenth-century villas set among palm trees. She was practically delirious with excitement. She didn't want to stay indoors and rest, or eat, or make love. She wanted to be outside, seeing everything.

13

He wasn't quite so enraptured. He hadn't realized it was going to be difficult to get his favorite brand of sourmash. And he said he thought the people were dark and dumpy.

"They're wonderful-looking," she told him. "Especially their faces. You aren't seeing them right. Why don't you like it here?"

"It doesn't seem all that romantic to me."

"Wait till we get to the pyramids. We haven't even started."

"I keep thinking what Ollie and Phil said about the flies. Sandflies everywhere."

"But that's later in the year, not now."

"And how sick they were with that gut-rot they picked up."

"You won't pick up anything if you dress right. That's what my book says: wear a heavy sweater."

"Not in the sun."

"All the time. Dress like the locals, and you'll be all right."

They went through the markets, where he was disappointed once more, because they couldn't find any sheets that were a hundred percent cotton. The only ones on sale were cotton mixed with polyester; the rest had been exported.

But he liked the fact that she had calmed down. She held his hand now as they walked, where back home she had always seemed to be slipping her hand out of his. She smiled at him, saying, "I love it here." He said, "And I love you."

They began the tours. Straight away they were put into the middle of the place where all the pictures came from: the sphinx, the pyramids, the vast space full of chairs for the *son-et-lumière* show. She was trembling with eagerness. She almost seemed to be a little crazed. He whispered, "Are you OK?" and she nodded vigorously, while motioning him with her hand to be quiet.

Their guide was a thin, gray-haired Austrian woman who had a thick accent. The other members of the troop were all American. Lily could see, as the guide took them from one spot to the next, how most of the little parties of tourists had been grouped according to nationality, so that the guides wouldn't have to repeat the same information in different languages; she wondered why their guide, Lisabette, had been chosen for an English-speaking group. Lisabette was definitely good at her job and made her subject sound interesting, but some of the others said afterwards that they were having trouble understanding her. Don said he'd heard her stating that one of the ancient characters on their list had had to "accept the inedible."

There were two old people in their group: Selma and Orville Potts. Selma had something to do with a cultural club back home. Orville was retired from the bank. They enjoyed everything and asked a lot of questions. They had also read a lot, unlike Don or the couple called Darrell—John and Patsy— who had a nine-year-old child in tow. The child's name was Cindy; she was orange-haired, freckled, and had white eyelashes and pale eyes. Despite the weak eyes, she was a determined starer. Selma had tried to make friends with the child, failed, and commented to the mother, Patsy, that, "I reckon it's real nice for little Cindy to get let off school to go on vacation with you." Patsy said, "Oh, Cindy's between schools at the moment." At the same time, John said, "They've closed her school for a couple of weeks, to fix the pipes."

"Well," Selma said brightly, "and are you having a good time?"

Cindy glared up at the old face peering down at her. Lily thought for a moment that the child was going to spit, but after a hesitation she muttered, "Sure. It's OK." Selma simpered. Cindy walked off, as if there were something a few feet away that she wanted to look at. Patsy and John seemed relieved.

Don and Lily moved ahead a few steps. They were followed by the other honeymoon couple, Ruth-Ann and Howie: she was tall, toothy and raucous; he was a tubby, high-voiced man. The idea of coming to Egypt had been his. Ruth-Ann didn't mind where she was, as long as they got away from the snow. She'd been thinking more of Hawaii, but this was fine. The only drawback was—

"No booze," Howie complained.

"You're kidding," Don said. "You at some kind of Temperance hotel?"

"Oh, they've got a bar, but not like a real American bar.

15

And no Jim Beam in the entire town, far as I can see."

"You've got to bring it with you."

"You're telling me," Ruth-Ann said. "We got so worried about rationing it for two whole weeks that we drank it all in the first three days. God, the hangovers we've had. It's like those stories about twenty people in a life raft and only one canteen of water. What are you doing about it?"

"Well, we just got here," Don said. "I guess we'll measure it out in thimbles till the week is up, and then go on to wine. At least they still sell the stuff. I've heard they're thinking of making the whole country teetotal."

Lily asked, "Were you here for the sandstorm?"

"We sure were," said Howie. "We went to this hotel to meet a friend of Ruth-Ann's mother, and suddenly everything started to get dark, and then—wham!—they pulled all the shutters down, and we were stuck inside."

"It can kill you," Ruth-Ann said.

Lisabette was looking at her watch. It was almost time to start the tour again. Ruth-Ann said, "Doesn't she look like something off of one of those tombs?"

Lily turned her head. Lisabette, small and emaciated, was adjusting the shoulderstrap of her bag. She still had her walking stick clenched to her, which made the operation more cumbersome. But when she finally straightened up, she put a hand to the piece of cloth wound around her head from the front to below the tight, gray bun at the back; she changed the stick over to her right side, then stood still. And it was true—she resembled some sort of ancient court official bearing a ceremonial staff.

"And what's the story with the kid?" Ruth-Ann murmured. "Jesus, what an argument for birth control."

Howie sniggered. Lisabette raised her stick a few inches and looked up. Her nine listeners grouped around her again.

At the next break, most people took photographs. Lily hadn't thought about bringing a camera. She'd said she'd rather have a good postcard. But Don had brought along a small, cheap, foolproof camera. He told her, "What I want are pictures of you." He took two of her, then they changed places. She clicked the button twice, closed the slide over the lens and handed the camera back. She looked past him at one of the pyramids. "The eternal triangles," she said, and laughed.

"They aren't triangles. They've got five surfaces and the base is a sq—"

"For heaven's sake. I know that." She turned away abruptly. She'd been careful for so long about not showing her true thoughts, that she was afraid to let out even a little irritation. When the outburst came, she might just start screaming, "Oh Christ, you're so boring," for half an hour. She was turning herself inside out to entertain him and knocking herself out in bed to please him, just because she didn't love him enough. And it wasn't his fault. He was a good, decent man; her mother was right. But it didn't make any difference. When she'd married before, both times, she'd been in love; she'd shared herself. Now she was only pretending. As a child, she'd loved playing make-believe. Now it wasn't for fun: now it was cheating.

She'd never be able to keep going. He'd be true to her—she was sure of him that way. And besides, he'd grown up in a family of ugly women who'd sat on him hard. The father had been the one with the looks, and had used them too, being unfaithful all over the place and finally leaving Don's mother. The mother and his two sisters looked like parodies of plain frontierswomen. They were also very concerned about all sorts of social, public and political issues that didn't interest Lily. They were the kind of women who would talk for hours about Vietnam at cocktail parties instead of getting married to somebody who'd die there. Don thought the way his sisters did, but he'd wanted to marry something different.

"What's wrong?" he said, hurrying up behind her.

"Nothing's wrong. I'm fine. She's going to start the spiel again, that's all."

Lisabette raised her stick and brought it down on the ground. It made no noise, but the movement caught the attention of the rest of the group.

"You aren't mad at me, are you?" he said.

"Of course not." She didn't take his arm or even look at him. She hated the way she was behaving.

"Egypt," Lisabette said, "is a marriage between the Nile

17

and the desert." She began to talk about the importance of the periods of inundation and about the special regard paid to the androgynous deity of the Nile, Hapy. Lily's glance moved across the other tourists; it stopped at nine-year-old Cindy, whose fixed stare was boring into the back of Orville Potts; she suddenly felt a horror of the child. Something was wrong with Cindy. The parents obviously knew it, too. The mother was a nervous wreck. And the father—it was hard to tell: he wouldn't have had to live with the worry, the way the mother would. He'd only have to hear about it in the evenings and say, "Yes, dear."

Don reached out for Lily. She jumped as he touched her. He was trying to slide his hand up under her folded arms. She let him, since other people were there. If they'd been alone, she'd have pushed him away and walked off. She tried to concentrate on what Lisabette was telling them. Lisabette actually looked less like a living monument to ancient Egypt than like someone who'd once been alive and was now mummified; "Hathor," she said. "The cow-goddess."

Cindy grinned. Her eyes began to rove to other people. Lily moved her head and looked somewhere else.

On their way back to the bus, Howie said, "You know what really turned me on to all this stuff? It was that big show from Tutankhamun's tomb."

"Yes, I saw that, too," Lily said.

Don pulled back on her hand. "You did?" he asked. "You never told me that."

She shrugged. "Me and about fifty million other people. Didn't you?"

"No, I missed it."

"It was something," Ruth-Ann told him. "Talk about gorgeous—you can have all that Greek and Roman stuff."

"Oh, I like that too," Lily said. "Only it never grabbed me the same way. It didn't have the philosophy."

"The what?" Don asked.

"Haven't you been listening to what Lisabette's been saying?"

"Sure. All about the Nile god and the cow-goddess, and that kind of thing."

18

"The first pyramids were built in steps, so the Pharaoh could go up there and into the sky and come back down again. After they died, they had their insides put into separate jars and they sailed across the sky in a boat. When they got to the other side, they went into the palace of death and answered all the questions about what kind of life they'd led. And if it was all right, then they started to sing chants to get back their stomach and brain and everything. The priest and the relatives of the dead person would help from back at the tomb. There were even little prayers for the heart, except that was the one thing they didn't take out. But I guess it had to be started up again. They called all the essential parts back into the body. And then the dead person would be whole in the other world." She stopped, breathless.

"That isn't philosophy," Don said.

"Hit him with your handbag," Ruth-Ann told her.

"I'll hit him with the guidebook."

"It still wouldn't make all that rigmarole philosophy."

"Well, religion. I like the way they thought about people and animals and kings, and all the natural elements: all in one big lump."

"They didn't think much of women, though," Ruth-Ann said. "You see these big statues of men, and way down near their feet is a tiny little figure of the wife—that's how unimportant they were."

"No, it's just the opposite. The wife shouldn't be there at all. If you see one of those statues, it's really just supposed to represent the man, but he's specially asked to have his wife mentioned—for luck, or for sentiment. It's like nowadays, if a painter did a portrait of a businessman and the man insisted on taking a pose where he was holding a photograph of his wife. See? It's a gesture of affection. Nothing to do with despising anybody. They told us that in the museum lectures I went to."

"There," Howie said. "They weren't so bad, after all." He patted Ruth-Ann's behind lightly. She shooed him away. "My wife's got this thing about victimized females."

"My wife. He keeps saying it like that. I feel like I've lost my name all of a sudden."

"I like the sound of it," Howie said. "I like trying it out. It's like driving around in a new car."

Ruth-Ann climbed into the bus. "Howie and his cars," she said. Don followed. As Lisabette gave the driver the sign to start, he said to Lily, "You should be hiring yourself out to one of these tourist outfits. I didn't realize you knew so much about the place."

"I just went to all those lectures and I remember what they told us. You know how it is when you really like something."

"Sure," he said. "I know how it is." He put his arm around her again and she relaxed. She'd forgotten her irritation. She was glad to be with him and to have him holding her close to him.

. . .

That night she had a dream. It began like the dreams she'd had before leaving on the trip: she was standing under the blue sky, with the sun pouring down, and she was looking at the hieroglyphics on the wall. But this time as she scanned the carvings, they began to form a story. The picture-writings seemed to be changing shape, running into each other and reforming. And after that, they became images that moved across the wall. It was like watching a film. In the picture-story she saw her first husband. He was standing on the bank of the river. Two servants were wrapping him in a length of white cloth that left him naked from the waist up. The material had been wound up into a long skirt. Then they continued. He raised his arms a little, while the men circled him with the bolt of material; they wrapped him to the midpoint of his chest, made him fold his arms, and proceeded to wind the cloth so that the arms were taped down.

She started to feel anxious. The place she was watching from began to draw nearer to the riverbank but she was still too far away to reach him. The long, white banner went around his neck. She could see they were going to bandage his face, too. She tried to call out, to move forward, to do anything to stop the men; but nothing worked. They wrapped her husband up completely, as if he'd been inside a cocoon. Only

20

his legs, under the skirt, were free to walk. She looked on miserably until the work was finished.

The two men turned her husband around and walked him forward—one on each side—to the river, where a boat was waiting for them. As she saw him going away from her like that—entirely enclosed in white, and because of that seeming to be blind all over—she grew frantic. She screamed, but no one paid any attention to her. Her husband stepped forward into the boat. The servants guided him to the central part of the vessel, where a curtain hung. He went behind the curtain and she couldn't see him any more.

She wanted to go with him. She tried to run forward. The boat floated off, carrying him away. She tried to call out again, and again no one took any notice. She woke up. Don was kissing her in the dark. They began to make love before she realized that they were in their hotel room and that it was in Egypt.

.   .   .

The tour took them to the Valley of the Kings and the Valley of the Queens, the Tombs of the Nobles. Lily held their guidebook in one hand and talked as fast as a racetrack reporter about deities, animals, heavenly bodies, cults. Strange-sounding names flowed easily from her. Sometimes it seemed that in her zeal she was getting everything mixed up—that she was repeating a lot of misinformation, jumbling thoughts, condensing centuries, forgetting who the real people were and who were the gods.

Ruth-Ann said that if she tried for ten years, she was never going to be able to pronounce the name Hatshepsut. "It's quite simple," Lisabette told her. "Hat-shep-sut. Repeat that." Howie went off into a fit of giggles. Don said in a low voice that he found all of those names a little weird and couldn't remember any of them.

"That's because you didn't study them beforehand," Lily said. "If you don't know the names, how can you tell one god from another?"

"I can tell which one is supposed to be some animal. The

21

cow-goddess and the jackal-god and the alligator-god." He laughed. "There's even a hippo-god, isn't there?"

"She's a goddess. She's a goddess of childbirth."

"That figures. I guess they thought she had to be pregnant if she was so fat."

"They didn't look at it that way." She was beginning to get annoyed with him again. "They thought that fat was a sign of abundance and good health."

"And a high social standing," Howie said. "You can't stay overweight unless you keep up the food supply."

"That's why the Nile was so important to them. They wouldn't have had any food without it." The wind blew Lily's hair back, the sun was hot on her face. You could feel it was a genuine desert air. And now that all the dust had settled from the storm, the clarity—the light, was like nothing she'd ever imagined.

Ruth-Ann rejoined them. She said to Howie, "Where's your sweater?"

"It's too hot."

"You know what Lisabette told us: you'll pick up one of those bugs if you don't keep it on."

"How could that help?"

"Well, she lives here. She ought to know."

Lily teamed up with the Pottses, while Don got into a discussion with John Darrell. Orville and Selma—Selma especially—shared Lily's interest in Egyptian art and mythology. Ruth-Ann and Howie kept to themselves for a while, occasionally bursting into laughter. Once Lily heard Ruth-Ann pronounce "Hatshepsut' again in a loud voice.

Lisabette concentrated on her three best students. Behind her shoulder, off in the distance, Patsy Darrell talked earnestly to her daughter; she'd come all the way around the world to do something she could have done at home—unless, possibly, the child was demanding the discussion in order to make sure that her mother didn't have the time to enjoy herself.

"I wish we were going to Saqqarah too," Selma said, "but we just don't have the time."

"Never mind," Lisabette told her. "You will be fully satisfied by Karnak, I can assure you."

22

"And Abu Simbel," Orville said. "I'm very interested in how they moved it. That must have been a magnificent feat of engineering."

"And of international cooperation. It shows what can be accomplished when people work together in a spirit of peace."

"And honesty," Orville added. "They tried to save Venice too. Pouring all that money into rescue funds—so now they've made about three people there into millionaires and the place is still sinking."

"It's such a shame to have just one week," Selma said. "Well, a couple of days over a week."

Lily agreed. She thought that she'd much rather go to Saqqarah than to Abu Simbel.

"It isn't on our tour," Don told her. "It's back where we came from."

"We could change. Just go by ourselves one day."

"If we took a whole day out, we might as well go to Alexandria."

"But there isn't anything there."

"There's a whole town."

"There isn't anything old."

"Lily, Abu Simbel's on the tour. You know it's going to be great. Haven't you seen the pictures?"

"Maybe we could stay on a little afterwards."

"Our plane tickets—"

"Just a few days."

"Maybe," he said. "We'll see." He wouldn't say no outright. He didn't want to start an argument with her. She could see he was hoping that by the end of the week she'd have forgotten.

She walked back to the bus with Ruth-Ann, who told her, "I was talking with Patsy back there. That's a real sick kid she's got. Jesus. She sets fire to things—I mean, like, houses. She isn't in school because—if you can believe it—she just burned it down. Honest to God. They keep moving all around. He's always got to find a new job, or get transferred."

"Isn't there anything—doctors? Psychiatrists?"

"They're spending everything they've got on the doctors already. Her parents gave them the trip."

23

Lily looked again at the Darrells, who were now standing near Lisabette. She wondered whether anything could help a child like Cindy. "And they don't have any other children?" she said.

"I guess one was enough. A brat like that—I'm telling you: I'd sell her to the Arabs."

"I don't know that the Arabs would like her any better than we do. I wonder if she was just born that way, or what?"

"You know what they say—some are born crazy, some become crazy and some have craziness thrust upon them. It all comes to the same thing in the long run."

"Yes."

"That's a real cute husband you've got there."

Lily smiled. "Want to trade?" she suggested.

Ruth-Ann shrieked with laughter. Howie came striding up to them, saying, "What's she done—forgotten that name again?"

. . .

That night Lily had the dream again. She stood in front of the wall, stared at the writing, and it started to turn into pictures that told her a story. It was the same story, but this time the man being prepared for the ride in the boat was her second husband. She watched, as before: at the beginning surprised and touched to see him, and wanting to walk up and talk to him; then, when it was too late, desperate to be heard—trying to stop the others from taking him away. And she woke up again.

"What's wrong?" Don whispered.

"Dream," she said.

"I thought you were in pain. You were making noises."

"No, it's all right."

"Maybe I'd better check everything, just to make sure. Does this feel all right?"

She put her arms around him and said that felt fine; and there, and that, too.

They went to Karnak. As Lily stepped into the ferry, she remembered her dream; but this was a modern craft, whereas

24

the one in her dream had been like the ones on the frescoes, ancient.

They both loved Karnak. Don took a lot of photographs and Lily changed her mind about the camera. She became interested in trying to get pictures of the undersides of the overhead stone beams. The intensity of light around them was so great that it was thrown up, illuminating the colors on the surfaces high over their heads.

"This place is gigantic," Don said. "I've never seen anything like it." He and Howie and Orville moved off together, leaving Ruth-Ann with Lily. Selma wanted Lisabette to look at something in her guidebook. Patsy, as usual, stayed at a distance from the rest of them, keeping watch over Cindy. John started to walk towards the group of men.

"Those two," Ruth-Ann said.

"Patsy and John?"

"Patsy and her child-arsonist."

"Poor woman. What can she do? All of a sudden when they're five, you find out you've got a bum one—you can't take it back to the store. She's stuck with that, I guess."

"And so's he."

Lily looked at the men. She noticed that Howie was in his shirtsleeves. All the others had on sweaters or jackets. John was gesturing up at the columns. "I don't know," she said. "He might walk out any time now. What do you think?"

"Oh? I guess it's possible. She can't have much time for him if she's got her hands full like that. Did you hear what happened when we were getting into the boat? Cindy said something to Selma."

"What?"

"I didn't hear. But I've never seen such a reaction. Selma and Orville, too. Then the two of them started to say something to Patsy and she blew up. John tried to calm them all down. And that horrible, rat-faced kid just looked smug."

"I wonder what it was."

"Something mean, I bet."

Later in the day, Selma came and sat next to Lily. They talked about the ruins. Lily admired the other guidebook, which was larger than her own, and full of color pictures. "I'll give it to you when we leave," Selma said. "I bought two, because I knew the one I'd be carrying around was bound to get all tattered. Just tell me the name of your hotel in Cairo and I'll drop it off there. If you don't mind it in this condition."

"I'd love it," Lily told her.

"I'll tell you something, though: a lot of the information in it is different than we're being told. Sometimes the change is just very slight, and sometimes it really contradicts what the book says. Makes you wonder."

"How?"

"Well, you know those two statues of the king on his throne? Here's the picture."

"The husband and wife in their chairs. Sure. The ones that had the singing heads till the nineteenth-century restorers filled them up."

"That's just it. That's so far from what the guidebook says that you could suspect she just made it up. First of all, both of those figures are the king: Amenhotep III. Then, it says here that one of them, the north one, was so badly damaged in the earthquake of 27BC that part of it cracked and fell. And that was the one that became famous for singing—because the sun used to heat up the cracks, or the wind got into it or something. But all that was way, way back. It was written about by the Romans. And the Romans restored the statue two hundred years or so after it was broken. So, Lisabette's story about how they were built that way in the first place— it just doesn't make sense. That's what she said, wasn't it— that they were part of the sun-worship?"

They were, Lisabette had told them, embodiments of conjugal love; although the seated figures represented a great king and queen, who were the guardians of their people, they were also just like anyone else: a husband and wife. They too obeyed natural laws and worshiped the gods. When the sun-god reached the horizon in his boat and prepared to sail across the sky, they would welcome him, praising him with their voices.

"They sang," Lisabette had said. "They were constructed

as musical instruments. A work of genius." Their heads were hollow, carved inside with a system of intricately fluted trails and passageways. When the morning sun struck their fore-heads, its heat activated the air within and made the stone sing—not singing according to a melody, but long, sustained notes that changed tone as the light grew stronger. In the last century, in order to preserve them, the statues were repaired, the heads filled with cement. And now they no longer made a sound. The two giant figures stared straight ahead, waiting for the sun, silent.

"Did you ask her about it?" Lily said.

"I told her my guidebook talked about reconstruction by Septimus Severus, and all that."

"And?"

"And she said that a lot of these books used different sources."

"That's probably true, isn't it?"

"But not that true. Not so you'd make a mistake like that. And anyway, you can certainly see they're both men—not a married couple."

"I think I like her version better."

"No, dear. Not if it's fictitious. The truth is always better."

"If you can tell what it is."

Selma sighed and said how strange it was to be in a modern country whose whole appearance was still dominated by the culture of its past. Cairo was a modern city, to be sure, but so much of Egypt seemed the same as in ancient days. Yet it wasn't the same, naturally. The only country left where you could say the past and present were still the same was India: she'd always wanted to go there, but Orville had this ridic-ulous feeling against it. He wouldn't go. "All the methods of making things, the craftsmanship, is still the same there," she said. "They still wear the same clothes. But above all, what makes the real difference is that they still believe in and practice the same religions. And that's all gone here."

Lily said yes, and thought again about the two statues. She looked up into the huge gatework of sunlit, painted stone, down at the canyoned pathways in shadow. "You can still feel it, though," she said. "Especially in a place like this."

"Yes indeed. It's like the travel people said: you can almost imagine the gods walking here."

Lily remembered the Englishwoman who lived in the house that was supposed to be dedicated to Isis. "There's something I've got to ask Lisabette before I forget," she said.

"Make sure you check it in a book afterwards. Unless it's something about herself. Now that's a tragic story. She told me her father was killed in the First World War, her first husband and her brother died in the Second World War and her son was killed in the June War."

"I guess that's one of the things that lasts longer than religions," Lily said. "People killing each other."

"I've never heard of one person having so much bad luck. Orville said how did I know she hadn't just concocted the story about her sad personal history—that's what he said: concocted. But I can't believe it. No. You can see she's had sorrows in her life. Maybe they've driven her to—you know, sort of invent things. Well, not really. They wouldn't hire somebody who did that. I expect she exaggerates a little, that's all."

Lily got to her feet. She said the thing about bad luck was that no matter what kind it was, a little went a long way.

She found Lisabette standing in the shade, not far from Orville and Ruth-Ann. "I wonder if you can help me," she began.

Lisabette moved her head stiffly. "Yes?"

"I've heard about an Englishwoman who lives in Egypt— I think maybe in Cairo—in a house she thinks used to belong to a priestess of Isis. I wondered if you'd know anything about her. Or even about the house."

"No, I've never heard of this."

"It was on the radio. She did excavation work on the house and found the garden, and that kind of thing."

"I don't know of such a person."

"Could you tell me where I could go to find out?"

"Possibly the embassy?"

Of course, Lily thought. She should have figured that out herself. The woman had been working with the British archaeological teams; the embassy would know how to get in touch with them.

"Isis?" Ruth-Ann said behind her shoulder. "She's the one that cut off her husband's prick and grew him again from it. That's some trick, huh?"

"It's one of the great pagan myths," Lisabette said curtly.

"And how."

"Containing profound observations on the nature of death, sacrifice and regeneration, life after death, and the power of love."

"And bereavement," Lily said. Lisabette's eyes met hers. The old woman's face lost its lecture look; it lapsed into a softer expression that made her appear even older and more exhausted. It reminded Lily of the way Don's small, ugly, buck-toothed mother had looked when she'd wished them both a happy marriage and added that her own wedding day had been the happiest day of her life.

"Just so," Lisabette said.

On the way back from Karnak there was a quarrel among the other passengers, or perhaps a continuation of whatever had already started between the Darrells and the Pottses. In the stark, offended silence that followed, Howie's voice could be heard announcing that he didn't feel well; he was sure it was the restaurant they'd been to the night before: the lousy, contaminated food they served you in this country. Lisabette threw a lizardlike look over the back of her seat and told him without sympathy that he shouldn't have taken off his pull-over while the wind was still blowing so strongly—it was no wonder he'd caught something.

"I really do feel pretty bad," he said a few more times. By the end of the ride he looked almost green in the face. As they left the ferry, Ruth-Ann told Lily and Don that if Howie had to change their travel arrangements, this would be good-bye, but she wanted to say it had been nice to meet them. Everyone offered to help. Ruth-Ann shook her head. She'd ask the hotel, she said; they'd find her a doctor if Howie needed one.

.   .   .

Late that evening Lily said that she wanted to go to Abydos and Saqqarah. And they should be staying on the other bank anyway, in Luxor.

"I guess we'll have to leave them for another trip," Don told her.

"When do you think we'd ever get back? It's such a long way from home. Doesn't it make more sense to go now, when we're here?"

"We just don't have the time, honey."

"And at Luxor: the temple. We're right here on the spot."

"We can't. We—"

She stood up and delivered a tirade about the importance of beauty to the development of a culture. He didn't know what she was talking about, and he didn't think she understood half of what she was saying, but in the end he agreed to change all their plans, so that they'd be able to get back to Luxor. Abydos was out, he declared. If she got Luxor, he'd be allowed Abu Simbel.

She then wanted to start telephoning the British embassy to find out where to get hold of the priestess of Isis. "Later," he told her: after they got back from the next day's sightseeing.

On their way out in the morning, the man at the desk handed Lily a package—a book wrapped in a piece of hotel writing paper that was held tight by a rubber band. On the paper was a short note from Selma, saying that they too had changed plans and were going to visit a shrine somewhere out in the desert. The book was the guidebook she'd promised to let Lily keep.

Lily's pleasure in the book was the only sign that she still considered the world worth noticing. She read while standing, sitting or walking. She read the book all through the journey to Abu Simbel and parts of the actual tour. She was in such a bad mood that Don was almost frightened for her.

They had said goodbye to Lisabette and the Darrells. Now they were with a larger group, of sixteen people: Americans, Australians, Britons and South Africans. Their guide was a young man named Franz, who came from a part of Switzerland that was mainly German-speaking. His accent was a

good deal better than Lisabette's, but he had a rapid-fire de-
livery that left many of his hearers mystified, especially when
he reeled off lists of ancient deities or rulers.

During one of the breaks when they were supposed to
wander around by themselves or take their photographs, Don
sat down next to Lily. He tried to coax the guidebook from
her. She dodged away. He dropped something into her lap.
"What's that?" she asked.

"A lucky stone. It's got a ring around it."

"Stones don't last long in the desert," she said. "They all
turn to sand." She picked the stone out of her lap and threw
it away. It bounced off the side of a larger stone and fell into
a heap of pebbles. The bright light made it indistinguishable
from the other shapes around the place where it had landed.

"I ought to hit you," he said.

"Go ahead. Go right ahead."

"You won't take anything from me, will you?"

It was true. She wanted to scream with rage, or get up and
start running, or hit him first. She'd never treated anyone so
badly. She was ashamed of herself, but she couldn't quit. She
even wondered if she'd married him because—believing that
there was a curse on her—she'd been willing to let him die.
She also realized that although she couldn't accept his love,
she wanted him to keep on caring. Her resistance to him was
like a lack of faith, an atheistic impulse; if there were suddenly
nothing against which to fight, she might be completely lost.

"Christ, what I'd like to do to you," he said.

She thought he really was going to hit her, but he turned
and stormed off in the direction of the river. He stood looking
out at the water, with his back to her.

She felt tears of stubbornness and remorse rising in her
eyes. Her throat ached. But she was also proud at the way
he was standing up to her. If he could hold out like that, he
might win her over and exorcise the curse. Or maybe it had
nothing to do with him; it might be more important that she
should talk with the priestess of Isis.

That night, as they were getting ready to go to bed, Lily
said, "I wonder where the others are now—if Howie's all
right."

31

"He'll be fine. People don't die of a stomach ache."

"I wonder what the quarrel was about. The one between Selma and that horrible little girl."

"What are any quarrels about?"

"Well, I guess each one's different."

"Your mother warned me about you, you know."

"Great," she said. "That's the kind of mother to have. OK, what did she say?"

"Oh, never mind."

"You can't leave it there. If you don't tell me, I'll call her up long distance, right this minute." Her mother; suddenly it was like having another person along on the honeymoon. Her mother envied her the two widowings. They were even more romantic and dramatic than Ida's divorce.

"She said you thought there was a curse on you."

"Oh?"

"Well?"

"Well, I sometimes feel like that, yes."

She got into the bed, taking the guidebook with her, but when he reached towards the lamp, she put the book on the night table. He turned out the light. She waited in the darkness for him to go on with the conversation.

At last he said, "You never talk about the others."

"What others?" she whispered.

"The other two."

She didn't answer.

"Your husbands," he said.

There was a silence again, longer than the first one.

"What for?" she asked.

"It's something important in your life."

She rolled to the side, to get near the edge of the bed. He put out his arm and pulled her back.

"It was a long time ago," she said. "They both were. I don't remember. And I don't want to. When people die, you get over it by moving forward."

"And I guess some people never get over it."

"I don't know."

I don't know what other people remember, she thought, *but I*

32

remember everything—every room we were in, every place. Love does that; everything new, fun, easy to remember. It was the only time I felt I was living. I just can't talk about it, that's all.

"If I died, you'd move forward?" he asked.

"That's a dumb thing to say. Besides, you had girlfriends before you met me."

"I was never married."

"It amounts to the same."

"No, it doesn't. It's completely different."

"I don't think so."

He said, "I used to have this idea that you were like one of those maidens in the fairytales, who had to have the spell broken."

"And what do you think now?"

"I think maybe you don't love me very much."

Here it comes, she thought. But no, he wouldn't really believe that. He'd just want her to say: *Of course I do.*

She said, "You don't have any reason to think that. It's because I get into bad moods, isn't it?"

He stretched and shifted his weight, moving his arm an inch higher under her back. He said, "Well, not exactly."

His voice sounded faint and sad. Suddenly she was weeping uncontrollably. "Of course I love you," she sobbed. "Of course I do."

·   ·   ·

Their time was running out. They could go back to Cairo and enjoy the town for a day, or they could see one other site and hurry back. Lily held the guidebook tightly and said that she absolutely needed to see Abydos and Edfu and Bubastis and Saqqarah: and after that, they had to have a few days extra in Cairo so that she could find the priestess of Isis.

"Say all that again," he told her.

"The sanctuary of Abydos and the sacred lake of—"

"No: the priestess part."

She told him about the Englishwoman who lived in Cairo and believed herself to be the incarnation of an ancient priestess of Isis.

He said, "Listen, you really want to see some old crone suffering from delusions? Didn't you notice, we've got plenty of those at home?"

"We don't have the temple of Isis or the house of the priestess."

"Well, we can ask somebody, I guess."

"I asked Lisabette. She hadn't heard of her."

"That settles it."

"She said I should try the embassy."

"Oh?"

"I did. When you went to see about the tickets. But I don't think I got hold of the right people. Nobody knew. They gave me a lot of names of different people and they turned out to be away on trips. But all I need to do is wait. Lots of people must have heard of her if she was on the radio."

"I'm not going to spend all the time we've got left, trying to track down some old woman. She's probably died by now, anyway. Why do you want to see her?"

Lily didn't know. There wasn't any reason, just the desire. She tried to think of something to tell him.

"I want to see her because she, um, lives in that place."

"Where?"

"Well, it's an ancient Egyptian house, with a garden in it. And anyhow, she's the priestess of Isis. That's why I want to see her."

"We just don't have the time."

"I want to stay," she said. "To stay here longer."

"Of course you can't stay. I've got to get back to the office."

Now he'd be saying to himself: who's footing the bill for all this? *Well*, she thought, *he offered*. She took a firm grip on the guidebook and looked up into his eyes. "You can get back to the office," she suggested. "And I could stay on here for a while."

"No." He said it so loudly that a cluster of other guests in the hotel lobby turned around to look.

"Just a few—"

"Don't push your luck, Lil," he said. He stared at her so fiercely that he looked almost frightening, but also exciting.

She leaned forward and put her hands on his arms, turned her face upward.

He grabbed hold of both her hands and began to pull her across the floor to the elevator. A group of people were standing in front of the doors. He started to drag her around the corner and up the stairs. "What's wrong?" she said. "Where are we going?"

"Upstairs," he answered.

"What for?"

"It's the only place I can get any sense out of you."

She tried to kiss him on the neck and sat down in the middle of the staircase. He piled on top of her, laughing. A woman's voice from below them called, "Hello, hello, you two. Did you drop this?"

They turned their heads. Down at the bottom of the staircase stood a woman who was smiling broadly. She was holding the guidebook in her right hand and waving it back and forth.

. . .

By mid-morning they were on their way to the ruins. Don seemed to be dozing behind his sunglasses. Lily sat quietly, the book held primly in her lap as if it might have been a prayerbook. Their new touring companions included two burly, gray-haired men—one Dutch and the other Irish—who were traveling together; an old Canadian woman on her own; and an American family of five: father, mother, two well-developed teenaged daughters and a son of about twelve. The son was interested in the height, width, and exact measurements of all the parts of every building they saw. He told Franz, the group in general and then Don in particular, that he'd worked out a theory about pyramidology that explained just everything you'd ever want to know. His two sisters had their eyes on Franz; the younger one, called Tina, was dressed—foolishly, so her mother told her—in a white T-shirt and red shorts. "They aren't shorts," the girl objected. "They're hot pants." The older sister, Lucille, was more conservative; she had on a pair of long trousers and a matching jacket.

Lily moved away from Don early in the tour. She told him that she wanted to read up on a few things. She sat down and looked out into the distance. Behind her people were taking photographs. The older American girl came up to where Lily was sitting; her face still covered by the camera, she said, "This is just great. Isn't it great?"

"Mm."

"The lure of the ancient world—I was always nuts about that kind of thing." She said that what had really convinced her parents had been her brother's insistence on his theory; he was going to make it his school topic for the coming term. She too had been thinking about Egypt for years, having been extremely impressed by an opera she'd once been taken to: Egyptian dress and scenery had figured prominently among the memorable aspects of the production. The name of the composer escaped her at the moment, though she hummed a little of her favorite tune from it, which she said was called "The Nuns' Chorus From Aida."

Lily said that was nice; her own introduction had been through the museums.

Yes, the girl told her, they were OK, but you had to get outdoors to see what was left of the buildings: she liked the temples and things best. She liked, she said, as she moved away with the camera, the way they'd built everything on such a big scale.

Lily closed the guidebook. She felt that she wanted to stay where she was for a long time, just sitting and doing nothing. She remembered a day at home, a few years back, when she'd gone for a walk in the park. It had been an afternoon in the fall—the distances full of hazy sunshine, the leaves gold, brown, coppery. Two young mothers had been sitting on a bench in front of hers, Each of them had a baby carriage nearby. Sometimes nurses and babysitters came to the park but these girls, she'd felt sure, were the real mothers. And something about the scene, or the season, or maybe just the weather, had made her think what a waste it was that people had only one life, that the choices were always so few, that you couldn't lead several lives all at once or one after the other.

But now it seemed to her that what remained of the past was just as much where she belonged as was the present. In fact, you couldn't help living more lives than one. Thought took you into other times. And there was always going to be so much to see and learn: you could never reach the end of it.

Don came and sat down beside her. "That kid's obsessed," he said. "Another one."

"Numerology?"

"Everything except spacemen. He thinks they had astronomical observatories and balloon flight and just about everything."

"I think the real facts are more interesting."

"The reincarnation of priestesses—that kind of thing?"

"Like the fact that all the lower-class people had broken teeth from eating stone-ground bread. Everyone I've ever met who's had a thing about health-food bread has chipped a tooth at least once."

"Is that in the guidebook?"

"That was in the lectures. They also told us: the men who worked in the mummifying business were divided into different classes, too. And the ones that handled all the poor people's trade considered it a privilege of the profession that they should be allowed to have sexual intercourse with the corpses."

"You're kidding."

"Apparently it's a well-known thing."

"Of course they were completely dominated by the idea of death."

"Most cultures are. Don't you like all this?"

"Sure. It's terrific. But I'm going to be glad to get back."

"Snow and ice?"

"This is fine for a time. But you know what it is."

"It's history."

"It's a graveyard."

"So's most of history. They lived a long time ago. And all that's left is what survived. This is here because it's stone. The houses where they lived were made out of wood and mud and plastery stuff. So, they're all gone. The tombs and

37

temples—the religious side of life—they were built to last. It's not so different nowadays; most old churches are made out of stone."

"Uh-huh." He took the guidebook out of her lap and flipped through the pages. "Franz says he's going on to Abydos with the group."

"Good. That's one of the most sacred places."

"It's too far away. It's got to be someplace nearer. We'd just have time to make Saqqarah, if you wanted to. I'd rather go straight back to Cairo and not have to rush so much."

"OK," she said. "Saqqarah." She breathed in and stood up, saying, "It's so clean here. The light's so wonderful. And the air—you can understand why some people decide they want to go off into the desert and never come back."

"Would you ever do that?"

"Not without a guidebook," she said, taking it back from him.

They strolled towards the others. Don said, "This is another funny bunch, though. We seem to end up with the oddballs."

"The family's nice."

"But a little weird."

"I don't think so."

"That boy?"

"That's just getting carried away by his ideas. And I liked the older girl. She loves everything about the place."

"I think maybe her sister's the one that's going to get Franz."

"Oh, no. If anybody's going to get Franz, I'd put my money on the mother."

He laughed and took her free hand. They were in tune for the rest of the day: all during the trip back to their hotel, through the evening and night, for the next leg of their journey and on their arrival at the new hotel.

In the morning they started to quarrel. It happened so fast that before either one of them knew what had led to it, he was hissing at her, "The minute you get out of bed, it's all gone. All I get is that silence. It's like you can't stand to be near me. You don't even look at me. You'd be that way in bed with anybody, wouldn't you?"

She wouldn't answer back. She just continued to put her

clothes on, trying to keep out of his way in the small room.

He came up to her and turned her around. "Tell me about them," he said. "Tell me about the other two."

She plunged away, furious, and said, "No." If it was going to turn into a real fight, she was all set to pick up an ashtray or a lamp and throw it at him. She went on getting dressed.

They didn't speak to each other on the way to the site, or when they got there. They sat or stood side by side, enraged and indignant. No one noticed anything wrong because, for the first time, they were in a large group of tourists—nearly twenty people—who didn't seem to have been brought together before. There was no chatting among the crowd. The guide was an Egyptian woman of studious appearance, who might have been a teacher or lecturer on the off-season. Her voice was rather soft, which meant that her audience had to crowd up close, to be sure not to miss anything.

They saw the frescoes, heard about the cult of the bull, passed by one of the most famous pyramids. The ancient Egyptians, they were reminded, called every pyramid "the house of eternity"; the king's statue would be seated inside, looking out on to the world through peepholes. If the statue was there, the king was there. The work of art had a purpose beyond mere decoration: it was a stand-in.

They walked in the direction of a huge mound of building rubble that looked like another, unfinished, pyramid. Lily had forgotten which places were ancient and which had been left by the excavators. Her strength began to recede as they neared the base of the structure. She thought how pointless her whole life had turned out to be. It was no use trying to fight bad luck; some people just had that deal from the deck. To consider marriage for a third time had been foolish beyond comprehending. She didn't feel that she could ever possibly get to know him, or that she'd want to; and she was suddenly so tired that she was ready to lie down in the sand and stay there.

He grabbed her hand. She looked back over her shoulder for the others; they'd gone somewhere else with the guide.

He started to tug her along the ground, yanking her hard by the arm. And he began to yell abuse at her. He was dragging her towards the pyramid-like hill—she couldn't imagine why. He said that she could damn well pull herself together and take an interest in their future and be a little nice to him sometimes and show that she appreciated it when he gave in to her—because that was what he was always having to do, all the time, and never getting any thanks for it, either.

When they came to the beginnings of stonework, he started to climb up, hauling her along with him. She had to follow. If she tried to sit down, she'd be cut and bruised. She called out for him to wait, but he wouldn't. "You're hurting my arm," she said. He climbed higher, taking her with him, until she thought her arm was going to twist out of her shoulder. And all at once he stopped, sweating, and faced her. He let go of her hand.

"You know what else your mother said?" he told her. "She said maybe it was a blessing in disguise that your first two husbands died so soon, before they found out what a spoiled bitch you really are."

She stepped back. She felt the sun shining on the top of her head, but she was cold. It was like the time when she'd lost her lucky-piece: the same terror. A few voices from below came up to her.

"Oh Jesus, Lily," he said. "I'm sorry."

She took another step back. She still wasn't able to answer, though her eyes hadn't moved from his face.

"Look out," he said suddenly.

She turned, knew that she was slipping and saw her foot skidding over the edge. She started to fall. He grabbed her by her skirt and slid past her. They tumbled downward for several yards and stopped a few feet apart. More voices came up from below them, shouting loudly.

Lily picked herself up carefully. Her knees and shins were scraped, her left elbow and forearm were bleeding. Otherwise, she seemed to be all right. She crawled over to where Don had fallen. He was lying on his back, looking up at her. She sat down beside him.

He said, "I didn't mean it."

"It doesn't matter."

"Are you all right?" he asked.

"I'm fine."

He said, "I can't move."

She called down to the people standing below. She screamed for them to bring help. They said that they were coming; several of them started up the rock surface.

She touched his cheek with her fingers and took his hand in hers. He smiled a little. Soon after that, he died. She was still holding his hand, so she felt and saw the moment when it happened. She hadn't been able to be with her first two husbands when they'd died.

.   .   .

At the airport both mothers were waiting: hers and his. Her mother began to cry straight away, loudly announcing, "Oh, poor Lily—I thought this time it had to be all right. But it wasn't meant to be."

Lily gave her a brief hug, pushed her aside and walked on, to where Don's mother stood. Lily embraced her, finding it strange that the one who was the mother should be the small one. "I was with him," she said. "He wasn't in pain at all." Her mother-in-law nodded. Lily said, "It was so quick. He asked me if I was all right. He was thinking of me, not of himself. And then he just went." She started to cry. Her mother-in-law too, wept. And behind her, her mother sobbed noisily, still saying that she'd been so sure everything was going to work out this time; that she couldn't believe *it had happened again*.

The funeral was down in the country at his mother's place, where they'd had the wedding reception. As Lily walked out of the front door and over to the car, she remembered the other time: when she'd emerged with Don from the identical doorway, to get into the car that was to carry them to their future as husband and wife.

She asked her mother-in-law if she could stay with her for a while. The two of them took walks together in the snow. Lily began to see more of her sisters-in-law; it was a large family and a lot of them lived near enough to turn up for Sunday lunch.

She kept expecting to have the same dream about Don that

41

she'd had about her other husbands: to see him being dressed in the winding-sheet and taken away in the boat. But she had stopped having dreams.

She was pregnant. She told her mother-in-law first. And she was thankful that her sister was planning to remarry near the end of September, so that her mother's attention would be deflected from her at the crucial time.

The child was born: a boy. She couldn't sleep. She couldn't concentrate on anything else. She forgot the pain and regret she had felt about not having been able to love her husband. The business of being a mother was harder than anyone had led her to believe. It was exhausting to the limit of her patience, and at times so far beyond that she didn't think she was going to get through it.

One day she looked at her son as he stood aside from a group of children he was playing with. He reminded her suddenly of a photograph she had that showed her grandfather at the same age; and also, she realized, of Don: the resemblance was so startling that it was almost like a reincarnation.

She confessed to her mother-in-law that she thought she hadn't loved Don enough—not as much as he'd deserved.

Her mother-in-law said, "That's the way people always feel. But I know you loved him. Anyone can see what a good mother you are."

She didn't think she was such a good mother. She thought she was slapdash and nervous, constantly fussing. The only thing she was sure of was that she loved her son. And she was delighted and extremely surprised that her father, who had always seemed hopeless as far as family matters were concerned, had fallen in love with the child: he'd turn up on the doorstep to take the boy for a ride, or to play outdoors somewhere, or to go on a trip to the zoo; they had private jokes together and stories that they told each other. She began to be fond of her father again, as she had been when she was young.

One day a reporter wanted to interview her. Her statements were to be included in a program about war widows, which was going to be broadcast as a companion piece to a docu-

(212) 688-4949

EXEL
COMPUTER CENTERS

Lois Lomangino
Sales Consultant

52 East 53rd Street
New York, New York 10055

mentary that dealt with veterans. The compilers planned to talk to children, too. They seemed irritated that Lily hadn't had any children by her first two husbands.

She told them that she was happy. It hadn't been easy, she said, and it had taken a long time, but she'd had a lot of help. She praised her mother-in-law.

Even if she'd been in the mood for it, she hardly had the time to dream. But she often remembered Egypt. One picture especially came back to her from the trip: of two immense statues made of stone—each out of a single piece—that were represented seated on chairs; the figures were sitting out in the middle of nowhere, side by side and both looking in the same direction: east, towards the sunrise. Sometimes she thought about them.

PEOPLE TO PEOPLE

Herb, Dave, Sherman and Joe sat around the table in Herb's hotel room. He was the only one who lived out of town. At first, after college, they'd all left. Then the three had returned. Herb had worked in Ohio for a while, and in Wisconsin, before settling in Illinois.

They had had wives and families, divorces, remarriages. Sherman was the only one whose marriage—so far—remained stable.

"I wish it was just to say hi," Herb said. "Have a couple of drinks, see a show, play a game of poker, talk about old times. I'm afraid I've got bad news. I've heard from Bill."

"So?" Dave said. "Last time I heard from Bill, he was campaigning to save the Indians or the jungles, or something like that. It's always bad news in his book."

"I've got the letter here." Herb pulled an envelope from his breast pocket, put on his reading glasses and took the letter out. *"Dear Herb,"* he announced, *"I've written this in my mind many times and I've wanted to, even more times. All those years I was in South America, the business about Carmen was preying on my mind."*

"Oh, Jesus," Joe said. "That son of a bitch."

"He spells it with an A," Herb said " 'Praying on my mind.' "

"Let's see that." Dave held out his hand.

"Wait . . . *on my mind. I never felt right about it, as you know."*

"That dumb bastard," Joe said.

"It was like a cloud hanging over my life. I think it was the reason why I never got married."

"Good excuse, anyway," Dave said.

"But now I've found a wonderful girl. We were married last month. I hope you'll believe me when I say my life is completely changed. I thank God that I have lived long enough to experience this great happiness and at last to know the peace and wisdom of the Church of The Redeemer, which we both belong to."

45

"Holy shit," Joe said. "One of those California cults."

"Wait for the punchline, kids. You want me to go on? *I have talked everything over with Nancy (my wife) and she agrees with me that we wouldn't be worthy of God and His gifts to us if we continued to hide the truth.*"

"Oh God," Sherman said. "Not at this late date. He can't do it."

"*I am sure in my heart that this is the right thing to do. But I wanted to talk to you first, because I think we should all give ourselves up together. Please let me know as soon as possible what your thoughts about this are, since I am not going to feel right till we get it straight.* OK. That's it."

"That dumb fink," Dave said. "He gets religion and they slam us in the can for the rest of our lives. After twenty years."

"He can't do it," Sherman said. "There's a statute of limitations."

"For murder?" Joe asked.

"It wasn't murder. It was an accident."

Herb said, "Right. Now, listen. I figure old Bill hasn't stood up and told the multitude yet, only Nancy. So, I wrote straight back and said: yes, I understood because it was preying on me too, but I hadn't even worked out how to tell my wife and I thought it would be a good thing for all of us to talk about it in private before doing anything. I asked him to set a date and to bring Nancy—she'd be able to give us the woman's point of view. And he wrote back to say fine: they're coming about a month after Easter. Here, a hotel right down the street. I've got them a room and everything. And now I want to ask you all: what do we do when they get here?"

There was a long pause while Sherman put his hands over his eyes and Dave lit a cigarette. Joe jumped up from his seat; he stamped his feet and shook his shoulders angrily. He made punching motions with his fists.

Herb put the letter back inside its envelope and into his pocket. "Well?" he asked.

"We kill them," Joe said.

"Don't be funny," Sherman told him.

"You got a better idea? What else can we do? They're religious nuts. There isn't any way you can deal with that. They're going to go to the cops and send us up the river to make everything jake with the Lord and save their consciences. We've got to."

"This is why I thought we'd better get together," Herb said. "The first thing to establish is whether the guy's serious, and the second is—if he is, how we stop him. I'm telling you: I don't intend to have all that brought up again."

"Me neither," Dave said. "Sherm?"

"No," Sherman said. "I don't think it's necessary to start talking about killing anyone, though."

"You wait," Joe said. "You'll come to it. You all will."

"I have a feeling," Herb said, "that a lot is going to depend on the girl. Nancy."

Dave said, "She sounds like a creep."

"How do you get that?"

"Some religious female."

"People can be religious for all sorts of reasons, and from a lot of different motives. This new-fangled church they belong to—the Church of The Redeemer: that should tell us something."

"He's a dope," Joe said flatly. "He always was."

"This isn't a traditional church. It's some kind of offshoot. On the perimeter."

"Ecclesiastically off-Broadway," Sherman said. "Back to hellfire and cleanliness. Come back, Darwin, and say it again, louder. Christ Almighty, they're taking over the country. Now they want to teach it in the schools."

"That's just an election gimmick," Dave said.

"We get a President who knows his way around the Hollywood back lot and he didn't even bother to see that movie about the monkey trial."

"What would you say he was like before?" Herb asked.

"Before getting to be President?"

"What was Bill like before this girl converted him? At least, I've been assuming she was the one."

"A worrier," Dave said. "Nervous and worried, and couldn't ever pull himself together when he had to, or couldn't relax

47

and enjoy himself. Had this thing about his parents and his childhood. No good with girls, either. Always worried everything would go wrong. Unless he was drunk. Then he was fine."

"Kind to animals," Sherman said. "Good with old people. Not so good with children. He froze up when people were rude to him. He ran on rails."

"He was scared," Joe said. "He was scared shitless all the time. He was the one that panicked."

"That was only once," Herb said.

"But it showed what he was like."

"Well, I sort of got the same impression about him: that he was somebody who was afraid of a lot of things. Stepping over his own feet half the time, afraid of living his life, of finding out what his possibilities were, letting rip. Which means, maybe he'd be easy to frighten."

"No good," Joe said. "You ease up for a minute on that kind and all of a sudden they're more afraid of somebody else instead and they're talking all about whatever it was you wanted to keep quiet. It's got to be permanent."

"What was he most scared of?"

"Carmen," Sherman said. "That's why it was so bad when it happened."

"OK. We wait till they get here. Or do we map something out? Like I said, it looks to me like it's serious. I wouldn't have gotten you all together otherwise."

"I could do it easy," Joe said. "I've still got my guns. But—"

"I don't like this kind of talk," Sherman said.

"But I'd want all of you to be in on it some way. I mean, I'm not going to go in there alone and come out with the scalps and have the cops saying, 'Where were you when the lights went out?' "

"You'd kill a woman?" Dave asked.

"If it's me or them, I'd kill anybody," Joe said. "Wouldn't you?"

"Bill is one thing. I wouldn't like it, but if he's really going to put us behind bars, so be it. But a girl—that doesn't seem right."

"She could go to the cops just like him. She's the one pushing him to clear his conscience. She's got it coming to her."

"I don't want to listen to this," Sherman said. He stood up.

Herb said, "Take it easy. We've got to decide something today. And we've all got to be together on it. We're all affected by this."

"I don't think there's any need to talk about killing."

"No, there may not be. But you can't afford to be so squeamish that we let the question drop till they're here in town talking about how good we'll feel when we go to the cops. Are you really prepared to let that happen?"

"I just think there's got to be some other way."

"OK. Sit down and think of one."

. . .

The five of them—Herb, Dave, Sherman, Joe and Bill—had had rooms in the same college dorm, on the same staircase. On the ground floor, down the hall from Herb, was a boy they hadn't noticed the year before, when they'd been in their freshman dorms. His name was Jeff and he was good-looking, rich, spoiled and a snob. He arrived in a white sportscar which was his own, not his parents', and had all kinds of expensive and desirable objects delivered to his rooms—the best ones in the building—which he occupied alone, and which looked out on the tree-lined street. He had visitors. While his neighbors were still trying to find girls to go out with who'd say yes, Jeff was entertaining women who were working, possibly even married, and who—since his suite of rooms gave on to the street—could actually climb in and out of the living room at night.

He didn't bother to get to know anyone he thought wasn't going to be important. The five other boys near him he evidently considered not worth noticing.

One day Dave and Sherman were looking out of the window and saw Jeff walking across the path below.

"Do you suppose Jeff stands for Geoffrey?" Sherman asked.

"I wouldn't put it past him," Dave said.

49

It was quite a while afterwards that someone looked him up in the freshman yearbook and discovered his first two names to be "C. Jefferson." After that, there were bets on what the "C" stood for. A friend of a friend, who had access to files in the Dean's office, did the rest.

They could hardly believe their luck. Joe actually didn't believe it for days. "It's a girl's name," he said.

"Well, his family's part Cuban or Spanish, or something," Dave told him. "It's probably one of those names that can be for both girls and boys."

Within hours they were calling the name at Jeff from their windows. He didn't react. The next time he passed by, it was, "Hey, Carmen Miranda." He shouted back, "Screw you." Over the next few days he called out other things, phrases not in common use at the time—obscenity and gutter-language that the middle classes hadn't yet taken up as a fashion. The five boys yelled it back.

But of course all the time they were leaning out of their windows shouting "Asshole" and "Shitface" and asking why he didn't do such-and-such with so-and-so, they knew the thing that hurt the most was simply his own real name: Carmen, which he'd tried to disguise and hide at the beginning.

The crowd of them battled along that way from September through to the spring. Then, just before exam time, everyone was busy. They studied and they went out, saw movies, planned parties.

There was one large panty-raid on a neighboring women's college. The raids were an imported custom from larger, rowdier universities that had already abandoned the practice and were more interested in reviving others, like goldfish-swallowing and crowding into telephone booths.

And the parties began. Some boys were drunk for days at a time. There was vomit on the staircases, loud music at night, mobs of talking, laughing, dancing people giving parties or looking for parties, or left behind. A friend of Herb's said he'd found the most beautiful girl one night, who couldn't remember where she was, and said she couldn't remember her name, either, and left before the morning without even giving him a phone number.

You were supposed to check people in and out in the usual way, but everyone knew that it was standard procedure to do both at the same time. Many girls were actually staying through the night, stealing out early the next day. There were a lot of girls in the building on the evening of Rockwell's party. Rockwell lived across the courtyard. The party was huge. There was hardly room to contain all the guests on his side of the building; most of them kept getting lost, anyway. Herb, Dave, Sherman, Joe and Bill weren't invited because they'd gone to the first one: Rockwell was giving three parties—one for friends, one for formal and family connections, and the last, and biggest, for acquaintances. All night long people were passing out in the corridors or asking how to get back to the party. They were screaming and crying, laughing and singing. Rockwell's phonograph played Chubby Checkers, Dixieland, big-band swing and barrelhouse.

The five boys tried to work but ended up breaking out the liquor and having their own party instead. Near midnight Sherman and Bill went out for food and brought back cheeseburgers, submarine sandwiches, french fries, doughnuts and cheesecake. After that, they had some more to drink. They considered starting up a poker game or going out somewhere, or crashing Rockwell's acquaintance-party, or sneaking into the gym and going for a swim. The swim won.

"But first we go wake up Carmen and Dolores," Joe said. "Give them a little surprise."

Everybody was pretty drunk by then and it sounded like a good idea. Dolores was the name they'd given Carmen's latest girlfriend—a redhead who wore high heels and, until the warmer weather had begun, a fur coat. The idea was to catch the two in bed. Everyone wanted to get a good look at Dolores.

"And we'll invite them along," Dave said. "Big swimming party in the buff. Dolores is a good sport, she won't mind. She's probably a call girl, does it all the time."

They charged up the hallway and pounded on the door. Herb turned the knob and pushed. The door opened. He switched on the light. They squeezed in through the corridor and living room, into the bedroom.

Carmen was standing in the middle of the floor. He'd obviously just gotten up out of bed, where he'd been sleeping alone. He was naked and angry.

"What the hell is this?" he asked.

Joe said, OK, where was she, and started calling names. Sherman and Herb were laughing. Bill sat down on a chair. Dave headed towards the bathroom, saying she was probably hiding in there.

"Get out of here," Carmen told them. He added a lot about their characters and at the same time picked up and threw a cushion that caught Dave on the side of the head and knocked him into a chest of drawers. He didn't seem to be afraid at all, nor in any way embarrassed about having no clothes on. He looked around for something else to throw.

Joe tried to tackle him at the knees. Carmen pushed him aside so he fell against a chair.

All five felt that the fight began because Carmen kept throwing things at them. Their only aim was to stop him. And since there were five of them, they soon managed to knock him down and sit on him, even though he was sober and they were drunk.

Sherman then said he felt terrible and needed some air. He wanted to go up on the roof. So did Herb. The others said they couldn't leave Carmen there alone. They decided to take him with them.

They dragged him up all four double staircases to the top, out the emergency door and onto the roof.

It was a warm night full of stars. The breath of greenery came to them out of the darkness, from the treetops around the building. Carmen, who had seemed for a while to be only semiconscious, came to. He started to fight again. He landed quite a lot of lucky punches and ducked out from under blows that then hit the others. For a while the five friends were stumbling around and fighting each other.

They caught him because he had no clothes. He had worked his way over to the edge of the roof near the front entrance. On one side below them was a large tree. Later it occurred to Herb that perhaps Carmen had hoped to be able to climb over the guttering, shinny down a few feet, grab hold of a branch and get into the tree, where he'd be safe from them until morning.

But they thought he was trying to maneuver them around so that he could start pushing them over. Dave and Joe began to mutter about what they could do to him to teach him a lesson. Herb and Sherman were still laughing, and Bill was in hysterics: it sounded as if he was crying.

The group struggled, fell, and lurched forward: grunting, laughing and swearing. And then, all at once, they lost him. "Look out," Sherman said, and it was already happening. They hadn't realized just how close to the edge they were, but they knew it the moment he slipped away. He gave a little cry that must have been just before he hit—the kind of sound a man might make if he'd bumped into the furniture in the dark—and then they heard the thump, and silence afterwards.

The entranceway to the building was paved stone and lit at night from the lights over the doorways. By leaning out carefully, they could see him below, lying face down.

He didn't move. They were all sure he was dead, but Herb said they had to call an ambulance right away, and Sherman said definitely: an ambulace and the police.

Bill went berserk: the police couldn't, wouldn't—to be mixed up with the police—his family, never. Joe and Dave didn't like the sound of it, either. "We just go back to your room and forget about it," Joe said. "It was an accident. They'll think he was taking LSD, trying to fly."

"We'd better get off this roof," Dave said. "He's lying in the light down there. Anybody finds him, they're going to come on up here."

They went back to Herb's room, had some coffee and talked about it. Joe socked Sherman in the jaw to stop him from telephoning. They had some more to drink and then had to prevent Herb from leaving the room. The ones who didn't want to get mixed up with the police began to find reasons why the others should stay clear, too. "It would ruin your career," Dave told Sherman. To Herb he said, "You don't think he's still alive, do you? Falling on stone? We get the ambulance and the cops, and there's some dead greaseball kid out there all beat up and no clothes on—are you kidding?"

"Son of a bitch had it coming to him," Joe said.

Bill stared down at the floor and said nothing. He drank three cups of coffee and fell asleep on Herb's fold-up sofa.

At about an hour before dawn, Joe and Dave went back to their rooms. Sherman and Herb slept. They slept all through the morning till noon, when there were loud knocks and poundings on all the doors in the hall.

The police didn't believe the drugs theory, although according to the rumors going around, they tested the body for all kinds of things. They also went into Carmen's rooms, where they found everything broken and about twenty girls and boys lying on the floor, in the bed, chairs, couches and wherever they could find space; they had moved in when someone saw the light on and the door open; their fingerprints were everywhere, their drinks all over the rug—they'd danced, made love, thrown up, smoked marijuana and left the shower on for six hours.

But despite the orgiastic behaviour of Rockwell's invited and uninvited acquaintances, what really shocked everyone speculating about Carmen's death was the fact that he had been naked. The bruises and scratches covering his body were incidental; they were evidence of violence, whereas the nakedness appeared to be a sign of erotic activity of some sort. And it was mainly as a result of the wild rumors which immediately sprang up that all five students were at first glad they had chosen to keep quiet. No one, they realized, would believe the truth. It looked too bad. It looked suspicious. It also, they came to see, looked deliberate.

.   .   .

They were never suspected, although they were questioned, but so was everyone else in the house. They said there had been too much coming and going to notice anything, that the racket had gone on just about all night, that they'd been drinking too and playing the phonograph, and that all they could say for certain was that when they went out for cheeseburgers and came back, there wasn't anybody lying on the ground in front of the entrance.

Carmen's uncle, a surprisingly young man called Earl-Somebody, came up to the college a few days later. He brought a dark-haired, intense-looking girl with him, who bore a slight facial resemblace to the dead boy; she was a cousin and her name was Lisa. Most of the time she sat in the uncle's car, or paced up and down. Whenever she had to wait for too long, she got up and walked around like an animal in a cage: on the sidewalk, in the corridors, in a room.

Earl himself came and asked them a lot of questions, among which were ones about friends, drugs, women, quarrels, money troubles. They told him they'd liked Jeff fine, only he'd kept himself apart from everyone else. The only close friends he'd seemed to want were the women they'd seen him with and they didn't know who any of those were, except to say that they hadn't looked like college girls—they'd worn a lot of makeup and had their hair all specially done; and the shoes . . . you know.

"Sure," Earl said. "I get you." He thanked them all, and, as he left, asked a couple of questions about traffic directions. Herb walked to the entrance with him and then out on to the street, where the car was parked. He told him how to get across town.

Earl said, "Somebody hated him a lot."

"How do you figure that?"

"He was beat up real bad."

"Maybe when he hit the ground—"

"No. The cops told me it was all done before that. And more than one guy, definitely."

"Well, as far as I know, everybody in the building got along with him. The only thing I can think of is something to do with his girls." Herb described how people could be let into those ground-floor rooms from the windows on the street. Then he said, "But you can't imagine what it was like with that party going on. There were fights and jokes going on all night long. The noise was just unbearable. We turned up the volume as high as we could, and the walls were still shaking with it. And everybody was pretty drunk. So, it doesn't have to have been on purpose. It could have been some kind of a dare that got out of control."

55

"Except," Earl told him, "that he hadn't had anything to drink. That seems strange."

"Yes, it does," Herb agreed. "The whole thing seems strange."

Earl held out his hand. Herb shook it. For the first time he realized that he had destroyed part of his life: from that point onward all mention of the incident, or the time surrounding it, would call up the fabricated substitute: the safe, untrue version.

There was worse to come. After a week, Herb and Sherman began to feel that the two guilty ones—the ones who had really wanted all along to kill Carmen—were Joe and Dave. And Joe and Dave felt that though they were all in it equally, the others were looking at them in a funny way and not really backing them up.

Bill started to have nightmares, or rather, one particular bad dream that kept repeating. In it, he was walking along without any worries until suddenly he came to the edge of a cliff he hadn't noticed at all, and he began to slide towards it. He started to go faster and faster, until he fell over the edge, waking up in terror. He went to the other four for help, but they only told him to relax and forget about everything. Dave gave him some sleeping pills a girlfriend had let him have. They didn't work when they were supposed to, but knocked him out the next day, taking effect so quickly that Bill said he was scared about what they must be doing to his brain. He stopped taking them, lost weight, and developed a nervous twitch in his chin. He said that all he could think about was that they were going to get caught, and then they'd be in a lot more trouble than they would have been if they'd reported the accident straight away. It was, he said, like hit-and-run drivers.

The five of them had many urgent, whispered arguments. Bill sat with his hands squeezing and squirming together while the others told him that if only he could pull himself together enough to get through the next couple of weeks, he'd be able to go away for the summer as usual, and from then on everything would be easy.

56

Suddenly the final exams were on top of them. Even Bill put aside the memory of Carmen. They all got through some-how. And afterwards, Herb called a meeting. He said they'd have to face it: they'd have to be careful. For the rest of their lives they would never be able to go on a real bender, in case they spilled the truth. They'd never be able to let their guard down completely with anybody—not with a girl, not even if they got married. You could never tell when somebody else would repeat a thing, and no one had the right to put the others in danger like that. "It's going to be hard," he said. "I hadn't realized how much I'd want to talk about it to some-one who'd be sympathetic and make it all right. But I'm telling you—never. Not to a doctor or your mother, or anybody. Think it over and you'll see I'm right."

They thought about the matter all summer long. They changed towards each other. It wasn't exactly that they began to think of the others with hatred, but the friendship was broken. Herb and Sherman still liked each other, as did Dave and Joe. But Bill ended up on the outside of both groups.

In the fall they all asked for different roommates. And right after college, they all moved away from town. It took several years before any of them wanted to come back.

.   .   .

Of course they told other people about it. Twenty years is a long time and it's possible to describe an accident as if you had been on the sidelines, rather than saying: *I helped to kill somebody*.

They told their wives. And their versions of the incident made it seem like a practical joke gone wrong, a group disaster that had taken place while alcohol had temporarily removed everyone's responsibility. By the time they were married, the event had decreased in importance, anyway. It had ceased to frighten them because of possible consequences, but it had also lost its power to make them afraid of themselves.

Only Bill was different. He didn't marry. He lost touch for many years. He never—so he said to them later—told any-one. He lived with the memory until he couldn't stand it any longer, and then he broke. What finally did it was the years he spent in South America.

He was working as an adviser on government agricultural schemes. Men he had known well would be missing from their jobs one morning and he'd assume that they had been arrested either by the police or the army, or a semi-official government organization—guerrilla fighters or small city groups of terrorists who had been at the receiving end of the official murder and torture squads. During his last two years, foreigners were particularly at risk, Americans more than others.

Perhaps Bill himself was left alone because he was withdrawn, didn't speak much, didn't have many friends. He had no religious thoughts, either—at least, he wasn't aware of having any, nor at that time did he have a regular girlfriend. Women had stopped wanting to know him at about the time when he had lost the ability to take part in his own life. He said later that it was like being a sleepwalker.

He was woken up by his sense of danger. Fear was all around; it was shining out of the streets. He knew all at once that if he stayed, they'd get him no matter how innocuous he appeared. Political groups like the ones around him were entirely uninterested in who was innocent or guilty, and of what. They were only intent on producing more fear. The falling-dream he'd had years before gave way to one in which people pounded on the door and called his name: coming to get him, as he and his friends had gone to get Carmen and found him naked.

He wasn't so completely panic-stricken that he was ready to abandon all his belongings. He spent two hours making arrangements to leave, telephoning packing companies, the bank, his employers. He told everyone that his parents—who had died five years before—were in the hospital, were badly injured and needed him to be with them immediately and take care of them for a while.

At the airport he was shaking all over. The fear was worse than anything he'd known before. He was prepared now to go to an ordinary American jail and give up a few years of his life; but to be beaten, tortured and humiliated was something he realized he wasn't going to be able to live through. He still had something of himself to lose; if it went, he wouldn't be human any more.

He had the jitters all during the plane trip. When they put down in Texas, he stood by one of the airport watercoolers and drank one paper cup of water after another. He collected his suitcases and sat in the airport for two hours. He had no idea where he should go.

At last he grew hungry, had a meal in one of the airport cafeterias and decided to take a bus out of town.

He spent over twenty-four hours on different buses. In the end, he couldn't go any farther. He sat down at a bus stop in the middle of a small town he'd never seen before, and collapsed.

He wasn't very loud. The tears poured silently over his cheeks. He sighed and swallowed and put his hands over his face.

After a short while someone laid a hand on his shoulder. A woman's voice said, "Are you in trouble?"

He gulped and breathed in. "I'm at the end," he told her.

"We're never at the end," she said. "You tell me about it."

He told her everything. He started to talk long before he had taken a look at her and seen how lovely she was, and with what sympathy she listened to everything—not just the death of Carmen back in his college days, but even before that: his family, and never being able to do anything right or get anywhere in life.

She listened to the whole recital with interest and understanding. He couldn't believe there were still people in the world who were nice like that—who would come up and try to help you and not be sure that you'd turn out to be a maniac or a bore or a swindler.

Her name was Nancy. She told him that he had suffered so much because he had tried to live a lie, and that God wanted to give him the chance to live with the truth and to be a free man. When he was free, he would be happy.

.   .   .

Herb wondered how many of the others had told someone, and who it had been. Maybe they had told more than one person. For him, once had been enough: it had relieved the pressure, and after that the memory moved away from him so quickly that though the facts were still there, he thought about the episode as if it had been something he'd once seen on television. He no longer had any sense that it had happened to him; it might even have been someone else's story told to him in a bar somewhere, but with such vividness and detail that he could imagine it was his own story.

He had told his first wife, Elaine. He hadn't mentioned his fear or guilt or the sense of shame and remorse that had come over him later; nor had he said anything about the occasional patches of dread he went through when he began to feel that some day everything was going to catch up with him. He gave her an unadorned but biased account and she had said what he had hoped to hear: that it was a accident and he shouldn't brood about it; he was being too conscientious, too good. She made him think that nothing bad would develop from the death because he didn't deserve to have bad things happen to him.

He hadn't stressed the danger he had felt himself to be in. And he didn't think any of the others—if they had talked—would have. That was an important point. Divorced wives could be vicious about not getting their alimony on time. It was possible, for example, that while not exactly blackmailing a man, you could let him know that you still remembered something he'd told you. Dave's first wife might be like that, or Joe's—except that Joe wouldn't have told a wife; it would have been more likely for him to tell a friend from his combat unit. And Sherman, dearly as he loved his wife he'd stayed with all these years, would probably have chosen one of his brothers, or a cousin.

So far, there had been no consequences. And if Bill went to the police now, the four of them could get together and say he'd always been crazy, or they could tell the truth and say it was an unpleasant accident. He didn't really think they'd be put in jail. Their youth, drunkenness and shock would be taken into account, as well as the fact that all of them had led respectable lives afterwards and had families to protect. Bill was the only one who didn't have children.

He didn't think the worst would happen, but it was just as well to look ahead. Dave, he thought, would do anything to avoid publicity. He was an advertising man, who knew the value of appearances; he lived by them. A spell behind bars would be the end of him. He might not take any action himself, but he'd back up anyone else who did.

Joe was the one to watch. He could be likable and charming, he could be a good friend. But he was stupid in so many different ways that you had to spend a lot of time putting things to him all dressed up, so that he wouldn't take offense or think you meant something else, or just get mad. He was also violent and his stint in the marines, when he was actually killing people every day as a job, hadn't driven the violence out of his system, only turned it into a routine.

When he thought about Joe, it seemed to Herb that he wouldn't be able to predict what would happen, even though he knew that Joe had a fear, a real mania, about being imprisoned or captured or in any way physically constrained. On the other hand, he did know about Sherman. Sherman, if he had to, would face the music. He wasn't really afraid of scandal or what other people thought. His family was right at the top. They could do just about anything and come out of it still admired. People would think he'd kept quiet only to save the others. No one would think badly of Sherman. Herb himself had always looked up to him, and still did.

Sherman would never raise his own hand against Bill. But would he allow somebody else to? That was going to be a tricky point. They had all heard Joe talk about killing. Not all of them would have taken it seriously. Herb did. He knew that Joe meant it, and would do it. And afterwards? Could you count on someone who was so ready to kill? And could you be sure that Sherman or even Dave might not go to the police? Whatever happened now, it wouldn't be the same as a drunken brawl.

As far as Herb was concerned, there had been a point after which the line was drawn and he decided: it must never be known that he was implicated in Carmen's death, or had even known anything about it. That point had come very early, at the moment when Carmen's uncle, Earl, had shaken his hand. He didn't understand why he felt so strongly, or what had happened to him at the time; but he knew that he wouldn't go back on that handshake. He had to be, forever afterwards, a man who was believed to be innocent.

He took his wife, Sue, out to dinner and talked about plans for the summer—what the children wanted to do, whether they'd visit her mother at the end of June or in September. The night was cool, though a warm spell had been promised. In another couple of months it would be coming up to nineteen years since Carmen had gone over the roof.

She said, "Everything in the garden's late this year. I'm sure it's making people depressed."

"Who's depressed?"

"Just about everybody I know except you. The weather's so important, even for people who aren't farmers or gardeners. There's a lot of truth in that biological clock theory."

"Keep winding it up every day?"

"You know what I mean. It's important to our state of mind. Light and dark, when we feel good, when we feel scared."

"But not so important as other things."

"Well, it's basic."

"The weather can be overcome. Unless you're making your living out of something that depends on it. It's less important to your moods than a good meal or a drink, or being with people you like, or having a broken arm or noisy neighbors, or feeling crowded, or—"

"All right, Herb," she said. "I'm not taking it to the Supreme Court."

It was his turn to drive the babysitter home. Her name was Cheryl and she paid him the great compliment of removing her Walkman earphones in the car; when Sue was driving, she kept them on. Between themselves, they called her Miss Sunshine, because she always looked so miserable. She seemed half asleep too, but if you could get her to talk to you, she usually had something intelligent to say.

He said, "Seen any movies lately?"

"A couple."

He asked her about them. She'd seen a science-fiction fable for children, a weepie comedy-drama about charming kooks, and a story about lust and adultery which he knew she was too young to have been allowed to see.

"I saw that one too," he said. "I guess that was a pretty good plot for a perfect murder."

"But they get her in the end. I didn't like that. I thought she was so smart she should have gotten away with it."

"Well, she escaped to—wherever it was. A different country."

"They get her with an extradition order. They can do that for murder."

"Don't be too sure. She had all that money. She could buy her way out."

"Maybe. I didn't think of that."

"Does that make you feel better about it?"

She laughed. "It's only a story," she said. "I just get mad when I keep seeing all this stuff on TV and everyplace where the women are always getting punished for practically breathing."

"Is this Women's Lib or a desire for poetic justice?"

"Poetic justice is the other way around. That's when they don't get away with it."

"Is it? I thought it meant happy endings. How would you commit the perfect murder?"

"I wouldn't plan it out too carefully."

"Why not?"

"You plan it too much, and if something goes wrong, the plan isn't any good, so what you should do is forget about it and do it some other time. But what everybody does is: they go ahead with the busted plan. Then something else in it goes wrong and finally it's a mess, the whole thing, and you're stuck with it."

"So how would you do it the right way?"

"That depends on whether I'd be a suspect or not. It's hard to murder anybody who's in your family, or an enemy, or a husband or wife."

"I guess so."

"Or if you'd gain from it—you know, if they'd left you something in their will."

63

"I guess it would be safer to be alone, too. Or for nobody to suspect you had a connection with the other person."

"Oh, you'd have to be on your own. Of course. And also, you'd have to choose your method."

"Like what?"

"Make it look like an accident. That's the best way."

"But not always easy to get an opportunity if you don't live with the person." He turned the car in to the street where she lived and stopped outside the house. "So, how would you do it?"

"I'd follow them around, and the first minute nobody was looking, I'd just run up and biff them over the head with a brick or something."

"That could take years," he said.

It could take a long time, and before you even started, you'd have to be willing to kill. Could he really do it? It had been bad enough the first time, when he hadn't actually been guilty of plotting a death, only of what was called manslaughter. This time, if he did anything, it would be murder. But, in his opinion, it would also be self-defense.

. . .

Dave picked Herb up on the street corner. It was raining lightly. As Herb got into the car, Dave said, "OK?"

"All set." Herb slammed the door. They moved off. "What about the place?"

"It's perfect, completely isolated. The builders finished last week. It's already bought. All the furniture's there, kitchen working, pipes hooked up, the whole deal. Two of the houses are still unsold, but they're way at the other side. Anybody who wants to look at them has to go with somebody from the firm."

"That's the kind of brother to have."

"He thought first of all I wanted it to fix something up with a girl."

"You need a whole house for that?"

"I got some food and liquor."

"Fine. You tell us how much it was, and we'll pay our share."

"This is on me," Dave told him. "I put it down on the squeeze-sheet, anyway."

It started to rain heavily. Herb wiped the palms of his hands over his thighs. He said, "Have you seen them yet?"

"No. Sherman's bringing them."

"He knows the way OK?"

"We all did some dry runs the past few days. That's all right. The only thing I'm nervous about is Joe. He's going crazy. He wanted to go get them straight off the plane. He's afraid they'll talk to somebody."

"We're the ones they want to talk to. They want to tell us why it's going to be good for our souls to do time in the State Pen. Jesus."

"I kept telling him: they could have talked to hundreds of people before they left their place. They could have told their whole religious club."

"And maybe they did. But I doubt that they'd give last names."

"They could look up the register of who was rooming in the same house with him sophomore year."

"Well, what do you think?"

"I think we're going to have to stop them."

"And how do we do that?"

"If it's necessary, an accident."

"That's what everybody always says. I've been going around in circles trying to come up with some idea. Seems to me that's the hardest way to do it. What kind of accident did you have in mind?"

"Car crash?"

"How?"

"They rent a car—"

"They aren't going to need one. But say we could talk them into it, then we've got the Hertz people and the insurance and everybody in on it. Police experts measuring the tire marks. That's no good."

"I don't know why we're talking like this. I'm sure we can persuade them. Especially the girl. She's bound to understand how it would affect the children."

Herb opened his side window a notch and wiped the back

of his hand down the windshield, where the glass was misting up. He said, "You're right, it's no use talking about it."

The other cars were waiting for them by the entrance of the estate. Dave honked his horn as they approached. He turned off on to the newly tarred drive. At the gatehouse he let down his window, leaned out and said to the guard inside, "Hi, Charlie. It's OK." Charlie waved his hand. The three cars moved on, coming to the end of the hard surface in the middle of a pine grove and reaching the old rocky dirt road, muddy from all the rain. They went slowly.

Dave pulled up outside the front walk of the house. Tall pine trees, which the architects had insisted on preserving, screened the other houses from them. The front lawn had been seeded with grass that was already growing. There were several bushes dotted around the brick walk.

They got out of the cars and raced for the house through the downpour. Dave unlocked the door with his keys and held it open for the others.

Everything was there: welcome mat outside, one inside to wipe your feet on, a stand for umbrellas, curtains on all the windows, new rugs wall-to-wall, lights and lamps, tables and chests of drawers, chairs and sofas covered in materials chosen to match the rugs and curtains.

Dave took the coats and said, "Go on in and sit down. Sherman, get everybody a drink."

"Gee, this is nice," the girl said. Herb looked at Joe, who had his face bent over the coat he was handing to Dave; he looked as if he were trying to concentrate on something different from his surroundings, trying to remember a phone number or repeating something to himself.

Dave went into the kitchen. The rest of them entered the living room. Sherman introduced everyone. He started with Joe, who put his hands in his pockets and said, "Hi, Bill."

The girl stuck out her hand to be taken by him. Joe ignored it.

"This is my wife, Nancy," Bill said. "Aren't you going to shake hands?"

"What for? You're the ones planning to send me to jail,

aren't you? That's going to be fun. A lot of fun for my wife and kids, too."

"Oh, I don't think it'll come to that," the girl said. "And if it did, it wouldn't be for very long." She had a flutey, pleading voice that went with her appearance: very thin, pale, with thin, mousy hair parted in the middle and dripping down her back; a narrow, almost noseless white face and eyes so light that the blue or gray seemed nearer to white. She looked undernourished, almost ill; or, if you wanted to think of it that way, ethereal. The expression on her face was sweet and enthusiastic, although not relaxed. She stood in a nervous way, too. Joe disregarded her. He walked into the kitchen by the other door.

Herb stepped forward. "Hello, Bill," he said. "It's been a long time." He held out his hand, knowing what he was doing. He'd thought about it ahead of time and he didn't mind.

"Sure has," Bill said. He took Herb's hand in a dry, desperate grip. "My wife, Nancy," he added.

Herb shook her hand, too. It was cold, reminding him of his first wife, who had always had cold hands, even—like this—in the spring; it was probably a matter of poor circulation. But she also failed to give any kind of returning pressure. She offered him the limp hand like a dead fish, and then tried to remove it quickly. He let her go, but smiled. He'd been careful not to hold on too hard. She returned the smile beatifically. He was puzzled. Most of the newly converted people he'd met went out of their way to pump everyone's hand like politicians. She had the fervor, all right, but she appeared to be averse to physical contact. He wondered if she was really, seriously, ill.

"And a new wife," he said. "A lot of water under the bridge."

Bill rose on his toes a couple of times and grinned. "Best thing ever happened to me," he said. He must have gone gray very early. He looked at least ten years older than the rest of them, and thin, and fairly bloodless, although nothing like his wife. That was what a clear conscience did for you.

Or maybe, Herb thought, they were on some kind of religious diet.

Dave came in from the kitchen, followed by Joe. They were both carrying trays. Dave nodded, said, "Hi, Bill. Hi, Nancy," and looked for a place to set things down. "What'll you have?" he asked.

"We don't drink alcohol," Nancy said. "Do you have any mineral water?"

"Tonic water."

"That's artificially sweetened, and it contains drugs."

"Drugs?"

"Quinine. Maybe just plain water."

"We've got tomato juice."

"That's got additives, too. It's artificial."

"Just plain, ordinary water out of the faucet?"

"That'll be fine," she said.

"Ice?" Dave asked. He was smiling a special, polite smile he used for idiots. Herb wondered if Bill would remember it. Probably not; he was beaming at the girl like a man who'd been hypnotized.

She did her own welcome smile back and said yes, please, ice would be wonderful. Joe's eyes flicked over to Herb; he looked as if he'd had a couple of stiff drinks out in the kitchen. So did Dave. Both of them were building up for an outburst or something—anger or laughter.

"Well, let's sit down," Sherman said. He mixed drinks for himself and Herb and sat in a comfortable chair that stood a little way removed from the surrounding furniture.

Herb said, "Well, it's nice of you two to come on out and get acquainted, let us talk everything over, put our point of view."

Nancy and Bill simpered. She turned to Dave and asked, "Where's your wife?"

"She's at the old house. I thought Sherm said: we haven't even moved in yet. It's going to take a couple more months still. I've just been using the place for entertaining clients, till we get organized."

"Oh," she said. She leaned forward and clasped her knees.

"You want to meet our families?" Joe yelled. "Jesus Christ.

Isn't it enough for you, you got us by the balls—you want to put the rest of them through it, too?"

The girl went gray. Herb, Sherman and Dave shouted at Joe.

He didn't pay any attention. "Me shut up?" he went on. "Why the hell should I?"

Herb stood up. "Joe," he ordered. "Just go sit it out in the kitchen for a while, will you?" He crossed the room and put his hand on Joe's shoulder. Nobody spoke. "Come on," Herb whispered. Joe stood up. They went into the kitchen together.

.   .   .

Herb held a finger to his lips. They could hear Sherman smoothing things over behind them. Herb pulled Joe over to a counter lined with stools. He pushed him down on one of the straw-woven seats.

"We aren't going to win against that one," Joe whispered. "I recognize the type. Power trip. She's got this thing in her head like a rear end, that just won't give up. Look at her: no tits, no ass—he's the one guy she could get. Old enough to be her father, too. Religion, my foot. She's just another ball-breaker, that's all."

"OK, OK," Herb said.

"Listen, you give me the word and I'm ready to do it, right now. Just go in there and chop them both."

"Let's see what we can do by talking," Herb said.

"Oh, nobody ever—"

"Hang on. Wait. We don't know yet. This may be a blind. They may be planning to hit us for a little loan, right? Wait till we know. If it's no good, I'm with you. I'm only worried about making it look good. We've got to be able to explain everything afterwards."

"Screw that. Knock them out, take them home to my place, cut 'em up with a power saw and feed the pieces into the disposal, burn the bones in the back yard."

"I guess Cathy's going to love that."

"I'll fix Cathy."

"We've got to plan it."

"You all are so worried about plans," Joe hissed, "you're

69

never going to do it. Let's do it first and worry about it afterwards, for Christ's sake."

"We'll see," Herb told him. "You stay here for a while."

He went back into the living room. Dave was talking about how the city had changed since their college days.

They all looked up. Herb took his drink from the table and sat back down. He said, "I guess you must have thought about this before you came. You don't have a family yet, but we do. All of us. We haven't told our wives. And we don't want to. It was only an accident, after all."

"We killed him," Bill said. "You can't get away from that. I tried for years to forget about it, but it wasn't any good. I don't understand how you can feel this way: just—let it go, think it was something trivial. That boy died, and we killed him. It was a terrible thing. I know now that it was the most important event in my life."

"But not in ours, Bill," Sherman said. "Herb's right. It was an accident."

"Maybe on the surface. But if it was really so accidental, why didn't we go to the police afterwards?"

"Because that would have been extremely unpleasant for us and for everyone connected with us; and we thought we could get away with not having to."

"And we were right," Dave added, "until you changed your mind."

"It was a change of mind and a change of heart, too. I kept having that dream again, falling."

"That was a metaphor," Nancy said delicately, "for sin."

"I kept remembering, too. That night. It was a beautiful night. Trying to keep him from hitting us, holding him tight. He didn't have any clothes on. All that noise from Rockwell's. And the smell of the trees, leaves."

"And you were drunk out of your mind," Dave said.

"I was so drunk I was ready to do anything. Really excited, and I hated him. I was ready to throw him over. I wanted to."

"You were giggling drunk," Herb said, "and then crying drunk. You weren't doing much of anything at all, either to help or to harm."

70

"It was a long time before I knew what a horrible thing it was. Then I felt pity. A young life like that."

"In the abstract," Dave said. "In the particular, he was a son of a bitch and we all thought so."

Joe came in from the kitchen and sat on the arm of the sofa opposite Bill and Nancy.

"It wasn't right," Bill said. "I had the feelings of a murderer."

"But not the deed," Sherman told him.

"I also had an erection. That made it worse."

"He remembers," Joe said, "every time he gets one. That must have been a red-letter day. Dear Diary: guess what happened today?"

"Joe?" Sherman said.

"We got to listen to this? He just wants to keep confessing till he runs out of listeners. He isn't going to be happy till it's in the papers. Public confession. You'll see. Just wait."

"We killed him," Bill said.

Nancy put a hand on his arm and said, "He's right. You know he is."

"How old are you?" Herb asked.

"Twenty-two," she said.

"And you don't have children. But we do. Think of our children."

Her face became transformed, as though something had been poured into it. "That's just what I'm thinking about," she told him.

Bill said, "Nancy's had more experience with children than any of you. She used to teach handicapped kids."

"Now she's stuck on handicapped grownups," Joe said.

"How would you like," she asked Herb, "those poor children to know their daddies were murderers?"

"It wasn't murder," Dave said. "Quit using that word. It was an accident. And nobody's going to know about it unless you tell."

"And," Herb added, "their suffering would be on your head. You'd be responsible for it. Why would you want to bring that on our families? If you don't tell, they won't know."

71

"When you tell the truth," she said, "they'll know you were big enough to own up."

Joe threw his glass across the room. It hit the side of the coffee table with a loud crack. Bill and Nancy recoiled into the cushions.

Joe shouted, "Oh, you dumb namby-pamby bitch!"

Bill jumped up. "You always did hate women," he said, "and anybody that had decent feelings. Anybody who's even slightly above your level."

Dave and Herb started to haul Joe out into the kitchen again. "It makes me sick," he said as they pulled him along. "You're going to tell me what's good for me while you ruin my life. To make you feel the truth's been told and everything's all nice and clean now, you bastards."

Bill called after them, "You always were an oaf." He sat back down and put his arm around Nancy.

She said to Sherman, "I think we'd better be going soon."

"So do I," he said, "but let's give it about fifteen minutes more. We'll talk about something else while they straighten themselves out, out there. Don't be too hard on Joe. He went through a pretty hard time in Vietnam."

"He was always like that," Bill said.

"I don't think so. He was very good to his family. He worked hard all through college, remember? And kept sending money home to help his mother and sister. He's a little unruly, but not as bad as you think."

"He was always like this," Bill repeated primly. "A violent man."

"We're all violent, Bill."

"No."

"Yes. We try to keep it reined in, that's all. To control it, and to put it to use. It's energy, and energy can be a good thing. All the vices can be used. Greed, for instance—greed can build a prosperous land out of nothing but forests and plains. It's the making of any frontier country."

"I don't know what you're talking about."

"I'm talking about tolerance. I think you should let other people lead their lives according to their own standards."

"We killed him. Whether it was conscious and deliberate or subconsciously desired and not admitted—that doesn't matter. Either way, he's dead."

"Of course it matters," Sherman said. "They're two entirely different things. Even the law distinguishes between kinds and degrees of motive."

"But does God?" Nancy asked.

"Well, as to that, God's got a tougher job. He's supposed to forgive everybody everything."

"Only if you repent," she said. She hitched herself forward eagerly. Once more her face became transfigured by the intensity of her beliefs. She said, "I know you're all afraid, but you don't realize—there isn't anything to fear. This is going to be a good thing. It isn't going to be easy, but when it's over, you'll be clean. You'll be free."

"We'll be in jail. We're free now."

"I mean, in your hearts. Better a free man in jail than a guilty one outside. Bill knows that."

"But Bill was that way before the accident."

"What?"

"How's that?" Bill said.

"You reacted that way because you brought it with you. When Carmen died, that just gave you something to pin it all onto. You know what I'm talking about."

"But I've straightened all that out now. And she's right. You can't be free if you're living a lie. I know you're scared of the publicity and all that. But the truth is more important "

"To whom?"

"To God," Nancy said.

"Well, God knows the truth already, and if you'll forgive me saying so, God isn't going to get thrown in the slammer and neither are you. The rest of us are in a better position to talk about how we feel about truth."

"God—"

"That's another thing. The god you keep talking about is your god, isn't that right? It might not be mine."

"Oh, He would be," she pleaded, "if only you'd open your

73

heart to Him." She held out her arms in a stagey gesture. She looked half-demented.

Sherman said, "That's going to take a lot longer than fifteen minutes."

"We'll stay," she said. "We've got all the time in the world for that. That's the truly important part. What does life hold for any of us, without the spiritual side?"

. . .

In the kitchen Herb moved the bottle away from Joe. Dave lit a cigarette and said, "I can't do anything against a girl like that. She's so frail and helpless. She's like a child. I hadn't expected her to be so pretty."

Joe snorted. "That whiney, rabbit-faced woman—you call that pretty?"

"Are we going to go to jail for the rest of our lives," Herb asked, "because she's pretty?"

"It won't come to that."

"Near enough. Whatever it comes to, they're both in it together."

"I couldn't."

"It's up to you, Dave. You know what it means if we don't stop them."

"If we all go to the police together—"

"Jesus, are you dumb," Joe said. "We aren't going to get away with this till we've been washed in the blood of the lamb and had the baptism of fire and all the rest of that crap. She's off her head. And she's got him right where she wants him."

Dave shook his head.

"I know what you mean," Herb told him. "I actually think she's the best thing that ever happened to him, like he said, only it's extremely unfortunate that we all have to get dragged in, too. She should have been willing to stick with just one."

"I can do it," Joe said. "I can do it tonight and I can do it right now. I've got everything."

"What?" Dave said.

"Knives, monkey wrench, couple of guns I brought back."

"No."

Herb said, "Dave, if you and Sherm could hold the fort here for a couple of hours, we'll take Bill and Nancy for a little sightseeing."

"In the rain? In the dark?"

Joe smiled.

"You don't have to do anything," Herb said. "Just keep Sherman happy. Get him to talk about their trip to Hong Kong." He stood up. "You go back first. I want a word with Joe."

Dave looked at his cigarette. He took three quick puffs, a long drag, and stubbed out what was left. He got up and went into the living room.

Herb stared at the door for a moment.

Joe said, "OK. How do you want me to do it?"

"Do you have a shovel?"

"Two. We knock them out, beat up the faces, take off the fingertips."

"Afterwards—what do we do about checking them out of their hotel, packing up their stuff, and so on?"

"We go in and pack it all up, take it away. Don't bother to check them out. We could be recognized later. Let the hotel think they've been bilked."

"We shouldn't have put them in a hotel in the first place. I didn't think."

"It doesn't matter. Main thing is, to do something about it. Not tomorrow: tonight. Now."

Herb hesitated. He had drunk enough to be confident about carrying out any scheme successfully, but he had also reached the stage where he thought he was having important revelations about life, becoming aware of things he'd never thought of before. He understood, for instance, for the first time that what had been so hard for Joe about the war was coming back to a place where he'd no longer be able to kill. He'd been trained for it, it was something he was good at, and suddenly nobody would let him do it. Or maybe he had killed people. Who could tell? There were always unsolved crimes. Joe seemed easy and relaxed now; now that he'd made his decision, he was looking forward to carrying it out.

Herb realized that he was breathing too quickly and sweating a lot. He thought that even if the whole plan went without a hitch, Joe couldn't be trusted. Because if he was the one to do the killing, he'd know that the others could give him away. And he'd wonder if they were asking themselves about him. Could you ever depend on a killer?

He felt his insides winding up tighter and tighter. There was no way to avoid what was coming. "OK," he said. "Count me in."

"Right. You drive left, go all the way down the side behind the houses that aren't finished yet. There isn't anybody around now. You drive into the woods there and stop when I tell you."

They went back to the living room, where Dave was talking about deafness, speech impediments and the parents of what Bill was calling "disadvantaged" children. He stopped when the others looked towards the door.

Herb said, "Well, it's getting late now and there's still a lot to talk about. I'd really appreciate it if you could come back tomorrow and continue the discussion. I sort of feel maybe we should get our families in on it, too."

"I think that would be a very good idea," Nancy said fervently. "I've thought that right from the beginning."

"Yes," Bill said.

"Right. Joe and I can take you back to town. Sherm and Dave, if you could clear up here, we'll see you later."

Everyone stood up. Joe was the only one who didn't say anything. Nancy and Bill didn't appear to like the idea of getting into a car with him, but the fact that Herb was there too seemed to make it all right.

"Well," Nancy said. "Well, it's been nice meeting you. I'll look forward to our next discussion."

. . .

Herb drove. Nancy and Bill sat in the front seat with him, Nancy on the outside. Joe was in the back.

The rain had eased off to a light drizzle. Herb took the path to the side and drove as Joe had directed.

"Is this the way we came in?" Bill asked.

"No," Herb said. "This way's supposed to get us out on

to a quicker way home." He kept going until the car wallowed through the mud into a clearing.

"OK, Herb," Joe said.

He stopped the car, keeping the lights on and the windshield wipers working.

Joe leaned forward over Bill's neck. "Out," he said. "We're going to talk some more."

Bill said, "No, we've talked enough." His voice was quavery.

Joe said, "Son of a bitch," and there was an explosion that threw Herb against the door. It took him a moment to realize that Joe had shot Bill in the back of the head. The bullet had gone through, drilling a hole in the safety glass in front and spraying blood and brains all over the inside of the car. The smell was like something out of a cage in the zoo. Herb opened his door and tumbled into the rain and fresh air. Nancy, on the other side, was screaming and trying to get her door open.

It wasn't what they had planned. The agreement had been for Joe to get the two out at gunpoint while Herb brought the shovels from the trunk; to threaten them with the gun in order to make them dig, and then afterwards shoot one apiece, dump them in, and cover them up. If they wouldn't both dig, Joe would threaten Nancy, to make Bill do the work, and Herb would take the second shovel.

"You want out?" he heard Joe saying. "OK, sweetheart."

Herb leaned over the hood of the car. He thought he was going to be sick. He could hear the two of them fighting, Joe beating her across the face with the pistol barrel while she tried to kick him and break free. Then there was a clunk as the gun was put down on the car, next to Herb's head.

He looked up. One of the headlights blazed into the rows of pine trees. The light from the other one came and went as Joe forced Nancy across the front bumper. He hit her in the face again twice and started to rip her clothes away. He shrieked at her, "This is going to be the best thing that ever happened to you."

Herb watched, dazed, as Joe tore off her skirt and slip and, still yelling at her, began to pull at her tights and underpants. Her arms made tentative pushing motions like those of a child in sleep, but she was barely trying to defend herself. She moved her blood-smeared face jerkily from side to side. Herb thought as he caught sight of her misshapen profile that her lips must be cut, her nose and some of her teeth broken. He reached for the pistol by his hand, felt that the safety catch was on, pushed it up, and held the barrel to Joe's forehead. Joe didn't look up; he called out, "Piss off—you can have her next." Herb pulled the trigger.

It was just like the movies, only louder. Joe spun backwards and down to the side and Nancy collapsed on top of him, whimpering.

He checked the gun. He put it inside the car on the front seat. He went around to the opposite side and got hold of Joe, dragging him to where he could heave him into the back seat. When he returned for Nancy, she hadn't moved. Her skirt and slip were lying in the mud. The coat she was still wearing was streaked and sodden. He shook out the skirt and slip, took them back to the car and started to clean up the inside of the windshield with them. Then he went back to get her.

He pushed her into the back with Joe, got into the front seat, turned around, and put the gun to her head. She opened her eyes and stopped crying. She said in an almost voiceless screech, "I'll never tell. Let me go and I'll never tell, so help me."

Of course she'd tell. She had started the whole business because all her thoughts had to be referred to an outside agency. She was incapable of judging a thing according to itself, only according to the rulebook, to the instructions her god was supposed to have laid down about the conduct of human affairs. She had never killed anybody—she just forced other people to kill. If he let her go, it would happen all over again. He shot her without thinking twice about it.

He drove back to the part of the site where their house was. It was the only one that had any lights on. He stopped for a minute to try to figure out what he should do first and whether he should drive home in Dave's car, whether he'd have to kill the security man at the entrance, whether he could walk back to town.

He decided to go back in Dave's car and take a chance that the man at the gate would recognize the car, and not him.

There was no other way he could cover himself. He had to have one of the cars to get back—that was certain. What else? He had to be safe afterwards. Sherman: he could count on Sherman, but not on Dave. There were three dead people now, and no way to stop Dave yelling about it. Herb could hear how it would sound: *I had nothing to do with this. I don't want any part of it.* He, Herb, would be standing there covered in mud, rain and blood, and the perfect person to take responsibility for everything, past and present.

But, if he did anything to Dave, Sherman wouldn't stand for it.

He started the car up again and drove it slowly forward, cut the engine, got out and let it roll down the incline towards the front of the house. He took the pistol with him and let himself in the front door.

He went through the hall, into the living room. Dave jumped up, saying, "Jesus, Herb. You scared me."

Herb circled around to the back of Sherman's chair. Sherman was his friend, the one he'd always liked best. He put the pistol to the back of Sherman's head and, as Sherman was about to turn, fired.

Dave screamed, "Herb, what are you doing? What are you doing?"

Herb said, "I can't figure out any other way, Dave." He came closer. He couldn't remember how many bullets ought to be left and he couldn't afford to miss. Dave was still too shocked to move away. He'd stood up, that was all. He had one hand on the arm of his chair. The other still held his glass and a cigarette.

Herb walked straight up to him. He said, "Just stay that way for a minute," as if he were a photographer, put the pistol against Dave's temple, and squeezed the trigger.

After that, he went crazy. He knew he had to hurry before anyone came, before he could be caught. He panted and talked to himself, his teeth chattered. He worried about all the noise there had been.

He threw the patio doors wide and drove both cars into

the living room, took the other keys from Dave's pocket, wiped his prints off the steering wheels and anything else he could remember touching, poured gasolene all over the rug and furniture and bodies, and spent nearly five minutes looking for Dave's cigarette lighter, which he finally found in the kitchen.

Everything looked ready. His eyes went around the living room, around and around. It looked all right.

He opened the front door, flicked on the flame, and threw the lighter into the room. Then he slammed the door and ran.

He was behind the wheel of the car and driving away within seconds. The light came up in the driving mirror and he could hear the glass go from the windows of the house. The place would burn for hours. And it probably hadn't yet been connected to any kind of alarm system.

The road going out was even worse than when they'd driven in. He approached the entrance booth cautiously. As far as he could see, the guard was still in his box; no warning had gone through. But the man wanted to talk to him. Herb pretended that he hadn't seen; he raised his hand in greeting, eased the car forward, then lowered his head and stepped on the gas.

The wheels gripped on the gravel beneath the mud and shot him ahead. He raced the car down to the highway and kept going for a long time at top speed. There was no one else around. He dodged down a few side lanes and made his way back to town by a different route. He was surprised at how well he remembered the old roads from his college days. He remembered lots of things from those times as he drove; they seemed to have come from someone else's life, not from his.

He parked the car in town, wiped the wheel, and examined his face in the mirror. He took the subway back to his hotel for a shave and a shower, checked out, got a cab to the airport and left for home.

On the plane he sat next to a girl who had brought two tennis racquets with her, which she'd stowed away in one of the top compartments. She kept asking Herb to get up, so she could see that no one put any heavy briefcases on top of them.

"You want the aisle seat?" he asked.

"If you don't mind."

"It's fine by me, but I think it's OK now. We're all packed up."

She said, "It's just so easy to damage them and it costs a lot to have them restrung. And they're never the same afterwards, no matter what they tell you. It's like putting new soles on a pair of shoes—it never works. They don't feel right. Not to me, anyway."

"Are you going to play in the tournaments?" he asked.

"No, just people to people."

"That can be the most dangerous kind."

"Why?"

"No rules."

She laughed. The rules, she said, were the same for amateurs as for professionals. "The only difference is that you're with your friends. And with your friends—well, you know where you are, don't you?"

"Exactly," he said.

INHERITANCE

When Carla's marriage broke up, everyone from her father's branch of the family felt obliged to load her with so much pity and advice that she didn't think she'd be able to last out the summer with them. Sometimes their kindness made her feel even worse: her Aunt Grace, for instance, had laid a hand on her arm and told her not to mind: time would heal the wound, and besides, think of how much worse it could have been—she might have had children.

When her grandmother died, that put the lid on it. She'd loved her grandmother. They'd always been able to talk together, rattling along like schoolfriends. In the last months of her life, her grandmother had done several things that other people considered eccentric, or even crazy. Carla knew better, because the old woman had explained to her beforehand: she'd said, "It may not come now, but if it does, I want to be prepared. I don't like leaving things in a mess. And legal formalities can be intimidating to simple people—to the kind of people who live around here." She was referring to old acquaintances; they included the cook, maid and handyman who had worked in and around the house over the past fifty years. She'd left most of them something in her will, but in addition she wanted them to have mementoes that wouldn't be taxable to the estate or come to them through the lawyers. She spent a lot of time on the phone, arranging for certain items of furniture to be collected and driven to the houses of friends. She sent cash through the mail—something everyone, even people not related to her, knew was crazy—and had it arrive safely.

Finally, one day, she asked Carla to get all the jewelers' boxes and silk pouches out of the safe. And she'd proceeded to put on every necklace, bracelet, pin and ring that she owned.

"Which ones do you like best?" she'd asked.

"The lizard pin," Carla had said, "and the gold link bracelet, and the ring with the tiny rubies—that's always been my favorite."

"It's not valuable. Very ordinary stones."

"I love it."

Her grandmother had put the brooch and bracelet into her hand and slid the ring on to her finger—the same finger on which Carla had worn her wedding ring.

"And it fits," Carla had said.

"Stop Minnie from being so scandalized. If you don't want to wear your wedding ring any longer, there's no reason why you should."

"I wouldn't want to. But even if I did, I couldn't. It broke. It broke in pieces on the day he walked out. I just put my hand up on the edge of the sink when I was reaching down to get my heavy frying pan out of the cupboard, just as usual, and the ring fell into separate pieces. There must have been a fault in the metal. It upset me so much—more than almost anything else. The exact same day: can you imagine? It's enough to make you believe—I don't know."

"Yes, there's no doubt these things happen. Nobody can explain them. I remember when Father was in the hospital; we were sitting together, waiting for news, and all at once there was a loud crash from the library: his portrait had fallen off the wall. Maybe you've guessed—we had the news shortly afterwards that he'd died, and it must have been at that very moment." She picked out several other small pieces of jewelry to present to Carla. "Promise me," she said, "you'll wear them or you'll give them away to somebody else who'll wear them. What I don't want you to do is to put everything in a drawer somewhere and save it. It's the same with life, the same with love. You've got to use it, enjoy it—be happy with it. And if you lose it, so be it: never mind."

"Oh, I'll wear them," Carla promised.

"It took me a long time to learn that," her grandmother added. "It was a conclusion I came to really rather late."

They got into the old Plymouth—the only car her grandmother still trusted—and Carla drove from one house to another. She'd stop the car, help the old woman out and then stand aside as the friend, ex-servant or acquaintance was asked,

"Which one do you like best?" As soon as the object had been handed over, her grandmother said that she had several calls to make and had to be going. Carla noticed that a nice etiquette was observed: towards the end of the day, the recipients were not asked to choose. Her grandmother would simply pluck some jewel from its place and say, "I wanted you to have this."

A few weeks later, she died. No pictures fell from the wall, nor were there other portents. Carla was desolate. The aunts and uncles started to divide up the furniture. She received instructions from her cousins about how to hang on to their share, too. Her father flew in for the funeral, but his wife didn't bother to attend. He looked and obviously felt uncomfortable, trying to give correct formal expression to feelings he hadn't possessed.

Carla felt sorry for him. They went for a walk through the woods on the trail starting from where the old stables had been. He asked her about her plans for the future.

"Go back to my job, I guess. I don't want to. I don't want to be in the same town with him. I'd like to make a complete break with everything, just go away somewhere. I really would."

"You could come stay with us," he told her. She was touched.

"In a year, maybe," she said. "I'd love to. I'll have to get things organized, think about money."

"Oh, I'm sure we could get you the ticket. And Marsha would love it."

Marsha wouldn't love it; she'd hate every minute, but she'd have to lump it. For a moment Carla thought she might take up the offer. She liked the idea, she said, but she wanted to wait a while.

Her grandmother had left her some money and a few stocks and bonds, which she could either save or use immediately. If she dropped everything and just went wandering around the world, she could probably last for three years. And in the meantime, the business she'd built up over the past five years would fall apart.

She was a designer. She'd started out with the idea that she'd go into textiles and end up with her own range of fabrics and clothes. But she hadn't been able to fight her way into the profession. She'd done a few magazine ads and cartoons for the newspapers, and got her first good assignment through a friend: illustrating birthday cards. That had led to the Kassels, who ran a toyshop that stocked the cards. From her first week with them she was designing the toys and overseeing their manufacture, and getting the coffee and sandwiches ready in the back room while first Mrs. Kassel and then Mr. Kassel came to her for advice: crying, telling her that the family was breaking up and their lives were over and why hadn't they had a daughter like her. The business was booming, thanks to Carla—or, rather, thanks to her work and the Kassels' ability to push it towards customers with all the enthusiasm they felt for it; she could never have done that by herself. The business continued to prosper while the family did in fact split and Carla had to take sides. And her husband began to feel that she wasn't paying enough attention to him. It was still doing all right when she set up on her own and it was her turn to cry all over both the Kassels about her husband.

And now her own business was a success, expanding all the time. She could send in work while someone else held the fort for her. But not for three years. Three months, maybe. She thought hard about where she could go for three months only. And suddenly she remembered the other side of the family: her mother's side. There was a little gang of great-aunts still living up in what had been her mother's hometown. They'd all be pretty old now. She thought she ought to see them.

She told her father the next morning, the day of his flight out, that she'd decided to use the next couple of months looking up her mother's relatives. "I've forgotten the name of the town they live in, though."

He told her the name and wrote it down. He even remembered the right street. "They're rather strange people," he warned her. "I thought so when I met them. Half of them can't even speak English."

"That's all right. And maybe we won't like each other, but I just feel that we should try; that I ought to get to know them

86

before it's too late." She didn't say that—beginning with the break-up of her parents' marriage—she had started to fear the weakening of any family ties. Her fear might even have contributed to the ending of her own marriage. Families should stick together, she believed.

When she left her grandmother's house, the others were already busy with their own affairs and hardly noticed her departure. Two of her aunts had stopped speaking to each other because of what her father referred to as a "misunderstanding." But there had been no failure to understand. The two women both wanted the same thing, that was all: they were fighting over who was to get the Chinese jade buffalo. Carla was glad that her grandmother had given her the special pieces of jewelry outright, with her own hands, on that day of presentations. Twice during the plane flight up north she stopped reading her book, held her hand up and turned it to the side so that the light from the small airplane window shone over the bracelet and ring. She could remember them both from all the way back to the beginning of her childhood.

. . .

The part of town where her great-aunts lived was a place of broad avenues, green lawns and big trees. The houses too were very large and decorated with banistered porches, balconies and verandas. The district definitely didn't look like one where you'd find people who, as her father had told her, could barely speak English. Nor had the letter she'd received read like the work of an illiterate. On the contrary, the language had been precise—in fact, almost stilted, although grammatically faultless.

She lost her way among the peculiar numbering systems of the neighborhood. As she was beginning to feel tired enough to risk the embarrassment of ringing a doorbell and asking for directions, she saw a mailman turn the corner and come towards her. He was a gray-haired man who looked as if he'd had the job for many years and knew all about the city. When she asked him, indicating her useless map, he said, "Oh, the Countess. Sure."

"Countess?"

"That's what she calls herself."

There was no way of telling if the man thought her great-aunt was pretentious, silly, or actually out of her mind. He told Carla that she'd missed one of the turns and was in exactly the right spot on a parallel street.

"Just one block away," he said, pointing. Then it was easy. She was held up only a few more minutes, and that was because she couldn't believe that the house with the number was the one she was looking for; it was about the size of a nice old country hotel.

She walked down the path, up the stairs to the porch, and rang the bell. The front door stood open, only the screen door was shut. Through it she could see a hallway, a table with flowers, the foot of a magnificent stairway; and an old woman tottering towards her, a uniformed maid at her elbow. The maid reached the screen door first and opened it. Carla stepped forward.

The old woman held out her arms. "At last," she crooned. "My dear little Carla. Oh, what a joy—oh, if only your mother were alive at this moment."

Carla allowed herself to be embraced, and she kissed the great-aunt on both cheeks. She also realized that she'd been led astray by what could genuinely have been described as a misunderstanding: there was nothing wrong with her aunt's education or upbringing—it was just that she spoke a different language. She was speaking German.

"Well," the aunt said. "Yes, lovely. Did your mother bring you up to understand German?"

Carla said, "No, she wasn't—I was with my grandparents most of the time."

"Of course," the old woman said, switching to English. "We tried to make them allow you to stay up here with us. But they wouldn't."

"I learned French and German in high school."

"Yes?"

"And I kept it up in college when I was bumming around Europe in the summer—"

The old woman lapsed into German again, asking questions.

"But I've forgotten a lot," Carla went on. "And I'm pretty

slow. I was always stumbling around, even at my best. My accent was OK, but I never got the genders right. And that stuff about matching up the adjectives in the dative—well, I sort of skipped that side of it."

"We'll have to do something about that. But not today— no, there's no need to be nervous. Now, where is your suitcase?"

"At the motel."

"We'll have it brought. You'll stay here, naturally. I'm your Aunt Gisela, by the way."

"You wrote the letter."

"I wrote it. The others didn't want to answer. Ridiculous. Come in here and we'll have some coffee and I'll tell you about it." She led Carla through a wide hallway, across oriental rugs, past furniture polished until it shimmered. In a far corner of the room where they sat down a grand piano gleamed as if made of patent leather.

The maid reappeared without having been summoned.

"Bring us some coffee, Agnes," Aunt Gisela said. "And the usual . . . sandwiches and cakes."

"Crackers?"

"Cupcakes. *Kuchen.*" When Agnes had gone, she said, "That's the one I still mix up. And she gets so angry if I want to send them back to the kitchen."

"This is a wonderful house," Carla said.

"Quite nice, yes. We had better in Germany. We had palaces."

"Really?"

"Didn't your mother tell you anything?"

"I was only ten when she died. I can't remember that she ever talked about her family at all, not once."

Aunt Gisela sat forward in her chair. She told Carla that she had come from an ancient, important and persecuted aristocratic family and that quite aside from the significance of being heir to a rich cultural heritage, there was the question of the actual property. Some of the buildings and estates were unavailable at the moment: they lay in Poland, East Germany and Lithuania. But there were others.

"One doesn't want things to go out of the family," she said.

"Of course, it's important to have museums, but it's better that all those objects should be in daily use."

Carla shifted her attention as Agnes brought the coffee. Her aunt said, "Would you mind pouring? My hand is still steady, but sometimes I pour a perfect cup just half an inch beyond where it should be. All over the table, over the floor."

Carla poured out the coffee and busied herself with the plates. She said, "My other great-aunts—"

"Gerda and Ursula. You'll have to discount everything they say. They're old-fashioned and absurd. There are so few young ones in the great families nowadays. We have to forgive and forget."

"That's what I think," Carla said. "Especially now. I wrote you: my grandmother just died. I think we should get together and be friends while we can. When people die, it's too late. But I wouldn't want to stay here in the house if they don't want me."

"You are my guest," Gisela said. In four bites she made a neat meal of one of the small iced cupcakes. She lifted her hand to the plate again. Her movements were exceptionally light and quick for a woman of her age. And she was extraordinarily thin for someone who was in the habit of gobbling cakes. Carla herself stopped at one and refused a second sandwich. She gave her attention to the family history: where they had all lived, how many houses and castles they'd owned, how many wars they'd been through.

"There aren't many of us left," Aunt Gisela said. She raised her coffee cup and added, "As you say: we can't afford to keep up family quarrels."

Carla smiled, but she suddenly felt less welcome. She was glad that for the first night at least she'd be in the motel.

After their coffee, she was shown around the gardens at the other side of the house. They were bordered by four noble trees and were full of flowerbeds. The beds were laid out in an orderly way that made the whole of the back yard appear clean and regimented.

"This must take a lot of work," Carla commented.

Her aunt nodded and said complacently, yes.

A little later, as the afternoon light was beginning to soften, she met the other two aunts: Gerda and Ursula. Ursula was tall, thin, dignified and not very talkative. Gerda was bunchily plump, had scanty brown hair, and stared at Carla, leaning close; in both of her eyes the iris was ringed in white. Carla wasn't sure what that meant, other than that it was something you often noticed in old people's eyes. It might just be a sign of age, not of disease or partial blindness.

"I see you're wearing the lizard pin," Gerda said. Her eyesight was good enough for that, at least.

"My grandmother's."

"I know. I remember. I have a photographic memory for jewels. If we'd been the right age, or from the kind of family that went into trade, I should have been connected with a jewelry business. Yes, definitely—I have a feeling for it, despite the unfortunate family failing. You too? You find yourself drawn to shiny objects and color?"

"Not specially. I just have this strong sentimental attachment for the things I saw my grandmother wearing when I was a little girl."

They sat down on the side of the room near the piano. Ursula began to play. She took every piece very slowly. Carla was invited to replace her at the keyboard; she had to explain that she'd never learned more than a few short works, had been bored by her music teacher, still couldn't read the bottom clef, and had begged to give up after a year.

"How you must regret it now," Gisela said.

"Not at all. It was completely wasted time. I never had any talent for playing. I like listening."

"One wouldn't expect you to be a Paderewski, dear. It's simply a necessary accomplishment."

"I don't," Carla said, "find it necessary."

"Ah," Gisela murmured.

Disapproval seemed to radiate towards her from all three women. She wanted to get up and go back to her motel and rest for a couple of hours. She'd almost reached the end of her time limit for chat with strangers. Having to do part of it in German was an added strain. "What's the family failing?" she asked.

"We're pearlkillers," Gerda said.

"What's that?"

"Did you know that there were such people?"

"No." She still had no idea what the phrase meant, either in English or in German.

"That's right," Gisela said. "It's true. Something to do with the chemicals in the skin."

"Oh?"

"But I don't think little Carla is interested in hearing about that kind of thing."

"Well, she should be," Gerda said. "It's a family characteristic. Did your grandmother ever wear pearls, Carla?"

"Yes, she had a long rope with knots between the pearls in case the string broke. She wore them all the time. One of my aunts has them now."

"She wore them all the time because you have to. Pearls need to be kept in touch with the oils of the skin in order to retain their lustre. They can dry out if you keep them in a box."

"There are some people," Gisela said, "who have a theory that you should also wear them when you swim in the ocean—to return them to their home—but I can't believe the salt would be good for them."

"Most of the ladies we used to know," Gerda continued, "had pearls. And when they weren't wearing them, they made the maids wear them, to keep the pearls healthy. The younger the skin, the better it was supposed to be. But there are some people whose skin produces a chemical harmful to pearls—if they wear a ring for a while, suddenly they'll notice that the pearls have shrunk and almost withered back into the setting."

"Pearlkillers," Gisela said. "Our whole family. You may be one, too. We had an aunt who didn't develop the symptoms till late in life; then she let one of the maids wear her pearls while she tried to find a buyer for them, and—guess what? The maid turned out to be a pearlkiller, too. We thought that was extremely funny."

"And very suspicious," Gerda added. "Sometimes servants acquire the family traits out of affectation or a desire to emulate. But to be a pearlkiller presupposes an inherited tendency. Doesn't it?"

"I don't know," Carla said. "She might have had a family with the same kind of thing."

"Servants don't have families. They're parasitic in that respect. They want the family they're working for. They love them and they hate and envy them. It's like biographers and the famous. What I could tell you about servants."

"Has Agnes been with you long?"

"Agnes. That slut. A real camel."

Gisela said quietly, "We've had a certain amount of trouble with Agnes."

"Oh?"

"She's been going out with some much younger man," Gerda said. "A fortune-hunter. He thinks we'd leave her our money. As if we would."

"He must be half her age," Gisela said. "There can't be anything in it."

"Don't deceive yourself. Agnes does it with anyone. She drinks like a fish, and then she doesn't care who it is. Yes, it's true. She goes to bars and picks up men and they go somewhere together. Some hotel that specializes in that kind of thing, I suppose."

"We have no way of knowing that," Gisela told her.

"Some of these old families, you know," Gerda muttered; "the servants even look a lot like the masters."

"That could be psychological," Carla said. "Or psychosomatic."

"Yes. There's also a word for family relationships that become substitutional."

"What?" Gisela said.

"Subst—"

"Yes, I heard it. I just don't know what it means."

"Ah. Let's say: the brother in a family commits a crime. He'd be punished, but then so would the other members— his parents and sister, and so on. They wouldn't be precisely what you could call guilty, but they'd be associated by virtue of their kinship. There would be a group liability. In German that would be called *Sippenhaft*. You understand?"

Carla said, "Sure—it's so they won't be able to take revenge for the brother being punished."

"I assume that's what's behind it."

"Primitive."

"And effective," Gerda said. "The cruel methods primitive peoples have of dealing with disease—they prevent it from spreading. There are other plagues, too, and epidemics. There are evil ideas, for instance."

Carla sighed. The muscles in her neck and shoulders ached from having to sit at attention. She thought of saying that the methods of primitive peoples hadn't saved them from being wiped out by measles and the common cold; but that would simply lead Aunt Gerda to some new topic. Did they always talk like that—jumping all over the place and never letting up? Or was it just because she was a new face? She said, "You know, I think I'd like to go back to the motel to rest for a little. I'm kind of tired out from the trip."

"Oh, you can't go till after supper," Gisela pleaded.

"Let her go," Gerda said.

At the piano Ursula stopped playing. She lifted both hands from the keyboard in a concert-hall flourish. She looked at Carla. "Your mother," she told her, "betrayed her family."

"She married an outsider, that's all."

"We always marry Germans."

"Or if you don't, you don't get married?"

"That's right. It's better than ending the way she did."

Carla stood up. Gisela, slowly, tried to follow; she scolded Ursula for her tactlessness.

Carla moved quickly from the room. Behind her she heard the piano starting again. Ahead of her Agnes—large-nosed, thin-lipped, with her hair scraped into a bun and a smirk on her face—reached for the screen door.

"Carla dear, please wait," Gisela begged.

As the old woman came wheezing up to her, Carla turned and held out her hands. "Aunt Gisela, it's been really nice meeting you," she said, "but not the others."

"They don't understand. They don't see anybody all year long. They forget how to behave. I'm the one who deals with everything. They haven't been out of the house and garden for over twenty years. I think your mother's engagement party was the last time they went out. And that was only to make a big scene and say they wouldn't come to the wedding. You have to understand. They're old."

"Were they wonderful and kind when they were younger?"

"Well, I suppose they've always been difficult."

"I'll see you tomorrow," Carla said.

"Yes, please. Please, Carla. I want to ask a great favor of you. There's something I want you to get for us. My cousin, Theo, took it. It didn't belong to him—it belongs to us. You will promise, won't you?"

"I'll come see you tomorrow," she said. "I've got to go now." Agnes swung the door ahead of her.

She ran down the steps and away.

·   ·   ·

She lay on the bed in her motel room and wondered if she'd have the nerve to pack up and just get out in the morning, leaving one of those messages that said, "Called away suddenly." But that was what other people had done to her all her life; she couldn't be the one to do it to someone else. She especially shouldn't do it to Aunt Gisela, who didn't deserve to be treated like that. Aunt Gerda would be a different matter. And the other one, Ursula: sane but nasty.

She also wished that she had a very large drink. She should have bought a bottle someplace. She wasn't the kind of woman who went into bars on her own. She didn't really want to go swimming alone in the motel pool, either, but if she just stayed sitting in her room, she might start thinking about her ex-husband again. She might even imagine how her divorced mother had felt after she'd left her child with its grandparents. Her mother had checked into a motel room—maybe a room very similar to that one—and had ended up cutting her wrists.

The view from the windows showed a parking lot and beyond it the old jetties. Across the river stood abandoned brick warehouses and behind them, pine trees. The sky was a firm, northern blue, only just beginning to darken. Even in her aunts' neighborhood, among the large houses and plush green lawns, the sky had that look. It reminded you that nearby were the lakes as big as seas, and the unbroken miles of evergreen forest that used to be the country of the Indians.

Her telephone rang. When she picked it up a man's voice told her that he'd had a call from her great-aunt Gisela and he'd like to talk to her for a few minutes, in person, if she didn't mind. His name was Carl Raymond.

"That sounds like two people," she said.

"What?"

"When did you want to meet?"

"I kind of thought right now. I could take you out for supper and we could talk. My uncle George is your aunts' accountant."

"Oh," she said. The information meant nothing, if true, but it persuaded her.

She took a shower and changed into a dress that was still slightly wrinkled over the skirt.

He was waiting at the reception desk. He'd been gossiping and joking with the clerk, who said to her, "I didn't know you were a friend of Carl here, Miss."

"We've never met," she said. She put the key down on the counter and held out her hand; Carl shook it. He said he was glad to meet her: they had a lot to talk about. "First of all, some food."

"What's wrong with here?" the clerk asked.

"Come on," Carl said. He took her by the elbow and led her out to a car. He told her, "It's a long story, and I've just come off work. I'm going to need a drink before I can get it straightened out."

"That's fine by me," she said. She began to perk up. Always, she thought, just when she was ready to throw in the towel, something nice turned up. And she still hadn't learned that it always would: the pleasant and unpleasant ran in tandem. But whenever she began to feel dejected, she forgot: the bad times seemed to be going on forever. Maybe it was possible that she'd inherited the predilection from her mother.

He parked the car and took her in to the kind of bar and grill that made the customers put on ties. The lighting was subdued enough to hide her badly-ironed skirt.

They each had two drinks. She got a good look at him while he was ordering the meal: he was tall and well-built, about her own age and had a squarish head, pale blue eyes, a strong-featured face, small regular teeth. His hair was straight and light, clipped short—almost like a crew cut, which made his ears appear to stick out a little. Most people would have considered him a good-looking man. She thought he was all right: nice but rather uninteresting. She'd grown too used to her husband's dark, frizzy-haired, ugly-romantic looks.

"Carl and Carla," he said. "That's sort of a coincidence, isn't it?"

"That's right. We sound like a comedy team."

"Well, some kind of a team, anyway. I'll drink to that."

"So you're an accountant?" she said.

"No, I'm in real estate. It's my uncle George who's their accountant. At least, he's still your aunt—your great-aunt—Gisela's, but there've been arguments with the other two. Maybe you didn't know it, but your aunts have a big reputation in this neck of the woods for—"

"Eccentricity?"

"And general cussedness. And when they don't have much to occupy their time with, they get on the phone and try to strike points against each other through a third person."

"Uncle George."

"And Uncle Bertram at the bank and my father, before he picked up and moved. He was in the same firm as one of their lawyers, Sandy Howe. Mr. Howe used to say it was a lean week when one of them didn't want to change her will. Anyway, I guess they're an institution by now. Life wouldn't be so colorful without them. And they went through quite a lot during the war; during both wars, there was a lot of anti-German feeling."

"But they've lived here for a hundred years."

"They didn't mix. They wouldn't talk English. They wouldn't marry anybody who wasn't from a German background. My family was mostly German, too. A lot of this town was. But nobody else thinks of it that way. We're all American. Your aunts aren't. They never wanted to be. And they told everybody about their titles."

"That wouldn't have made them disliked. That's something everybody laughs at. Even the mailmen."

"It isn't democratic."

"If it's true."

"Oh, it's certainly true."

"Really?"

"Without a doubt." He began to tell her about the family's holdings in Eastern Europe.

Their food came and he continued to talk. She could see he was a man who could be driven to frenzy by the idea of large stretches of salable land. She wondered if perhaps the three old women had decided to bamboozle him just for fun.

Over coffee he went on to tell her about the houses and estates they still had in countries that recognized their ownership. "They're millionaires," he said. "Multimillionaires."

"Nice."

"I just wanted you to know that if there's any difficulty about the estate, you could fight it."

"What do you mean?"

"You're the heir, aren't you?"

"No."

"Surely."

"Not at all. They cut my mother right out of their lives when she married."

"Your mother, but not you."

"Me too, I'm sure. It's what they call *Sippenhaft*."

"I think you're the heir. And if you weren't, you could claim it. You could certainly claim it against the parlormaid."

"Agnes? What's she got to do with it?"

"She's one of the ones who's put into the wills and taken out again every week. It's how they keep her there. They make a promise and then they fight and they break it, and so on."

"What a life. How can she stand it?"

"Not much choice, I guess."

"But how can she believe it? Obviously it's a game they play."

"Nope. If they sign all the right stuff, it's real. It's binding. You could try to prove afterwards that the way they kept changing their minds was a sign of mental decay, and that they were being taken advantage of; but you'd have to fight it through the courts. You couldn't just throw it out."

"Well, it's no stranger than anything else. I don't think it has anything to do with me. But thanks for the information."

"Right," he said. "Just thought you ought to know."

He took her back to the motel, walked her to her room, waited till she'd unlocked the door, and then pulled her back and kissed her on the mouth before saying goodnight. She went inside, shut the door and stayed looking at it. It was too short an acquaintance for him to be kissing her. And it was a long time since anything like it had happened to her.

· · ·

As she was getting ready to go in to breakfast, her phone rang. Aunt Gisela was on the line. She sounded a lot more quavery than Carla remembered.

"Please, dear, I know it must have been upsetting yesterday, but I'm not feeling very well—I don't have the time to smooth things over the way I used to. Would you come over, please?"

"All right," Carla said. "After I've had my breakfast. But just you. Not the others."

"They're very sorry."

"I doubt it."

"What's that?"

"I said I don't believe it. Ursula did the dirty work and Gerda thought it was a scream. They got a lot of pleasure out of hurting me. And I'm not letting myself in for a second dose."

"Oh, no. I'm sure—"

"I mean it. If I see them, I'm walking out again. Agreed?"

"Yes, dear," Aunt Gisela said.

Carla felt that she had taken action and made everything clear. Before the divorce she'd never spoken harshly or even decisively to anyone. She ate a large breakfast. Over her last cup of coffee she remembered that the evening before, she'd been ready to get out altogether. Now she really didn't know what she was going to do except that when Carl had kissed her at the door she'd been given the impression of having a lover again. She could even have asked him in. It all started so easily, she thought. Again. She'd been sure she never wanted anything else to happen ever again.

Aunt Gisela arrived panting in the front hall. She hadn't been quick enough for Agnes, who whipped the screen door open and afterwards deliberately slammed it so that it twanged like a harp.

"The humidity today," the old woman said, her breath whiffling; "or perhaps the pollen." She drew Carla down a side corridor and into a pleasant study overlooking part of the garden.

"This used to be Albert's room," she said. She waved her hand at a leather armchair large enough to have been the favorite reading chair of a fairly big man. Carla sat down in it.

Gisela seated herself bolt upright in a straight-backed wooden chair. "I must tell you some more about the family," she said.

Carla leaned forward. Her aunt's narrative came out without pause, partly in English, partly in German, both broken by labored breathing and a whistling from the lungs. Carla didn't dare interrupt. It seemed like the kind of speech people gave when about to be executed—it appeared to cover everything Gisela had ever thought or remembered about the family, and included statements to the effect that: they were all under a blight; they had done many great wrongs to several other large and important families hundreds of years ago; they had lost kingdoms, or places as good as kingdoms; they were of royal blood; some of the family, led by cousin Theo, had managed to swindle the others out of a very great deal of money and property and were living it up on their ranches in South America; Theo had absconded with something called "Count Walter's Treasure," but it belonged to her—Gisela; he had ruined her when she was a girl and then laughed at her, and if there had been any consequences, she'd have had to—well, Carla knew what she'd have had to do. "And now getting old," she sighed. "But if you get the Treasure back, Count Walter's, I'll be well again. And it's yours after me, you know. A part of your German inheritance."

"I'll try," Carla said. The old woman was in such distress that she'd have promised almost anything to calm her down.

"I'll pay all expenses, naturally. Carl is seeing about the tickets now. And he's agreed to chaperone you. It wouldn't be right for you to go alone."

"Where?"

"He'll be in Germany at this season. Or possibly in one of his Italian villas."

"But—"

"Then it's all arranged. I'm so glad."

"Aunt Gisela, I don't understand."

"Priceless. I'll be well again when you've got it."

"I don't even have my passport with me."

"You remember the number?"

"Yes."

"Good. We'll be able to do something."

"How? That kind of thing takes time. And doesn't Carl have a job someplace?"

"He's saved up a lot of vacation time. You don't understand about Theo. Soon it's going to be too late. I'm too old now. We've got to have it."

"Why?"

"If we die without the Treasure. . . ."

"Yes?"

"I don't want to tell you."

"When you say it's going to make you well: how's it going to do that?"

"By touch."

"Is it a kind of relic or something?"

"Exactly. That's the word. Isn't it stupid—when I forget a word nowadays, I lose it from both languages. Occasionally I can get it again through the French or Italian. The mind is so weak, Carla. When you start wearing out."

"And Carl would go, too?"

"He handles a lot of our business affairs now."

"What happened to his father?"

"I believe they call it 'mid-life crisis.' He started to want young girls instead of his family."

"Is Carl the only one?"

"There's another boy and a girl."

"And their mother?"

"She's still here, complaining. You can see why he went. But she wasn't like that before he left. She's become a different person."

Something made of metal clanked on to the floor just outside the door. It sounded like a bunch of keys. Aunt Gisela rose with an easy smoothness surprising in her condition. She opened the door.

Agnes stood outside, not looking in any way bothered; she said, "Are you going to want lunch or what?"

"A light luncheon for two, Agnes. In here. And then you may leave us."

"OK," Agnes said. She slouched away.

Carla was on her feet, protesting that she had to go, she had to make phone calls about her business, she certainly couldn't spend more than a week on vacation.

Gisela overruled her. She said quietly, "Yes, dear, yes," patted her had, smiled charmingly and added, "but you know that I'm the one who really doesn't have time. I can see it running out as clearly as if it were sand in an hourglass. Just this one thing for your old aunt, little Carla."

. . .

The phone woke her up early. She'd swum back and forth in the motel pool for twenty minutes the evening before, had had a large drink with her salad-bar meal and slept like a log. They weren't supposed to give her a morning call; she had an alarm clock with her. It was still almost dark.

"Yes?" she said into the receiver.

"It's Carl. I've got some bad news."

She thought something must have happened to Gisela—a stroke or collapse of some kind. Or, maybe after all the excitement of the day and the amount of talking she'd done, actually her death.

"Didn't you hear the sirens?" he asked.

"What?"

At some time around midnight, her aunts' large house had burst into flames. Carl had been wakened, since his family lived so near. Half the town had been there, and the whole of the fire department. The house had burned for hours. In fact, it was still on fire. And as far as anyone knew, there were no survivors. That meant her three aunts, a cook, two parlormaids and Agnes, who—the police were assuming— had been the one who had started the blaze.

"Oh," Carla said in the dark. "Oh. I can't take it in."

"Go back to sleep. I only called up because I didn't want you to hear through somebody else. My uncles are going to be handling most of the paperwork, I guess."

"Shouldn't I go out there?"

"No. There's nothing you could do. There's just a big crowd of people watching the place burn to the ground. It's OK about the passport, by the way. Or maybe you won't want to go, now that they've passed on."

"I don't know," she said. "I'll have to think about it." She said goodbye and lay back in the bed. She wondered about Agnes and whether the act of arson had been revenge for being cut out of a new will. She thought about the three old women surrounded by fire, then she pushed that thought away and went to sleep again.

. . .

In the first week they covered north and middle Germany and were headed towards the south. Uncle Theodore was always at some new address; he'd also sold a lot of his former property. Gisela evidently hadn't kept up with his movements as well as she'd imagined. All the telephone numbers Carl had unearthed were out of date. Even the exchanges were different. Sometimes the new occupants they met would become interested and dispense friendly information and advice, none of which was of any help in tracking down the missing relatives; or, at least, not during those first few days. But Carl usually managed to get another address out of the people they interviewed—his German was better than hers —and so they moved south.

"It's like the treasure hunts my grandfather used to invent for us," Carla said. "At Easter, when we were children: you began with a poem that was a riddle. It led you to a certain place, where you'd find the next clue. And at the end there was a present."

"Lots of candy? A chocolate egg?"

"No, we had that anyway. The present was usually a book."

"Bavaria next," Carl said. "We've even got castles on the agenda."

"Aunt Gisela told me the really big estates were in the east. Some of them were in Poland and Czechoslovakia."

"So they're all collective farms by now?"

"One of them's a sanatorium and another one's a kind of health farm, where people can do their exercises in beautiful surroundings. It had a famous park."

"Doesn't it make you feel strange to know that your family owns those places—that they're actually part of your inheritance?"

"No," Carla said, "definitely not. One ordinary apartment is going to be plenty for me. What makes me feel funny is knowing I've got all these relatives like Uncle Theodore and Aunt Regina, and I've never met them. And now I can't even find them."

"We'll get you there," he assured her. "Plenty of time. I've got six weeks."

"Five, now."

"And we've got two good clues: Munich and Naples. Maybe we should split up for a couple of days. That might cut down on the time. How's your Italian?"

"It isn't. Only phrases from operas: *Ah, patria mia. Perfido amore*. And so on. That's about it."

"And I can ask what time the train goes and how much things cost. What do you think? I could go there and phone you in Munich. OK?"

She thought it over while they ate lunch outdoors on a terrace crammed with iron tables, each of which had a striped parasol sprouting from a central bar that went up through the middle of the tabletop like the trunk of a tree. They were surrounded by Scandinavian and American tourists. Carla figured that she could find her way around another German city all right, but she wouldn't have any idea how to go about making a phone call from one country to another, between two languages, neither one of which was her own.

"All right," she agreed.

"I'll miss you," he said.

She smiled. He meant that he'd miss sleeping with her. All the time they were still in America, nothing had happened. And on the first night they'd spent in Germany, he'd come into her hotel room and that was that.

They'd visited one or two places not on the list: she'd always wanted to see Heidelberg, so they'd gone there and had their picture taken together with what seemed like hundreds of other tourists; there were Americans all over the town, even though the summer was almost over.

And they'd made a detour to a little church they'd been told about, which was supposed to be architecturally interesting. As they'd approached the place in their rented Volkswagen, Carla had suddenly seen the building; it stood on the top of a hill, among other gently rounded slopes planted with wheat that had already been harvested. The stooks were lined up in the fields, the sky embellished with puffy clouds, and the whole day was like an illustration from a volume of nursery rhymes. The church itself was of a dark, honey-colored stone; the front looked like a Carlsbad clock one of her father's aunts had owned.

Most of the other tourists there had been German. They were taking photographs of the outside, and talking in lowered voices inside. As she and Carl entered, the change from bright light to the murky interior was abrupt. Carla had stood still. With one hand she'd held on to Carl. With the other she'd twiddled nervously at the small ruby ring her grandmother had given her in the spring.

"This way," Carl had whispered. She'd followed him until they stood side by side, looking into a glass box let into the church wall. Inside the box was what Carla at first took to be a ceremonial robe laid out in splendor. And then all at once she realized that within the robe was a corpse. There had been fourteen of the things, each in its private showcase, all around the inner walls. They were supposed to be saints.

"I'll miss you, too," she told him.

She got so lost in Munich, and so often lost, that she ended up taking taxis everywhere. It was pointless in any case; the two houses she was looking for, and of which she had several fine photographs, didn't exist. In one instance, the street itself was no longer apparent. Everything had been bombed and built over.

She walked around the museums and in the evening went out to a performance of a ballet. When she got back to her hotel, there was a message that Carl had telephoned. He called again at midnight.

"Any news?" she asked.

"Lots. And I've talked to Uncle Theodore."

"Well, finally."

"Not completely. I talked to him on the phone. He's in South America."

"I don't believe it."

"And he wants us to come see him."

"Just hop across—"

"And he's arranging the flight and paying for everything. And," he added, "he says he's just dying to see you."

.   .   .

They walked out of the airport into a thrashing crowd as noisy as a political demonstration. A lot of the people looked as if they were in fancy dress. Everything suddenly seemed utterly strange to Carla—almost as though she'd been put into a different century. She didn't even have the sense that she might have known the place from pictures in newspapers or on television.

Carl held her by the arm. He had a way of nipping her upper arm with his hand so that his thumb made a large, painful bruise. She didn't complain. She thought that if he let go, they might become separated. And if that happened, she wouldn't stand a chance. The noise and crowd and heat would over-whelm her. She felt nearly ready to pass out as it was.

He found a porter and then a cab. They drove away from the airport, through part of the city and to a highway. She sat silent, his arm around her shoulders. The taxi turned off the main road and started to climb. They were going up into the mountains.

"Look," he said.

She made an attempt to take in the landscape and the views, but she was too tired to appreciate anything. She tried to sleep. She wished they hadn't left Europe.

It was evening when she woke. The taxi had stopped and their luggage was being moved to a horse-drawn carriage. Carl shook her as she began to close her eyes again. When she saw the horses waiting and got a second look at the carriage, she said, "My God, it's like one of those fairytale things."

They both wanted to sit outside, up with the coachman, who kept signalling back towards the doors with his whip and repeating some instructions.

"What's he saying?"

Carl told her, "He wants us to get in."

"Why?"

The man put the whip down and made flapping movements with his hands.

"Owl?" Carl asked.

"Bats," she said. "I'll bet that's what it is. Let's go." She climbed into the coach and sat down on the seat. As soon as Carl joined her, the wheels rolled forward. She said, "This is unbelievable."

"I guess the roads aren't very good."

"If they're no good for a car, they'd be a lot worse for one of these things."

"Pretty comfortable, actually. If Clark Gable could do it in a phone booth—"

"We could fall out on the doorstep before we realized we'd arrived. I could have bruises in a lot of new places."

The night came down around them, the road grew bumpy. At one stage, while they were negotiating a sharp turn, something slapped hard against one of the windows from the outside. Carla was suddenly wide awake.

"A bat," Carl said in a sinister voice. "Coming to get you."

"Couldn't have been. It was huge. Maybe it was a condor. Or a big rock."

"A rock would break the window."

"It's so dark," she said. "There isn't a light anywhere."

107

They drove for half an hour more before they saw lights, which seemed from the outline to be coming from a castle of some kind.

"They don't have castles here," he told her.

"Well, a big house. An enormous house. See?"

Carl put his face to the window. He didn't speak.

She said, "I've got a feeling it's like something I've seen before. It looks a little like one of those photographs. Maybe they built it that way on purpose, as a copy of what they'd left behind. Carl?"

"It's big, all right," he said.

.   .   .

"You slept well?" her great-uncle Theodore asked. In daylight he didn't look so peculiar. When she'd arrived—cold, sleepy, stumbling into the light—he'd struck her as odd, and incredibly old, and irretrievably foreign. She and Carl had been introduced to the entire indoor household, who were lined up in the front hall to meet them. The other great-uncle, Erwin, had appeared senile and dwarfish rather than—as now—diminutive and charming. And her great-aunt Regina, in a floor-length green and black dressing gown, had given an impression of dramatic malevolence; she now seemed merely grumpy and theatrical: a heavy-faced old woman who dyed her hair black, as she must have been doing for nearly forty years. She also wore, even at breakfast, a great deal of strong-colored makeup. Another woman—a frail figure in white, who had gestured tentatively from a landing the night before—still hadn't come downstairs.

"I slept like the dead," Carla said. "Isn't Carl up yet?"

"Roderigo is showing him the estate. He woke early, with the others."

She sipped her coffee. The first thing they'd done as she'd sat down was to warn her about the strength of their coffee.

She wondered why Carl hadn't come to her room. She didn't even know where he was sleeping. As soon as the servant had shown her to the room she was to have, he'd hurried Carl down the corridor, and that was the last she'd seen of him. She thought it was strange. He was only a recently acquired boyfriend, but the others didn't know that; they had been told that she and Carl were engaged. That was supposed to make the whole question of bedrooms easier and perhaps less offensive, if anyone thought that way about it.

"Was Roderigo the man with the moustache?"

"The manager, yes. They'll be back for lunch. And in the meantime, perhaps Kristel—"

"Kristel is in her study," Regina said.

"Or Regina?"

"I have to do my exercises."

"And I, unfortunately, am occupied with business matters, but—"

"I should be delighted," Erwin said, "to show little Carla the house and gardens."

Erwin was waiting for her in the hall when she came down from brushing her teeth. She was beginning to get a better idea of the structure of the house. It was built in stories, on several levels of the mountainside. The gardens too climbed up and down screes of rock into which stone steps had been cut. There was a wooden handrail that would have been useless if anybody had really needed to lean on it. Uncle Erwin skipped along nimbly at her side. For a man of his age he appeared astonishingly agile and supple in his movements. All the great-uncles and aunts of the family must have been hitting eighty at least, possibly ninety and upwards.

"Did the family build the house?" Carla asked.

"No, it was here before. It was a convent, or a monastery, or something like that. And a fortress. So often these places are like that: they have some treasure, and so they have to be in a position to defend it. There are a great many sacred buildings in the area from the same period. Most of them are partly ruined. They were lucky to have water here. That's why they survived so long. We added a lot, of course. Look." He raised his arm towards the windows and towers above them. He started to explain which walls had been added when. Carla lost interest.

He went on, "There are three main gardens. Everything else is extra. The vegetables are over on the other side. Now, be careful and watch where you put your feet. The mist comes up and makes the rock slippery. And there's a kind of moss—that can be just like ice when it's raining."

He led her down a stone staircase between two walls dappled green and gray with lichen, and into an arcade of white-blossomed bushes. Everything in the first garden was white. The second garden was almost all full of red flowers, though there were pink and orange shades too, and some yellow. The last garden was purple, blue and gray. "We wanted black," Erwin said, "but so few flowers are truly black and the only ones we could think of won't grow here."

"A black garden? Why?"

"Because of the flag, of course. Red, white and black."

"I thought the flag here was—"

"The German flag, Carla dear."

"Oh? Well, I guess now you've got the American flag instead. And England and France."

"Yes. Unfortunate, but it will have to do."

He walked her down to the front of the house, where they climbed into a carriage. The sides of the vehicle were open but there was a canvas top. Erwin gave orders to the driver in a language Carla didn't understand. As they started to move, she told him about the night before and about the bird, or whatever it was, that had bumped into them.

"Probably an owl," Erwin said.

"We thought it might have been a bat."

"Bats never make a mistake like that. They have their own system of radar. But an owl, or another kind of bird, might have been caught by the shine of the windows."

"Do you get a lot of bats around here?"

"Thousands. And they're the real thing, you know—the vampire bats. They come into the fields at night and attack the cattle. And also the horses. We have to be careful. Of course the local people here say that we're vampires, too— our family."

"Why on earth?"

"It's a figure of speech. Because we're rich. We suck the blood from the poor. At least, according to them. The truth is that we're civilized and educated and they're just ignorant peasants. And we pay them to do work for us."

"You own the land they live on?"

"That's right. And so do you. You're a member of the family."

She was shown a model village, a rug-weaving factory and a fish farm. The workers were Indians of all ages. A lot of them were very light-skinned. Most of the adults, both men and women, had a scar on their foreheads. Carla didn't hear a single laugh, or even any talking, among them. They worked slowly, with concentration.

Erwin made a detour so that she could see what was happening in a pool at the other end of the hatcheries. He led her up close. A large, jittery crowd pressed forward behind her. When two men emptied a pail of scraps into the water, the pool appeared to boil with activity. The crowd moaned, at once sickened and gratified. "It's the fish," Erwin said. "They're like piranhas."

"You breed them?"

"Not really. We like to keep the pool full. Everybody knows what can happen to whatever falls in. The idea of being deliberately pushed in, or even thrown, is one that fascinates our employees. They seem to regard it as a form of insurance we hold over them—a warranty of their good behavior. I understand that mothers even threaten their babies with it."

"But, that's terrible."

"No, no. It's like a legend now. It's, ah, a focus of attention to which other things are referred. You understand?"

"I don't think so," Carla said.

"Well, it doesn't matter. Let's just say—everyone would miss the pool if we decided to get rid of it. And the people who'd miss it most of all are the ones who are the most afraid of getting thrown into it."

They spent the rest of the morning looking at meadows and pastures and views that spread away from them like an ocean of cultivated land. The family holdings appeared to be of about the same acreage as the state of Connecticut, or possibly even more extensive than that.

"And the forests," Erwin added. "We sometimes speak of

111

them as the jungle. And all the places where you can find butterflies. Kristel is our great lover of butterflies. She can show you."

"Was that the woman in the shawl?"

"That was the housekeeper, Maria. Kristel didn't come downstairs last night. She hasn't been well."

"Oh? I hope it's not serious."

"It's never serious," he said. "She likes the pose. Her mother was an invalid—romantic and glamorous: had hundreds of lovers. One always assumed that her fatigues were brought on by an excess of amours. Or perhaps a heightened artistic sensibility. I remember her very well—a marvelous woman. Poor Kristel isn't quite up to that standard. And she doesn't have the acting talent."

"Oh," Carla said again. Erwin gave directions to the driver to turn the horses and they went through a gully that was bursting forth in yellow bushes even high up, where it didn't look as if the roots would have anything to hold on to.

They reached the house again and were let off near another walled garden, so that Carla could be shown the vegetables. She stepped over a low-growing branch of pink flowers and clutched at the corner of a stone outcrop. They had followed the paths around to the other side, where the vegetables joined up with the flower gardens. The blue air beyond rose above them like another mountain. The combination of flowers and talk and the steep climb between dangerous turnings was beginning to confuse her. She said, "You know, I think I've still got a little jet lag left over. I feel sort of dizzy."

Erwin put out a hand to steady her. "How selfish of me," he said. "I should have thought. It's probably the altitude, too—most people feel that straight away."

She didn't see Carl until just before lunch. He was coming down the main staircase as she was going up. She asked, "What happened last night?"

"There you are," he said. "This place is driving me crazy. I couldn't find my way back to your room, and then I almost got lost again when somebody turned out the lights. Jesus, did you hear the crying?"

"No."

112

"Roderigo says everybody thinks it's a ghost."

He started to tell her about the tour he'd been given. She thought how healthy he looked, and how happy. He even seemed a little too cheerful—like a commercial for a cereal. He told her, "This place is fantastic. The whole thing. It's like a private empire. Really."

"And by rights Aunt Gisela should have had her share of it. Maybe it was all hers."

"First I've heard."

"She told me that. She said: 'Theodore stole the Treasure from me.' "

"She was kind of gaga towards the end of her life."

" 'Count Walter's Treasure'—that's what she called it. At first I thought it was her way of alluding to something else, like her emotions or her honor. You know. But she would have been almost a generation older—well, not quite that much, but I think she was too old to have had any kind of an affair with him when she was young. She was way up in her nineties—at least ten years older, so it couldn't have been in her youth: he'd have been too young for her back then."

He said, "I know these older women that keep on moaning about being ruined by younger men."

"Is that right?"

"Wishes."

"Carl, has Uncle Theodore said anything to you about how long we're invited for?"

"It's indefinite."

"My work isn't indefinite," she said.

Over luncheon Uncle Theodore talked about the history of the estate and the founding of the family fortunes in that part of the world. Regina listened to him without comment. She shoveled her food purposefully into her mouth and chewed. Aunt Kristel had risen from her sickbed in order to attend the meal. She had shied away from both young people, saying, "Please—if you'll forgive me: my hands hurt today." And she had placed the hurting hands in her lap. "Some days," she murmured, "are worse than others." Carla was just as glad to avoid the physical contact. Kristel's whitely desiccated face and hands were alarming: they had a leprous look.

113

She shot a glance at Carl but he was turned to Theodore in an attitude of interest and expectation. She looked down at her plate. The meeting with her aunts and uncles was one she'd felt she had to have, but it was hard for her to believe that she was related to these people. They seemed grotesque. She couldn't understand how Carl was able to play up to them, unless he was simply impressed by their wealth. *To the end of the week,* she thought: and then she'd be saying goodbye.

"Goodbye?" Uncle Erwin said. "But—we shouldn't dream of letting you go so soon."

"I have to get back to my work."

"Yes, the child is right," Theodore agreed. "We're retired. And the young have their own lives." He sighed. "But stay to the end of the week at any rate. We'll have a few parties. Show you around the neighborhood and boast a little."

"Yes, parties," Kristel squealed. The onrush of gaiety made her look momentarily imbecilic as well as ill. She raised her afflicted hands in the air and made a few dancing movements with them.

"I'll send someone down to the village," Theodore said. "Have you any preference for a day? I'm afraid the best we can do is Tuesday or Thursday. Let's make it this Thursday. Then we'll be able to keep you a bit longer."

"All right," she said. Everyone around the table smiled. She wondered why she'd ever had the feeling that they might not be willing to let her go.

That afternoon she and Carl had tea with Theodore, who talked about the duties of running such a large estate and the difficulties of growing old without heirs. "You have to leave everything to foundations," he said, "and do it in such a way that the next generation won't be forever quarrelling about what you really meant."

Carla said that she agreed with her grandmother: you should just give your possessions away and let the other people do what they liked with them. She twisted and turned her grandmother's ring as she said so. It wasn't easy to speak up against Theodore.

"One or two trinkets," he told her, "are hardly to be compared with a huge amount of land."

"But the principle's the same. The future may be completely different. The way people live, the circumstances of their—"

"The future," Theodore stated, "can be controlled from the past. Good planning ensures that the future will be as one wants it. We have to look ahead, that's all."

"No one's ever been able to do that."

"I agree with your uncle," Carl said.

"Oh?"

"Certainly. It's only a question of organization. It's political."

"Really," she said.

"That's right. And," he looked at Theodore as if for confirmation, "the systematization of heredity."

"What does that mean?"

"It means: the great thing about graduating from the Neanderthal and Cro-Magnon stages is that once you've got a good brain, you can get the people with less brains to work for you. And if you're only reproducing with your own kind, your people become more and more intelligent, while theirs become progressively stupid and degenerate, and finally unable to run their lives without being governed by someone else."

"But does inheritance operate like that? I thought it was supposed to skip around; you know—the similarities show up on the tangent and between generations that are three or four steps apart."

"No," Carl said flatly. "All you have to do is look at greyhounds and horses. It's a matter of breeding."

Uncle Theodore nodded. He looked approvingly at Carl. It was easy to see where the theory had originated. Carla said, "Even if that were true—which I don't believe—would it be right to deny people equality just because they're stupid or underbred?"

Theodore took over. "It's definitely right," he answered, "to prevent them from taking up a position of power for which they're completely unqualified."

"If you change people's circumstances and upbringing and education, you change their qualifications."

"No. There's nothing you can do with poor stock."

115

She was irritated enough to push the argument further, even though it would break up the tea-drinking. She opened her mouth to begin and then saw that the others all sided with Theodore. It was better to drop the subject. She said, "Well, I don't agree."

Kristel giggled and said she'd always felt that debates on these big political subjects were best left to the men. Regina threw her a look of contempt.

"The future is our job," Theodore said. "As well as the present."

Carla raised her cup to her lips. Maybe the mania for control—like the whole line of reasoning—was connected with the fact that these people had no generations to come after them. The future meant children. Now, at last, she was glad she didn't have any. She remembered one of the quarrels she'd had with her husband; suddenly she could even recall, as if echoed intact, the tones of their voices as they'd yelled at each other. "When are you going to get pregnant?" he'd shouted. And she'd screamed back, "When you stop sleeping around." "I'm not going to stop," he'd told her. "I like it. It's a hell of a lot more fun than you are right now." And so forth. It had gone on and on. And all that time she'd wanted children, yet she'd known that no matter what he said, he'd walk out on her as soon as she had any. She hated him more than anything in the world and wished that she could kill him again and again—once wouldn't be enough.

She was gripping her teacup tightly and staring down at the rug. She still loved him, which made it worse. The marriage couldn't have ended any other way, but she kept catching herself at wishing: if only things had been different. The future might be determined by the past, but the present seemed to her always uncontrollable and chaotic.

Kristel finished her last cup of tea as she pressed flowers into the pages of a book for Erwin's collection. Regina occupied herself with some kind of crocheted scarf. And while Theodore took Carl upstairs to look at some old papers that concerned the estate, Carla walked up the opposite staircase, to her room. On her way she passed the three paintings that gave her the creeps: a landscape of blasted trees and ruined temples lit by a livid glare that made the stone columns look like old, naked legs; a still-life vase full of rotting flowers, with a cup and saucer sitting on the table in front of it; and a mythological scene that showed a convocation of centaurs: these bearded, hairy creatures were grouped in a circle, though most of them had their muscled backs towards the viewer, and within the tight huddle they formed, appeared to be doing something singular, perhaps unpleasant, possibly unspeakably gross.

Regina had told her the names of the painters, who were apparently well-known. Regina was extremely proud of all three. They were, she said, prime examples of German culture.

·   ·   ·

Carl came to her room before they went down to dinner. He said, "I won't see you tonight. Your uncle is initiating me into some kind of ceremony. It's for men only."

"What kind of ceremony?"

"I don't know. Some club the ranchers have, maybe."

"I hope it isn't anything political. From the way they've been talking, you might end up covered in swastikas."

"Don't be silly." He sounded as pompous and didactic as Theodore, but unlike Theodore, he wasn't the kind of man you could be afraid of. There was a hint of shiftiness about him. He'd probably done something crooked with her great-aunts' money, she thought. He'd probably been friendly with Agnes.

"What are you looking like that for?" he asked.

"I was remembering what you told me about older women," she said. "How they fell in love with younger men."

"It isn't just the older ones here. It's all of them. Haven't you noticed? There are a lot of blond children on the estate. And grown-ups, too. Theodore told me: it's in our interest to have as many workers as possible. And it isn't as if they mind."

117

"Who mind?"

"The women. They come to us naturally, of their own free will. They reject their own men."

Us? she thought. She said, "Why do they do that?"

"Because," he said, perfectly seriously, "we're superior."

It wasn't worth getting angry about, but the effort of putting up with him was beginning to wear her down. He was still good-looking and she still felt tolerance and a certain affection for his body, but not so much now for his face or voice. And all at once she wondered about the fire at her aunts' house: how it had really started, and if someone had deliberately set it, or had even been told to.

"I guess it's like the lobotomies," he said. "They think of it as medicine."

"What's medicine? Are you talking about sex? What does lobotomy have to do with it?"

"When you took the tour with Erwin, didn't you see how many of the Indians have a scar right here on their foreheads?"

"Yes. It's the way they get rid of the poison from some kind of insect. It's trepanning, not lobotomy."

"Whatever you want to call it. They go to Erwin, crowds of them, and ask him to do it. Theodore, too; Erwin taught him how. No insect bites, no infection—they just want the operation. And afterwards they feel better. A lot of them want it done over and over."

"There isn't any reason for it? They aren't sick?"

"They're all completely well. I told you: they just want the operation. Apparently it goes way back. The Incas used to do it, too."

"The Incas used to cut the hearts out and eat them."

"That was the Aztecs."

"I can't believe it."

"It's all in the history books."

"Jesus," she said.

"I don't know. They really do feel better afterwards. And a lot of civilized people believe the same: they want somebody to run their lives, fix them up, change their luck."

"That's horrible."

"If it makes them happy?"

"It can't," she said. "To have an unnecessary operation can't make them happy."

"But it does," he told her.

. . .

Carla sat between Regina and Kristel on the back seat of a horse-drawn carriage. They were shielded by screen curtains and covered with a green canvas top, in spite of which she'd already been stung by a gnat.

They had a driver named Eusabio. He'd stopped the horses so that the ladies could admire the view. In the distance, outcrops of rock massed together into a chain of spiky hilltops. At the top of one of the high peaks was another monastery, they'd seen three already.

"Now, this is really interesting," Regina said.

Kristel murmured, "I don't feel well."

"I've got a bit of a headache myself," Carla admitted.

"Nonsense," Regina said. "You'll both feel better once we've had some exercise."

"I'm not walking all the way up there," Kristel wailed. "That's how Frieda got sick. You kept pushing her."

Erwin turned around from the front seat and smiled at Carla. "You mustn't think we're like this all the time," he said.

"Oh, shut up," Regina told him.

"Usually," he added, "we're much worse."

Regina rose from her seat. She climbed down to the ground. Erwin followed, saying that they'd be back soon. Eusabio drove the carriage forward slowly and stopped under the shade of some trees. They waited. Carla fanned herself with a piece of paper she'd found in her purse; she always kept a supply of paper by her in case she wanted to jot down an idea for a design.

"I hate these places," Kristel said. "They aren't my idea of Christianity at all. I remember the way churches used to be —the way they still are, on the other side of the world. God knows what the people here really believe. They're all like animals."

"I got the impression they were very devout."

"They like ceremonies. They love all these ceremonies about death and entombment. The ideas, the ideals, mean nothing to them."

The glare coming off the rocks was beginning to make Carla sleepy and slightly dizzy. She looked down at the fan she was holding, and noticed that on part of the paper she'd begun a picture of one of her cat-boxes; the paper must have been in her bag for months: the drawing divided the sitting cat at a point lower than the one she'd finally chosen. And the completed boxes had been put into production before the previous Christmas. She considered telling Kristel about the German church of the fourteen saints. But it wasn't worth trying to shock these people.

"I feel sick," Kristel said.

"Was Frieda the one who couldn't walk? Was she always—"

"Healthy as a horse till her eighty-sixth birthday, when she made a pig of herself on Elvas plums and brandy."

"Didn't she have a disease like—"

"Oh, everybody knows what was wrong with her. Disappointed in love, that's all. And Regina—well. She was the scandal."

And you? Carla thought.

"Regina would still be a scandal if anybody'd take her. It's a disgrace. And now she's so righteous."

"And you?"

"Me?"

"Do you like living here?"

"Oh. Of course. I'd rather be back home, naturally, but this was where Theo wanted to take us."

"Where's home?"

"Berlin, Dresden, Leipzig."

"And the last time you were there?"

"I went back once on a visit with Erwin in 1931. We had a lovely time."

"I see," Carla said.

"I love parties. Are you looking forward to yours?"

"My what?"

"Your initiation ceremony."

120

"Oh? Initiation into what?"

"Into the family."

"Is that the same kind of thing Carl was doing last night?"

Kristel looked suddenly as if she'd said more than she should have, and knew that it was too late to do anything about it. She flapped her hands, laughed, and said she had an idea that the business with Carl was some sort of contest that had to do with the Indians.

"Like what?" Carla asked.

Kristel shrugged. She didn't know, she said. And maybe, Carla thought, she didn't.

"But I've seen your dress, and it's beautiful. It's just wonderful. It's silk and satin and all covered with little glittering jewels and shining white, like a wedding dress."

"Oh?"

"Yes. Right down to the floor. And there's a veil that goes with it."

Carla turned her head. Kristel was looking straight out into the landscape; her face glowed with eagerness. It was impossible to tell if she was lying, or remembering some other event, or imagining a thing that had never been.

"And you'll be wearing the family jewels. Including the Treasure—they had such a time getting it away from Gisela before we left home."

.   .   .

She caught Carl as he was turning out of the hallway leading from her landing. "What's going on?" she said.

He was in evening clothes. Something about them didn't look right. They fitted perfectly, but seemed antiquated, especially the jacket. "Aren't you ready yet?" he said. "I thought you were trying on your dress. We aren't supposed to see each other."

"Carl, what is all this?"

"It's just to make them happy. Some kind of pageant-thing they do. The Indians believe it makes the grass grow, or something."

"You're kidding."

"Anyway, hurry up, will you? We don't have much time.

And I want a drink first." He ran on down the stairs, moving easily, his head up, not having to look down at his feet, which she always had to do on staircases.

She went to her room and began to pack. She started with the dresser drawers and the medicine chest in the bathroom. After that, it was only her two dresses and the trousers and extra skirt.

She opened the wardrobe door and stepped back. A mound of shiny white material bounced out at her—part of the lower half of a very long dress. It was like uncovering a light. And there seemed so much more of it than should belong to a single dress. She tried to push it in again, so that she could get to her clothes. The voluminous heaps of it sprang back at her. The whole garment reminded her of a filled parachute and a newsreel she'd once seen, that had shown a landed airman who'd had to fight with his still-billowing chute. It was all over her. But as she reached up to squash some of the material into place, she caught sight of the bodice, still on the hanger, and stopped. She'd never seen anything like it: delicate lace, interwoven with tiny pale jewels in leaf and flower patterns, crisscrossed by knotted and curled ribbons in all shades of creamy white: tinted in pastel colors like the dawn.

As she stood there examining the workmanship of the dress, there was a knock at the door and Regina stepped into the room. "I'll help you with it," she announced. "You'll need someone to snap up the inside straps, otherwise the folds won't lie right. The others are no use—they always get so hysterical about parties."

"This must have taken years to make," Carla murmured. "Hundreds of people must have worked on it."

"Only about ten, I think."

"Where does it come from?"

"From here. It's been in the family for generations."

"When was it—"

"Hurry up," Regina ordered. "Take off your clothes."

The door opened again. Kristel and the housekeeper, Maria, burst in. Kristel looked even more sickly than usual—her skin was almost like a cheese going bad; but Maria was grinning with excitement. She made a grab at the buttons of Carla's blouse. Carla pulled away.

"Calm down, Maria," Regina said. "Here, hold the train free."

Carla began to undress. She kept her underclothes on, and her sandals. Regina and Maria stood on chairs and lifted the dress down over her head.

"The shoes," Kristel pointed out.

"Nobody's going to see the shoes," Regina said. "The dress is too long on her, anyway."

"And the Treasure. My God, how could we have forgotten it?"

"I didn't forget," Regina said. "Hold her hair up, will you?"

They dragged her hair up and back, and began to stick hairpins into it. They jammed the veil comb on top and batted the netting out of the way; it floated backward like a ghostly shadow of herself. Kristel turned around and took a bottle and glass from a bag she'd left near the door. She poured out a liquid that looked like sherry, and handed the glass to Carla. "Drink this," she said. "It's traditional."

Carla was reluctant, but the drink smelled good.

"Go ahead," Regina told her. "Be careful not to spill."

Carla drank.

She drank three glasses while the other women fussed over her—shoving rings on to her fingers, skewering diamonds into her sleeves, pinning and clipping sapphires across the headband of her veil. When they were ready at last, she felt drunk. They guided her out of the room, holding her skirts to protect them as she squeezed sideways through the doorway. They led her along a corridor, down a staircase and to a landing bordered by a balustrade. Down below she could see a congregation of people and heard the hum of their voices. Far off in the background she picked out Carl, who was talking to her great-uncle Theodore. She felt like yawning. Over in the right-hand corner a group of men with musical instruments sat in chairs. Such a large gathering, she thought: what was it about? And what was she doing there at all, surrounded by these weird old women? She should be at home, designing toys. Any minute now she'd begin laughing the silly laugh that came over her when she hit the best stage of inebriation—the first, where she felt terrific.

"You wait here with her," Regina said. "I'll be right back."

"Where are you going?" Carla asked.

"To get the Treasure."

"Better hurry up, before I fall asleep."

"You shouldn't have given her the third glass," Regina said to Kristel. "Idiot." She stomped away, turning abruptly and entering a room just beyond the corner. The band started to tune up. Kristel sniveled miserably; she muttered that her hands were hurting.

Carl looked up. Although he was so far away, Carla could tell that he was staring at her with an especially expectant, approving look. Some of the other people below had also caught sight of her, or rather, of the dress. The band gave out a few screeching chords, pulled itself together and swung into a jaunty tune. Regina came swishing back around the edge of the banisters. She was holding a box covered in black velvet. She handed it to Carla, saying, "Here. Put it on."

Carla lifted the lid. It snapped open so that the contents were hidden from the others, but she could tell that in any case their attention was all on her face. She stared downward. "What is it?" she asked.

"The largest pearl ever discovered," Regina said importantly. "Absolutely perfect, unique, and—of course—priceless."

Carla smiled drunkenly down into the box, at the black velvet stand, the heavy, glittering linked chain, the elaborate gold and enamel setting, and inside it the large sunken blob of shrivelled brown matter that resembled a piece of burned meat.

"Well?" Regina said.

"Wonderful," she answered. "Priceless."

CAPTAIN HENDRIK'S STORY

Captain Hendrik's property extended to the bay. In the twilight of dawn or evening you could imagine the house as a large, white ship stranded there from another age. Far behind it began the dense pinewoods that covered all the islands of the archipelago. Nearer to the house were ornamental lakes populated by ducks and swans. And in between lay what had once been famous sunken gardens full of exotic plants that generations of Hendriks had brought back from the New World when it was still considered new.

They had been explorers for hundreds of years. An offshoot of the family had even been related to the Dane, Vitus Bering, after whom the Bering Strait was named, and who—while in the service of Peter the Great—had proven that the land-masses of America and Asia were separated from each other. Hendriks had discovered rivers, islands, animals, fish, orchids, trees, and given them names as Adam is said to have done in Paradise. They were, of course, the men of the family. The women stayed at home.

The women were brought up to be good listeners. From childhood they were used to seeing great-uncles push the saltcellars and pepperpots around the tablecloth in order to give a picture of where the cavalry had been or how the ship had come about close to a treacherous sandbar lying just off the hidden rocks. They learned how to do all the secondary work: making neat copies of the notes and logbooks, mounting the sketches, collating the figures, planting the tubers and bulbs. They were glad to do it. They admired their manly, adventurous relatives.

And for a long while all branches of the family flourished, as did the transplanted tropical seedlings. But then, suddenly, there was a period of financial experimentation which turned out badly, unrestrained speculation to gain back what had been lost, and subsequent safe investments that diminished every year. Some of the land was sold. Huge tracts of the mainland went, to be forested by lumber companies and turned into paper. Many fine pieces of furniture and silverware, and also paintings, were taken from the house to the auction rooms.

And the great source of wealth, the men, came to a stop. All at once the family produced only daughters.

It was at this point that Captain Anders Hendrik decided to mount his own expedition. He was thirty-eight years old, had a young wife, Lina, and two small daughters, ten and eight years old. His mother, her two sisters, and his two great-aunts—sisters of his grandfather—all still lived in the house, together with his widowed sister, Elsie, and her nine-year-old daughter, Erika. After plans for the voyage had been drawn up, his wife's younger sister, Louise, joined them, and his own cousin, Sophie; both of the girls were attached to young men who would be accompanying the captain. That made twelve: twelve female members of the family in one house. In addition to them, there were six maids, a cook, a butler, a gardener and a gardener's boy, and—farther away, out in the forest—three gamekeepers.

Anders expected to be gone for at least two years. He was counting on that. Before anything happened, therefore, the lies had started: he lied about simply wanting to be free from so many women. And they lied about not being hurt by his actions. Without anyone saying anything on either side, it was understood that the women were prepared to forgive him if he managed to make them proud of him. That would mean success, and one which probably ought to entail some kind of replenishment of the family coffers.

He was taking five other men with him. Martin Brandt, a friend from his schooldays, had gone into the navy with him as a cadet and then changed his mind and become an astronomer instead. He had suffered a series of reverses and misfortunes during the past three years and had seized on the idea of the expedition as his last hope for an active life. Anders' sister-in-law, Louise, was engaged to one of the younger men, a scientist named Ib, interested principally in the history of medicine, who saw in the trip a good opportunity to establish a name for himself. The Germans and English had long since sent out explorers, who had reported back that Central and South America were virtually untapped, even unstudied. Perhaps the Indians in the part of the world they were going to had drugs and potions unknown to Europe and the north of the continent; he would be able to try out new cures. He would have plenty to do, even though his field would not embrace so much new information as that of Cousin Sophie's young Count, Johann Hellstrom, who was the botanist of the company. He was bringing along many large and splendid manuscript books and boxes of paints, as well as a great store of tubs and protective crates for the collecting of specimens.

The crew had been picked by Martin, so they were all right. And the ship was of a very dashing appearance—just like the white seabird of Anders' dreams. He had insisted on the look of romance, despite the fact that the yacht had steam power. Actually it had both sail and steam. It had everything. But it seemed to be exactly as if it had come from the boatyards a hundred years before. You had to look carefully, and in the right places, to see just how modern and scientific the design was.

When Anders first saw her, his heart turned over. Already he imagined her anchored off tropical shores or racing before the winds. His mother had told him, "It's like the boats in your grandfather's day," yet everything was as fresh as the instant. To see such a ship in the water was like being present at the return of an exiled ruler.

His officers approved. And they liked the combination of the out-of-date, which was lovely, and the brand new, which would be safe and efficient: the result disappointed no one. But the builders had been chosen by Anders' cousin, Gustav, and everybody should have known better than to depend on any object or person of his choice.

Gustav was charming. Everyone liked him. He'd been a beautiful child, and extremely alert—so bright and clever, in fact, that it was a long time before anyone realized that he wasn't really very intelligent. He'd start an idea and drop it halfway through. It was generally held that that was a sign of frivolity—that Gustav was a natural dilettante; but it would have been truer to say that his mind, his heart, his attention just didn't have the staying power. Single-handedly he had run his fortunes into the ground; luckily the rest of his family were a good-looking and attractive set of people who found no difficulty in making friends, so that before he ruined everyone completely, the other men acquired professions and the women husbands; they had their small apartments and houses, although the great estates were gone, as was the old mansion up in the north, which had been—of all the houses the captain had ever visited—his favorite. He himself still enjoyed Gustav's company; he would ordinarily never have considered taking him on any voyage, but Gustav had written to him and asked especially: he was in some sort of trouble again, naturally. They were the same age, but Gustav had had three wives and nearly a dozen children, all of whom always needed money, and as soon as they had realized that application to Gustav was useless, they had transferred their attentions to any relatives who would listen. Hendrik's wife, Lina, was of the opinion that Gustav's *ménage* was partly responsible for the fact that their own bank balance was sinking. But one couldn't, he kept saying, let people starve.

Gustav arrived five days before the expedition was set to depart. He brought too many belongings, which he insisted were essential to his comfort, as well as a servant—a dark, curly-haired, gypsy-like boy named Sten. Sten, it appeared, was also indispensable. Room would have to be made for him on board.

"This is a scientific expedition, Gustav," the captain told him. "Everything we take with us has to be used. If we transport a jar, it should contain food on the way out and seeds on the way back. We've got to take drinking water. We don't have room for extra boxes—certainly not for another person, who's going to be eating and drinking all the way across the Atlantic."

"But Sten is my right-hand man," Gustav said. He smiled in the same agreeably infectious way in which he'd greeted Anders when they had met for school vacations at their parents' houses. He said he was writing a "history of the world," but that he could never arrange his thoughts satisfactorily until he'd first explained them out loud to Sten. Sten was the perfect listener: he'd changed Gustav's life. "You can't turn him away," he added. "He's had such a hard life. You can't imagine how he was mistreated before I hired him. It's no fun to be a servant in this world, Anders, you know that. You and I have been fortunate."

"Yes," Anders agreed. Gustav could always bring up the right subject at the crucial time. Sten looked at the two of them as they stood talking at a distance from him. His mournful, small-featured face showed patient hopelessness.

"He was a circus boy," Gustav said. "They trained him brutally, to be able to do all the tricks. They broke his back, Anders."

"Is that possible?"

"To make him capable of doing those running backbends—you've seen them. All his joints. His own father did it. It was a large family—they needed the money. And when they moved on, they sold him. He stayed with the circus in Hungary. He's never had a friend, Anders."

The captain had reached the stage of nervous excitement and physical exhaustion where he had stopped measuring and counting and wondering if one more of this or that would make a difference. If his friend, Martin, had been there, neither Sten nor Gustav would have set foot on the boat; as it was, Anders finally allowed both of them to come along. And all their luggage was stowed, too.

He didn't want a big ceremony. "Let the celebrations wait for the homecoming," he said to Lina, but she insisted. All the children in the district had been looking forward to it for weeks, she told him—and particularly his two little daughters, Hannah and Astrid, and their cousin, Erika.

A gigantic quayside party was arranged. It went on for three days. The whole of the town seemed to be there, including every newspaper reporter in the country. Waiters and waitresses distributed food, beer and wine. The captain couldn't imagine who was paying for it all.

He was unhappy about the festivities. If people wanted to go off and enjoy themselves, that was fine, but in the meantime, let him get away to the New World without fuss. It was always a mistake to drum up interest like that for a departure; after everyone got ready, there was sure to be a delay—sometimes it could be a matter of days or weeks, depending on the ship, the winds, the settling of the cargo.

But this time everything went beautifully. The yacht pulled away from the harbor like a swan gliding across the surface of a lake, and all the relatives, reporters, tavernkeepers and other townspeople waved frantically. The band played, voices sang, handkerchiefs were held up and fluttered, people cried. The weather was perfect; the day all blue and white, sunlit and sparkling. And the captain soon got over the sadness that had come upon him as he'd said goodbye to his children. His younger daughter, Astrid, who usually liked the ritual of farewell just as much as that of greeting, had begun to cry piteously into his neck and to tell him over and over again in a heartbroken voice, "I don't want you to go."

.   .   .

He was away for years, during which time the family fortunes fell even lower. The great quayside party had, of course, been paid for by Anders himself, although he had known nothing of the arrangements. Lina and his mother had organized everything with the help of the bank, who were very glad to give them a loan. Before the ship had disappeared over the horizon, the women had spent all their extra money for emergencies and some that should have been used for repairing the house. The ordinary running costs would be taken care of, but there would be no summer holiday, no treats nor new clothes, fresh tutors for the children, trips into town to see the theater, parties for friends. They still thought the voyage would last between two and three years. They expected news within four months at the latest. But nothing came; and nothing, and nothing.

.   .   .

The silence lasted ten years. Anders' mother died, and her sisters, his two aunts. The two old great-aunts lived on, but the middle generation was gone from the house. One of the gamekeepers got an infected foot and he too died. Two of the younger housemaids married and moved away. The family quarreled with all of Gustav's relatives and severed communications with them. After the first three years, the Hendriks seldom heard from anyone connected with the other men who had sailed on the voyage.

And then at last there was a letter, or rather, a brief note. It came from Portugal, where it had been brought by a cargoboat from South America. It was from Anders. All he would say was that the expedition had suffered privation, sickness, death and massacres. They had re-formed themselves several times, using local labor and studying the unmapped interiors of several different countries. They had been through epidemics, battles and accidents. And he was the sole survivor. He was shipping out as master on a Dutch freighter and hoped to be home shortly before the end of the winter.

Lina prepared to travel with Anders' sister, Elsie, to Cherbourg, where he was to land, but another letter came to forestall them: Anders had had luck—the ship had achieved record time and he would come overland and then by ferry and so on to Stockholm. They were to stay and wait for him.

"Well," Lina said, "we've had enough practice."

"He still doesn't say anything about Ib," Elsie said. "Or even Johann."

Lina stood with her hand on the strap of her basket trunk. She murmured that he didn't say much of anything and that it wasn't like him: he was usually so mindful of others and had a thought for everyone.

She didn't stop to consider as she talked. It had been ten years without a word. They had had him, she only now remembered, officially declared dead—and the others. Sophie had married someone else three years before; what would she do now if Johann came home?

"They're dead, Elsie," she said.

"Anders is alive, at any rate."

"I mean the lawyers. Don't you remember?"

"Oh, good Lord."

"And I sold most of his grandfather's library—the books with all the French bindings. Elsie, what am I going to do?"

"We just wait, dear. That's all we can do. He'll understand that you acted for the best."

Lina wasn't sure. The children, at first so delighted by the news, picked up her apprehension. The two daughters, Hannah and Astrid, now twenty and eighteen, were told, as if still children, to go off into the park and amuse themselves somehow, while their mother and aunt discussed matters of business.

.   .   .

The three girls strolled down to the boathouse, which had been converted into a study for Erika.

Johannah, the eldest, was positive that her father had come back with a wonderful secret about the fountain of youth or the herb of life, or something along similar lines.

Astrid wanted the treasure to be gold, or pearls at the very least.

Erika expected him to have brought back a knowledge of the customs and languages of the people who lived in the region of the Amazon. She hoped for an advance in scholarship and some kind of national or international recognition of his work: a medal, or a citation or award, a special degree issued to him by the universities. "But the others?" she asked.

"All dead," Hannah said. "They wouldn't let us look at the letter, but Ingrid was listening at the door."

"All of them?" Erika said.

"Well, in ten years. A lot can happen."

"Or all at once," Astrid suggested. "Eaten by cannibals."

"Mother," Erika said, "was interested in Uncle Anders' best friend, Martin Brandt. She doesn't say anything, but I wonder if he's alive. I can still remember him."

"I remember the party when they left," Astrid said.

"All of them. All dead," Hannah repeated. "That's what Ingrid said."

"Well, we'll have to wait and see," Erika told her.

.   .   .

He arrived late in the evening, brought by the two-horse carriage that worked from the train station. He didn't say

132

hello to anyone, nor did a single person greet him. He went unrecognized. The porter and cabdriver loaded his three large trunks and two boxes at the back and on top, and they started off. The driver made some conversation about the weather, but that was all.

It was still cold. At the Viking stone landmark Anders stepped down and rode the rest of the journey inside, braced against an old cord-bound bootbox that was being delivered to some house in the neighborhood. He closed his eyes. It had taken him a long time, nearly two years, before he could decide to come home. For a while he had really wondered whether he might not stay away forever. He'd been living under a different name, he was speaking another language, he'd read the announcement of his presumed death. He looked different.

He looked so different that old Ingrid at the door failed to recognize him. He asked for his wife, stepped into the flagged hallway, and stood alone there as the old woman's footsteps went on, fainter, behind closing doors. He knew exactly where she was going and what she would pass by: all the corridors, the paintings hung along them, the rooms, chairs and tables.

He remembered the hall itself from his childhood: the hexagonal flagstones, the whitewashed semicircular wall with the straight-backed wood chairs set against it; the antlers and heads of deer and elk mounted high up on the wall. His eyes traveled to the long curve of the banister and the first flight of the staircase, which was all he could see from the level where he stood.

Lina came from downstairs, out of the little room his mother had used to write her letters in: the room off the passage that led from the drawing room to the library. And Elsie was rushing right behind her.

They both stopped still when they saw him. They thought they must have made a mistake. He'd had smooth, brown hair when he'd gone away; now it was bushy and gray. And he had a gray beard, too.

"Anders," Lina said. "Oh, my dear." She walked slowly to him.

Everything, he thought then, was worth that moment, no

matter what happened. He opened his arms and folded her up in them, bowing his head.

His sister withdrew for a while, until she could hear that they were moving off towards the drawing room. Then she ran after them and threw herself at him, giving out a cry as if she had suddenly hurt herself.

.   .   .

There was a big family gathering at which he met and embraced his relatives in almost total silence. At first there had been a laugh or a sob, or a silly remark about how things had changed; but as the minutes passed, a funereal quiet spread through the company. They didn't know what to say, nor did he. Two extremely pretty young women pounced on him eagerly and wanted to kiss him over and over: they turned out to be his daughters. He shook hands with the servants; one of them said something about what a pity it was that his mother hadn't lived to see the day. He felt his mind beginning to spin and the room seemed too crowded wherever he moved. He stepped back beside his wife and sister. He motioned them out into the hallway with him and towards the library. He asked that he should be allowed to rest for a time.

"Of course, dear," Lina agreed. "We'll have a quiet meal together."

"Just the three of us," he said.

"Lovely." She hadn't thought that he'd include Elsie. "But at some point, you must just go up and say hello to the aunts."

"Aunt Emmelina and Aunt Irmintrude?" he said, as if hauling the names from memories of a book read in his childhood. "I'm surprised they're still alive. They must be nearly a hundred by now."

"Aunt Emmelina is ninety-seven," Elsie told him. "Aunt Irmintrude is ninety-nine."

"Are they still up and about?"

"Yes, indeed," Lina said. "They're wonderful old dears, really."

"Getting very doddery," Elsie added, "and can be nasty as toads when they like. But fortunately most of their energy nowadays is taken up with hating each other instead of the rest of us. Ingrid won't go up the stairs any more."

"She's getting on, too," he said. "I thought so when I saw her in the hall."

"But she's strong. It's the spiteful things they say that she can't stand. She says that in her day only peasants had such bad manners."

"What a shame it is," he said. "I remember them as such charming ladies. A breath of the old world. As it was. Before everything changed."

"I suppose you have to think of it as an illness," Lina said. "Old age."

"Ninety-nine is certainly very old."

"You must just look in. They'd be so pleased."

"Yes," he said. "But first, before anything, I have to talk to you both."

. . .

"As I wrote you," he said, "the others are dead. We traveled through so many places and lived through such dangers— ten years is a long time; sometimes I wonder at the fact that I'm still alive myself. And sometimes I look back and think: did that happen? There's another thing, one that frightens me now: I'm actually pretty sure that there are times I don't remember exactly. Some of them I may even have falsified— not meaning to, but simply in the course of time, as people do—as you'll notice happens if you ask ten eyewitnesses to describe an accident or even an opera. I realized it first five years ago, when a few of us were comparing notes about the arrival in South America; and we couldn't agree about any- thing at all."

"But why didn't you write?" Lina asked.

"Wait," Elsie said. "Let him take his time."

"We wrote. Of course we wrote. All the time. But, after the initial flow, we wrote sporadically. And then, some of the others stopped. Wait, and I'll explain why.

"We hit calms, we ran into storms, we foundered off a cluster of islands not far from the African coast. We lost our navigating instruments, our wonderful special equipment for jungle travel and research; we lost some of our men. We almost lost our lives. We took to the boats in a big sea.

"Then we were on the beach for about a week. And damn thankful to be there, I can tell you. Better than drowning. But eventually it did begin to seem that we might never get back to civilization: that we might die out there, forsaken. A ship went by in the distance and we signalled like madmen. They let down anchor, put out the boats for us and, hey presto! we'd been captured by a gang of desperadoes, the like of which I'd thought hadn't been seen on the high seas in a hundred years at least. We were prisoners."

"Good heavens," Lina exclaimed.

"My gracious," Elsie said. "In this day and age?"

"We were chained. Yes. And nobody was writing letters. We stayed on that rotten tub for over a year. The pirates quarreled and fought among themselves so much that at first we hoped they'd kill each other off and leave us to take over the vessel. But then our own men began to die; of disease, of bad food and water, of being wounded—getting in the way when the fights were raging. At last the captain—if you could call him that—made for the West Indies and there the pickings were so good that they overreached themselves: they took too many prisoners. While they were drunk, we mutinied and gained control of the ship."

"Ib and Count Hellstrom?" Lina asked.

"They were both still alive. But Cousin Gustav's servant, Sten, had his head taken clean off with a cutlass and Gustav was wounded so badly in the leg that we thought we might have to amputate. He was ill for weeks. And when he recovered, he walked with a limp. He wasn't much use after that—I think the death of his servant unhinged him slightly. He'd been very fond of the boy."

"I always remember Gustav joking and laughing," Elsie said. "I don't like to think of him in pain. He wasn't meant to lead a serious life."

"We decided to try to mount an expedition anyway. We had quite an amazing store of gold and pirate treasure on board, and we put in at Venezuela to set about outfitting another team."

"But you didn't let us know anything," Lina said.

"Of course we did. I don't know what happened—letters go astray all the time, boats sink every day. And I wasn't thinking clearly or I'd simply have gone to a consulate at the beginning and told them everything—or had advertisements put in the papers. That's how I found out that I'd been declared legally dead: from reading a newspaper."

"You can't blame us for that," Lina said. "We never heard."

"I'm not blaming you. Not at all. It could have been worse. You could have remarried."

"Sophie married somebody else finally."

"But Louise never did," Elsie told him. "It's ruined her life."

"If he hadn't been a Count," Lina said, "Sophie would have found another man much sooner."

"But you didn't," he said.

Lina looked down at her hands. She said, "No."

"Well, if I'd been thinking, as I said, I'd have done it through the papers. But we waited too long, so that soon it was no use calling on the official bodies, because we'd broken the law in so many directions, we weren't sure how far we could be protected. We had contraband goods that we were in the process of turning into equipment for scientific exploration, we'd taken part—although against our wills—in piracy, we'd committed murder. There's a limit to the lengths your country can go to in giving you assistance among foreigners, even if you're a *bona fide* gentleman. Wherever we went after the first week on land, and whatever we did, it seemed to us likely that if we notified any ambassadors from home, the local governments would find it much more to their taste to shoot us as outlaws and confiscate our possessions. We couldn't. We didn't dare to.

"It was a terrible time," he said. He bowed his head. The two women could see that his hands, gripping each other tightly, were trembling. "The sense of isolation," he said, "was appalling. The impression that it's never going to end."

Lina and Elsie had also suffered from what he called a "sense of isolation." But they said nothing. They didn't even bother to exchange a look. It was over now.

"We still had a long way to go," he continued. "We had

137

to cross many hundreds of miles to get to the beginning of the lands we wanted to study. And only a few of us wanted to keep going. I knew I had to, for all your sakes, and for the family—naturally. Ib and Johann felt the same. But Gustav was ready to quit. And—he threatened to tell all sorts of things that weren't true: to say we'd been the ones to attack ships and turn pirate, that we'd—oh, all fantasy. He demanded things: villas, riches, dancing girls—that's what he said. He seemed to have a picture in his mind of some kind of Turkish harem set in a South American garden. He wasn't himself, but he wasn't sick. I don't know what it was. He sometimes seemed to have gone completely dotty, like his great-uncle Svensen.

"We had long discussions as to whether we could afford to leave him behind. We decided not to; he had to come with us. There was no other way we could prevent him from seeking out an embassy or even the police—no. Everything else was going wrong at that time, too. For instance, the men we still had were getting drunk as pigs every night and going on the town. We didn't know how much they were talking, or to whom. Martin said they were always too drunk to talk, even in their own languages, but I couldn't believe that. I wanted to get them out of the cities as soon as possible. Martin had the bright idea that we should pretend there was no more money but that we were going to combine our scientific expedition with a hunt for gold. So, that was what we did. And we persuaded what was left of the crew to come with us, into the jungle.

"Into the jungle, yes. My God, what that was like."

Both the women had been thinking and dreaming about the jungle off and on for ten years. Now they were silent. They already knew from the thoughts and dreams what it was like.

"We had it all: mosquitoes, spiders, insects, plagues of boils, Indians blowing darts at us, animals attacking at night, poisonous fish, forest fires. Everyone started to die. Ib first, from a gangrenous thigh—it had been a small cut he'd made by accident when he'd wiped his knife across his trouser leg;

then Johann, of a fever. We'd had fevers all the time. When he died, we were stunned."

"Did you give them good, Christian burials?" Elsie asked.

"Of course, as well as we could. We didn't remember all the words, but we recited as much as we knew. I told you, I'm too tired out to go over this a hundred times, so if you could tell the girls, the—everyone in the house."

"Yes," the two women answered together.

"Cousin Gustav was stronger than both of them, in spite of his limp. He even began to apply himself to drawing the shrubs and flowers we encountered—the work that Johann had been doing before he died. And Gustav's drawings weren't all that bad. I was surprised. He'd never had any scientific training, only fiddled about a bit in Paris and Rome at the art schools years back. I don't know why I mention it; all the books are lost. It's all eaten by beetles and worms by now, down on the floor of the jungle with the rotted leaves."

"Don't," Elsie whispered.

"He was bitten by something. That was another thing we lived with: infected bites, ulcers, eczemas, insects that bored under the skin and laid their eggs there. I thought I was going half blind myself from a swelling in my right eye. But his didn't heal. It got bigger, and it opened; it began to ooze pus and to stink. And he was dead in four days. We buried him too; Martin and I."

"Then Martin is alive?" Elsie asked.

"No, he was the last. He was killed by the Indians, just near the end, as we got out. They tied him to a rock. It was some sort of ceremony. I'd hidden and followed to where they took him. I was going to creep forward and let him loose in the middle of the night, but when I touched him, he was cold. They must have given him something to eat or drink before they began. It went on for hours, with chanting. I watched from where I was, and waited. I couldn't do anything until it got dark. When they went away, they left him without a sentry, but they'd put hundreds of little statues around the rock; in rings, like the circles from a whirlpool. I think they were intended to be spirits standing guard over him. I picked one up and took it with me to use as an extra weapon. If I'd known what it was, I'd have taken more than one. Look.''

He reached for the carpetbag he had carried with him and put down on a chair. From an inner compartment he took out an object the size of a closed hand. He set it on the table in front of them, to the side of the tea tray.

"How hideous," Lina said.

"Is it an animal?" Elsie asked.

"It's a woman," he told them. "Perhaps a goddess. And very heavy. It's solid gold."

Lina reached for the statue and then withdrew without touching it. The thing was foreign to her understanding of what a work of art should look like. Elsie stretched out her arm. She moved the figure closer, tried to pick it up, and expressed astonishment at its weight.

He stared at the gold. The statue was almost square, the head and body appearing to be one. The eyes were rectangular slits, the lips drawn back over large, ferocious-looking teeth. The two breasts and swollen belly bulged from the point where a neck might have begun. And underneath, it ended. There were no hips, legs or feet. It was like a fist seen from some odd angle that prevented it from being recognized for what it was.

"Barbaric," Elsie said.

"I suppose so."

"Wonderful, in a way. Very strong-looking."

"Horrible," Lina said. "I don't like it."

"There's more to come," Anders told her. "Oh, yes. I lost the expedition but I came back with a good deal of money. And I earned it quite prosaically: I got a job as a riverboat captain and then I gambled with my earnings. Unbelievable, really. We're worth millions now."

Elsie squeezed his right hand and put her head against his shoulder. Lina, on his left, burst into tears and threw her arm around his waist. His eyes remained on the squat idol in front of him. In all the time he had carried it with him, he'd been unable to determine whether it had the face of a god or goddess, an animal, or even the face of an enemy.

140

.   .   .

He waited until the next day to visit his grandfather's sisters. Although twice his age, they were so tiny and shrunken now that they'd almost regained the look of youth. And it seemed strange to him that in a way they had hardly changed, whereas he felt himself so greatly altered by the intervening years, and also thought of himself as having grown old. In their long dresses with the lace sleeves and collars, the old ladies looked like dolls, or children dressing up, or—he was reminded—like a couple of chimpanzees he had seen in a German zoo that he'd been to as a child.

They recognized him. Emmelina said, "You haven't been to see us in a long while."

"Oh, it's Anders," her sister said.

"I've been away," he told them.

"That's no excuse," Irmintrude shot back at him. "What did you bring us for tea?"

"Cream cakes, I think. Is that all right?"

"We used to have lovely cakes in Paris," Emmelina said. "Remember?" Both sisters had once taken him out for a stupendous tea party in a restaurant, where he'd eaten everything in sight and been sick afterwards. The aunts at that time had been plump and tightly corseted and had disposed of nearly as much as he, but had held on to it better.

"I remember," he said. "With the pink sugar-mints in the shape of strawberries."

"And the walnut cake with stripes of butter icing," Irmintrude added.

"The chocolate mice," her sister recalled.

"That was a great day," he said.

"For all of us," Emmelina told him.

He left them, feeling that he had made them happy, but thinking that as soon as he walked out the door they'd forget that they had enjoyed his company, or perhaps forget that he had been there at all. And the next time they saw him, they might spend all the time bickering, or accuse him of saying things he hadn't said, or mix him up with someone else—his father, or even his grandfather, which they'd been in the habit of doing long before he'd set out on the expedition: so frail was one's hold on age, memory, character, consciousness, sanity. He was exhausted by the meeting. He wanted to sit down somewhere and cry.

He put on his warm clothes and tramped out to the boathouse. It was the place he used to go to when he wanted to be alone.

He was astonished when he let himself in and found that the building had been turned into a one-room house: the kind of bohemian barn full of curtains and paintings and cushions that he had hankered after during his years at the naval academy, when what he'd secretly longed for was escape to France and to the life of an artist in an atelier.

"Oh," he said. "Oh, my. What have we here?"

Erika stood up from a desk at the far end of the room. She said, "Of course, this is all new since the last time you saw it. Come in, Uncle Anders."

"This is just the way I used to dream about student life."

"Good. Sit down over here and we'll make it even more like the real thing: we'll have a long discussion. I keep looking for people to talk with. They all seem to peter out after five minutes or so."

"I'm not such a great conversationalist myself."

"But you have a great story to tell."

"No. I've told Elsie and Lina already—I can't keep going over it. I don't care to think about it much, either. I've got to start moving forward again. What I'd really be interested in is hearing about you."

"I want to be a doctor."

"What kind of doctor?"

"A doctor of thoughts."

"A difficult profession. Would you use bandages or pills?"

"That's just my joke. I'm studying pharmacology. I'd like to know all about the vegetation—everything you saw, and the arrow poisons they're supposed to have over there."

"I don't know about the poisons. They exist, all right, but I've no idea which plants they're extracted from. I brought back some drawings. I don't think they'll be any use."

"Of course they will. Why not?"

"Because they're mine. I don't even know how to draw very well. I did them to pass the time on the river."

"When can I see them?"

"Any time. After luncheon." He looked around, as if dazzled. "Everything's so bright here."

"Mamma says it's gaudy."

"I like it. I like colors. I used to think I'd had too much of the sun, forever blazing—it never stopped; you thought it was going to burn out your eyes. But in the jungle there isn't any sun. At least, not in the part we were in. There are different kinds, you know: the rain forests of the East, the African jungles, and so on. Where we were, everything was covered high up. The light doesn't penetrate very far. It's gray. Or dark; black-green and purple, blue. It's almost like being underwater, but hot."

"Marvelous."

"Terrible. It was terrible."

She put out a hand and touched his arm, saying, "It must have been terrible to lose your friends. I was sorry to hear that."

He dropped his eyes. He thought for a moment he was going to faint. He muttered, "Thank you, my dear."

"I should brew you some of my special tea. I've got dozens of different kinds. Each one cures some particular ailment."

"They really work?"

"Oh, yes. All based on old wives' tales, and they're all true."

"That's sometimes the way with folk remedies. Brown paper and cobwebs still do the job, no matter what the scientific journals say nowadays."

"But that's probably because there's some scientific principle at work that we don't understand yet."

"Are you really studying the subject—going to lectures, that kind of thing?"

"Of course."

"But I expect you'll get married in the end."

"I expect so. Why not? I can do both."

"Yes, well that's the new way now, I understand. Do you have a young man?"

143

"I've got three."

"One for pleasure, one for duty, and—what else?"

"One for show, of course. We attend all the right dances together. We make a lovely couple. He's like a plaster mannequin in a tailor's window."

"And the others?"

"For duty—that's easy. The family chose him. And for pleasure, that's secret."

He went for a short walk by the side of the lake. The wind ruffled the waters. It was cold, but soon spring would change everything: there would be swans on the lake, the grass would come back, the leaves. The only trees that didn't look like skeletons now were the pines. Spring would change the world and money would change it, too. He could buy back the lands, the paintings. He could add to what there had been before. For the first time since his homecoming, he gave a long sigh of relief.

In the afternoon he went to the top of Sightseer's Hill, from which he could see the bay, the islands and the town inland, and he made out a trace of smoke coming from the game-keepers' cottage. He set out to walk there, but well before he reached the hut, he was challenged by Haken, who didn't recognize him, nor for an instant did he recognize Haken, who had become an old man. He knew him only from his companion, Erik.

The three of them walked back to the cottage together. They sat around the tiled stove and drank aquavit.

Haken said, "We've had some bad years since you left us."

"So have I," Anders said.

"The fourth winter—was it? No, the sixth. It was so bad, the wolves came back."

"There haven't been wolves in these parts in over a hundred years."

"Well, they were here four years ago. Weren't they?" He kicked Erik's chair.

"That's right," Erik said. He'd been a boy, almost still a child when Anders had gone away. Now he was a surly young man, held down and criticized and taunted by Haken, who used to be a giant of a man but was now aging fast and losing his strength. Ten years had turned the apprenticeship into a slavery. Now the old man was jealous and the younger one hated him.

"Big, fat wolves," Haken said.

"How were they so fat, if it was such a hard winter?"

"Eating people, of course." Haken crowed with laughter. He took out a pipe that Anders suddenly remembered. Erik stared into space as if he were trying to deny his presence in the room.

"Looks so dazed like that," Haken muttered, "I sometimes don't know if he's right in the head."

Erik paid no attention to him. Anders said, "I used to think sometimes about the bear hunts. Do you remember?"

"Oh, those were the times," Haken said. "I recall your grandfather telling us how he'd been on the bear hunts in Russia and how they'd be all lined up afterwards, the dead bears. They'd get dozens. Really big hunting over there."

"But I remember it here."

"A little. Two or three at a time, that was something exciting for us."

"I thought even one was exciting. I was just a little boy. I was scared of the bear. And I thought the hunters were such romantic characters."

"Rogues and villains. Paid in drink."

"I dare say. But they looked like wild men, with their long hair and their headbands. One of them had a bearskin cloak, I remember. And they all had their rifles decorated in special ways. I thought they were like the tales I'd heard about the American Indians out West."

"Yes, I expect so," Haken said. "They weren't much use living in the towns, though. They didn't know anything but the forests."

"The dogs were wonderful, too. Grandfather knew every one by name."

"That's what counts—the dogs. We've still got the men, Master Anders, but not the dogs. They've died out of this region. There isn't a decent strain anywhere near here. You have to go miles to the north for them."

"My cousin's got some good hunting dogs," Erik said.

"Your cousin couldn't find his face in a looking-glass," Haken told him. Erik's head moved slightly, but his eyes were still dulled and inattentive. He didn't glance directly at either of them.

This is the way it happens, Anders thought. *Two people tied together for one reason or another, tied by work or love or blood; they don't speak what's in their minds, just pester each other from dawn to dusk until one day the more persecuted one—or perhaps the other one—goes berserk. Maybe soon it will happen to Haken: Erik will just pick something up and hit him or stab him.*

He walked back to the house, breathing deeply, thinking about the spring.

In the late evening Lina said she wanted to go to bed early. He put down his newspaper and stood up.

"You stay," she said. "I'm just feeling tired, that's all."

"So am I," he said. He kissed the others goodnight: Elsie, Erika, Hannah, Astrid; and Louise, who had wept hysterically when she'd heard of Ib's death, and whose eyes were still red. He would have thought she'd guess after all that time, or be able to imagine it, but apparently the blow had come as if totally unexpected. There was no telling what people kept locked away as hopes or dreams. Sometimes they really thought the impossible was only a matter of faith—that it would happen because they wanted it to, or that they could escape it simply because they hated the idea of its happening.

He climbed the stairs after his wife, his eyes on the silk hem-flounce of her black dress. They were all still in black after three years. It was the way people lived out in the country.

He shut the door behind them.

"I really am tired," she said.

"We can sit here and talk. You can tell me what's on your mind. Or we can plan the renovations. And I was just thinking how solemn you all look in your black. You and Elsie need some new clothes, don't you think? And the girls too, of course."

"That would be nice." She stood rigid against the windows, looking into the green pattern of the drawn curtains. He had to go up to her, take her by the arm and steer her to the couch. She sat down without resisting, but she sat, as she had stood, stiffly.

He seated himself beside her, leaning lightly against her, and said, "Tell me."

She unclasped her hands, pressed them together again, and sighed. He thought about how well she knew all the bankers and lawyers in town and how often she'd had to visit them while he was gone. There was no knowing what a woman could get up to if she needed money badly enough.

"Something that happened while I was away?" he asked.

"Not really. There was enough, but most of it unimportant now. The bank, the lawyers, the formalities when we had to have you all declared dead."

"Yes?"

"It's what didn't happen. You could say that I've been on an expedition, too. Ten years. My youth left me in those ten years."

"No. You're still beautiful."

"I'm no longer young. Physically: my body, my hair, my teeth, my eyes. For ten years I was a woman without a life. Like a fly in a bottle."

"Oh, Lina."

"You spoke of isolation. Well, I was waiting so hard for you that I didn't notice. But now—did you know that when Sophie got married to that man, we all disapproved so much that we couldn't bear to be near her? We were glad when she moved to her in-laws' before the wedding. We attended, but we all still disapproved. And when I think of that now—after all, she waited till he was declared dead. Even his parents didn't hold it against her, but we did. And now that you're back, I know why we did. Because it was so hard for us to remain, willingly, in isolation: just to wait. Of course there was the threat of public opinion, but that's always there."

"Not if you'd remarried. Why didn't you marry someone else after I was declared dead?"

"Once was enough."

"Do you wish you'd had a lover?"

"Yes," she burst out. "I wish I'd had them all the time, for the whole of the ten years. Anyone, no matter who. You know how I've loved you all these years, every moment; but I wish that now."

"Maybe if you'd gone ahead and had the lovers, you'd have felt sorry for it later. Or maybe you'd have stopped loving me and begun to love somebody else instead. That's how it starts."

"And you? Didn't you love anyone in ten years?"

"Not enough to worry about," he said. "Hardly enough for me to remember."

She relaxed a little. She leaned back and said that soon they had to have a talk about the children. "Sometimes they seem complete savages to me. They haven't been given the training they should have had, they don't take anything seriously and they don't have the kind of strength that can keep them steady without supervision. Erika's different: she's an unusual girl. But our two, I'm afraid, are two ordinary flighty young things."

"But rather nice."

"Oh, enchanting. But utterly lacking in polish."

"That too can have its charm."

"No, dear. That must be seen to as soon as possible."

She nodded her head once, decisively, as he could remember seeing her mother do when she had made up her mind. Her mother had also used a fan to great effect, tapping it on chair arms to drive home a point, flicking it from side to side when she was being flirtatious.

"This houseful of women," she said. "We should have had a son."

"No," he told her. "Think of the burden that would have fallen on him while I was away. I had enough of that myself when I was the only one. I know what it's like."

.   .   .

He went into town to make all the formal declarations. Elsie and Lina went with him. Often they stood or sat so that he was in the middle, they remained for long periods on either side of him. It was like being in the center of a triptych or having guardian angels the way they were drawn in the old

148

book his grandfather had had of the lives of the saints. He couldn't have gone through the business alone. He was surprised at how readily they seemed to understand his need to be reticent, to get through all the explanations as quickly as possible, and then to forget.

The snows melted, the skies took on bluer shades. Plans were made to send the girls to Paris at the beginning of the summer. It wouldn't be the right time of year to go, but the trip might be the better for that and, as Elsie said, it was in any case a great deal better than not getting to Paris at all. All the women in the household were to go along, except the older servants and the great aunts. And Anders might either accompany his family, wait till they were settled in and then join them later, or stay at home, seeing to the estate. He hadn't made up his mind yet, but he was already looking forward to being on his own for a while.

His children were beginning to swamp him with their idolatry. They gazed huge-eyed at him and he, who had found their womanly faces and figures such a shock at first sight, was doubly embarrassed. They fawned on him like worshipping little girls, yet also like lovelorn young women. He felt much more comfortable with his niece, Erika, in her boathouse study.

"You really should do something with the sketchpads and notebooks," she told him.

"There must be any number of books like them already published," he said. The continent's been open to all the nations for a very great while now: the Spaniards, the Portuguese, the Germans. When I was there, I met Greeks, Frenchmen and Italians. You couldn't move without tripping over half of Europe. They were building banks and opera houses hand over fist. I'm sure the flora and fauna have been done to death."

"Then why did you set out on your expedition?"

"Oh, the interior—that's a different story. I told you: all the notes were lost. It's as if it never happened."

"But what you've got right here is fine. It's also good about the river and how it changes. And about the different tribes.

149

And what the other travelers have to say."

"Most of it made up, undoubtedly. It's great country for alcohol."

"People would be interested," she said. "You know they would be. Did mother tell you—she turned away some journalist the other day, who said he'd come from the newspaper office in town? 'A beady-eyed young man,' she said."

"Oh? What did he want?"

"He'd heard that a dead man had come back to his home, and he thought it was a good story."

"I see." Anders flexed his right hand, which had begun to stiffen in the cold weather. He spread out the fingers, curved them, made a fist and relaxed. It was becoming a habit to do the exercise at odd moments.

"He's right, too. It's a very good story. And I think if anyone's going to print it, you should tell it yourself. Don't you?"

"Perhaps," he said. "I'll have to think about it."

She smiled. She wanted to encourage him—and everyone—in everything. And like most others, he responded.

He thought at first that it could do no harm. It would keep his family quiet. And he could shut himself away in his room downstairs, where no one would disturb him because he was "working on his book." But then he really did begin to compose a narrative. When he'd break off between sentences, he'd sometimes find himself looking into the fierce stare of the pagan statue. He'd grin back at it, mimicking its expression. His younger daughter, Astrid, hated it, despite the fact that it was made of gold. "It frightens me," she had said.

"You shouldn't be frightened," he'd told her. "If a bad thing is going to happen, fear won't keep it away. Or do you enjoy being frightened? I think some people do. Perhaps it's a habit they're taught early."

"I just don't like the way it looks," she said.

He was frightened too, although not of the statue. He didn't know what of. The past was more terrifying than anything he could dream up, but the past was over. He worked at his book in order to keep away the dread, to push back the sense he had when he looked outdoors or went for a walk, that the thing—whatever it might be—could fall on him suddenly from the sky above.

. . .

He worked and he planned and he scented the beginning of spring, which was followed by a spell of clear weather. It turned very cold. Erik and Haken knew for certain that the cold temperatures came straight from the Arctic. They had seen that kind of thing before, they said; they had long experience of just such weather changes. Then the air grew warmer and the rain started. No one in the house liked that; it meant a constant changing in and out of boots and cleaning off the splashes afterwards.

During the first week of the rains both old aunts, within forty-eight hours of each other, died; the younger one—Emmelina—first. Irmintrude didn't begin to sicken or apparently to notice her sister's illness until the other members of the family gathered at the bottom of the stairs to come up and pay their respects to the corpse. It was as if the loss itself took her away—as if the two had been attached to a single line of life. The only one at the funeral who was really in tears was old Ingrid, who had had such troubles with them, but who could still remember them as they had once been: young and beautiful women.

Lina said afterwards that she wished both aunts had waited till autumn. "It seems wrong for people to die in the spring," she told him. One morning while he was working on the book, she wandered into his study and stood behind him. He turned in the chair to look around, and smiled, though his mind was still on his work and automatically he had put a hand—and then gradually slid the whole of his lower arm—over the page he was correcting.

"How's your writing coming along?" she asked.

"It's all right. What did you want?"

"Nothing, really. I was thinking about the aunts."

"A long life," he said. He put down his pen and hitched his chair a little to the side. "Stay and talk, Lina. Sit down."

"No," she said. "I don't want to disturb you. I should find some occupation of my own." She continued to stand in the same place, while he held his smile and waited. Her eyes went to the statue on the desktop.

"A long life," she said, "but how they changed during it."

"It's unavoidable."

"Yes, I see that now. I've realized that it has nothing to do with whether you've been good and followed the rules or whether you're pretty and clever, or anything at all. At the end, you become what old age makes of you. It's like being melted by a great heat. There's nothing you can do about it."

"It's still a long way off from you," he told her. "And we'll be together for it. The children would help us. It would only be really bad if you were alone. Or to be in the poorhouse, in one of those hospital wards."

"Is that what the gods are like?" she asked. "Look at it: an intelligence lower than that of the animals, more brutish than beasts."

"Astrid doesn't like it, either. But it's got something, you know. It's a different style of beauty, that's all. And it's seen me through a lot."

"When I was a child, they told us that the gods and goddesses—the Greek and Roman ones—were lovely to look at. They were like people: beautiful-looking people, like the statues and paintings of them in the museums. Even the Biblical pictures of the Old Testament characters looked wonderful and romantic. Now I can see that they were all just based on the models used by the artists: athletes, dancers, actors, ordinary people. The gods are different."

"It's a way of representing an invisible power. They simply give it a shape. It's like trying to draw a picture of the wind; you show the effect: the trees bending, the hat blowing away. A god of youth or beauty can be pictured in the form of some beautiful being."

"And this one?"

"I still haven't decided what this one is supposed to be, but I imagine it's got something to do with fertility."

"Is fertility so ugly? So murderous?"

"So strong: I think that must be the idea. The animal-like head is there because wild animals are strong and fast and can do things that would be miraculous if they were demanded of the natural capacities of man. And then the breasts are there, and made large, to show that there's a source of nourishment."

"For whom?"

"For the believers."

"I find these ideas disgusting."

"Why?"

"Because it took us centuries to get away from them and now people are trying to pretend that there's really some special sort of wisdom in this primitive ignorance."

"Your father was a great Darwinian."

"That's different. I'm speaking of civilization's progress towards moral and ethical standards that are no longer founded on superstition."

"I remember. It was one of the subjects we talked about at dances. Out in the gardens, looking at the stars and the moon. I finally got you to agree that Christianity was like any other religion."

"But we all still go to church, even you. And you believe."

"I never believed, Lina."

"Of course you do."

"Not even when I was a child."

"I know you've always said that. It only means you believe in a different way."

He nodded towards the statue and said, "I can understand that this is what the gods are like."

"God is love, Anders."

"Love?" He reached out and touched her dress. He took hold of a pinch of the material and tugged gently.

"I'll leave you to your work," she said.

.   .   .

He had no idea of publishing anything more than Erika's improved watercolors of his already faded pencil drawings. The narrative account he worked on was to be merely for the family archives, although at Erika's insistence he did compose a few additional notes to go with her paintings; these concerned the plants: how he had found them, where they grew, what their seasons of fruition were, and their uses; to some he had appended brief stories and snatches of folklore.

In between bouts of writing he looked at catalogs for wallpaper, furnishing material, paints, garden landscaping equipment. Hannah and Astrid were interested in dresses. Lina and Elsie spent their time making lists for the inside of the house; and he helped to compile a series of plans for the gardens, which they were going to talk over with Louise. Everyone, especially Erika, had suggestions about what flowers would look best where, and at what time of the year. Anders and Lina were the only ones who thought of consulting the gardener, Ekdahl. And all that Ekdahl would say about the arrangements was that if they wanted to go ahead with half the things they had on their little pieces of paper, he'd need a much bigger work force. Wilhelm was a good lad, willing but not very useful—you had to tell him everything and keep repeating it all day long; they'd need to hire at least three more men. And if the mistress stuck to this proposal for new greenhouses, that would mean more still.

Anders went to Louise and asked her to help. Her mood was improving with the warmer weather. In fact, the aunts' funeral seemed to have brought her back to life. According to Lina, she had spent nearly a week composing a long letter to Sophie; apparently Louise had been the most vehement of the disapprovers at the time of Sophie's wedding. And after she had sent off her letter, and rested, she stopped looking as if she cried every night. When the reply came, you could almost say she was back to normal. She began to take jaunts into town with Hannah and Astrid. One weekend they spent two days away, coming back with stories of everything they had seen and done and heard.

He had had money distributed, invested, put aside for particular purposes, talked about, given away. He had written to Martin's wife and arranged for a modest annuity to be handed over to her and the two children, now also—as his own were—grown up. She was another who had married, but she wrote back a letter that told him she would accept the offer because Martin would have wanted her to. On the evening after he received her letter, he sat for a long time at his desk, letting the room grow dark. He had always liked her. And she was the kind of woman, he thought, who could marry two men and be good to both of them without betraying either. Somehow she would manage to make everyone friends in the end. That was the kind of woman they needed in the diplomatic service, in the government, anywhere. But there was no method of training people to achieve those qualities. You had to be born that way.

He didn't worry about the others, except that he sent Sophie a letter. He hoped that they would meet soon, maybe in Paris when he joined the three girls and their mothers. Louise had relented about that too: she would travel with the party to France. Sophie had plans to visit Rome in the spring, Germany in the summer. On the way back, perhaps they'd all meet. The house was lively with voices discussing the future. Lina said she'd seen Ingrid smile for the first time in eight years.

"You're the one I want to see smiling," he told her.

"But I do. You haven't been looking."

"You need to get away, and come back to see everything transformed."

"Nonsense. I want to be right here to make sure the work's done exactly the way it should be."

He came to what he could see was the last chapter of his book, and on the same day a letter arrived for him from a man named Petersen, who had been the author of a small paragraph in the papers about the odd fact that a man who was presumed dead could come home after ten years. The letter said that there had been such interest in the expedition ten years before, no word about it since, and didn't he—the captain and instigator—think it was the public's right to know what had happened?

Petersen, Erika told him, was not strictly speaking the "young man" her mother had described to the rest of the family. He was in his late thirties, had worked on a paper in the capital and had been demoted, if not actually thrown out, for something-or-other, probably political. "They always say it's because of their integrity, or they got hold of some important truth that people wanted to hush up, but my experience of that crowd is that half of them are so drunk they don't know

155

what they're saying; they slander and libel people without ever checking the facts, and they'll write reviews without bothering to see the plays. That really did happen to me once: the man took me to a first night where we were given a marvelous party of champagne and little hors d'œuvre beforehand, and we started to have such a good time that we decided to go on to dinner somewhere instead. I read his review the next morning—he said he'd just asked his friends about the plot and scribbled down something based on what they told him. I think this Petersen was like that, but he got caught doing it."

"So he wants to get back into the main stream," Anders said. "And he's looking for a story that will put him there."

"Once you talk with him—you can if you like, but you know how it's going to turn out. He'll ask you, 'Don't you think such-and-such,' and you'll say, 'Maybe, but what I really believe is so-and-so,' and when you see it later, you're saying his words, not yours."

He took a long, early-morning walk around the far side of the lake and into the woods. He sat for a while on the bench at the lookout point on Sightseer's Hill. And he remembered what that first day had been like ten years before.

The Vikings spoke about the highways of the sea; that was how he had thought of the wide stretches of water around him on that day of departure: the roads that would carry him away.

The bands played, the people cheered, the handkerchiefs waved in the sunshine. He stalked up and down the deck restlessly, waiting for the right moment to get away from land and from the expectations of everyone still on shore. Ahead of him lay all the oceans, pulling him forward as if on a path created by his own eagerness. He turned his face away from the crowd.

He wrote a letter to Petersen, as short as he could make it without being rude, to say that: yes, there has indeed been an interest taken in the expedition, but unfortunately the venture had miscarried. He had already written to the relatives of the men lost; as for anyone else's right to know, the undertaking had, after all, been a private one. Perhaps some day he might write about it himself, but the years had taken their toll of him—at the moment he was simply trying to get back his strength and begin his life again.

Petersen wrote once more, to say it was all very well to be so vague about these extraordinary events, but unless every rumor was false, the captain had returned—alone—with a vast fortune, had he not? And didn't the captain think that he would like the world at large to feel clear about the way in which he had acquired the wealth?

Anders let his lawyers answer. He outlined the reply he wanted them to send: a formal request for Petersen to present any proof he had in his possession that could have given rise to the assumption that the captain's wealth had not been honestly gained. They were prepared to take the matter further unless they received an apology and assurances from Mr. Petersen and his employers that the captain would no longer be troubled by insinuating letters.

Petersen was almost out on his ear after that. It turned out that the editors hadn't known about his attentions: he'd been angling for a story on his own. Anders got the apologies. He also, he realized, got an enemy, although Petersen appeared to be one of those men one couldn't help antagonizing—someone like a village gossip, whose envy and jealousy extended to everyone, and who was always looking for a victim; nobody would ever like him and he'd never be a success, but he'd have a great many different reasons why important people had conspired to prevent his rise.

Anders sat at his desk, looing into the golden face of the idol that grimaced back at him. It was definitely the kind of god you'd want if you had to deal with people like Petersen.

· · ·

The snows retreated. The first flowers were out, white like the snow that had been their background and protection. There was work to do everywhere, repairing fences and roads. He never saw the gamekeepers any more; they had no time to sit in their huts and drink with friends, to imagine stories of impossible encounters with animals, or to remember the real hunting in the time of their grandparents.

He went into town a few times to hear concerts. At first he

felt awkward. He couldn't rid himself of the idea that people were staring at him, stealing looks at him and his family as soon as he turned his head. But once the music began, he forgot. His self-consciousness was lost in the flood of singing, speaking notes and it seemed to him all at once that part of the despair of his missing years had been the lack of music. He had craved it without knowing what the deficiency was. It had been like starvation: a hunger so dangerously advanced that the pain and desire had vanished. It had been like an absence of love, unrecognized for what it was.

The second time he went, with Louise and Elsie, he had to get up in the middle of a string quartet and leave. No one took much notice, as it was at the end of a movement. He had to walk out because he knew that if he didn't, the tears would begin to run down his face. It was all right for the women: Louise always cried and nobody minded. For a captain, a man of nearly fifty, it wouldn't have done.

He leaned against a pillar outside the concert hall and thought that that was what people's lives should be like—like music, harmonious and unhindered; not full of disruptions, torn and twisted, or—as his had been—so shattered that no matter how well the break mended, he would always be reminded of where the weakness lay.

He waited till the intermission to rejoin the others.

"I thought you liked Schubert," Elsie said.

"Very much. I just sometimes find him unbearable."

"But beautiful," Louise insisted.

"Yes," he said, "it's the beauty that does it."

.　.　.

He read poetry and the newspapers. He sent away for books—history and biography—to put back on the half-empty shelves. He made plans to have a boat built—a small pleasure craft that he could sail through the islands in the summertime and use to take the family on picnics. That would be the late summer, after the buying sprees and the sightseeing. And after that—

"Parties," Hannah demanded.

158

"Dinners and luncheons and dances," Astrid said, "and treasure hunts and everything."

"We should be doing all that this summer," Lina said, "but I suppose we'll need that time just to paint the place up. It's been falling to pieces. I hadn't thought it was so bad."

They had two days of still air and brilliant light. He walked around his property in the morning and at evening. He especially liked to see the last of the sunshine on the house. There had been so many years when house, family, friends, country had been lost to him, that he wasn't yet easy in their possession. He still didn't feel that he had them all back. And some things were beyond remedy; there were acquaintances and friends of his who had died in the meantime. For years everything, the whole of his life, had gone. Now it lay before him again, with the sun touching it.

· · ·

The brighter flowers came; and the bulbs that had had an early bloom indoors were out in the gardens. Lina and Elsie put on aprons and talked to Ekdahl while Wilhelm carried loads of heavy sacking from one corner of the terrace to the other. From the drawing room windows Anders could see Ekdahl shaking his head. The ladies had set their hearts on a system of sunken pools.

He found himself more and more often wandering down to the boathouse to have a cup of mid-morning coffee or afternoon tea with Erika. He was a little in love with her, but so many others were too that no one thought anything of it.

They talked about the book. She would show him her copies of the drawings he'd made, and she'd ask him about his notes: Could he remember at which time of the year the berry appeared on this particular plant, and was it a hard or soft fruit, what size was the seed in the middle of it, was this leaf as prickly as it looked or did it have a smooth texture, was this a stringy stem or would it break cleanly, and, above all, were the colors right? He himself had never thought to ask so many questions, although if he concentrated, he was able to answer most of them.

They also talked about mesmerism, a subject in which Erika had expressed an interest. "It's a hoax," he said. "It's more of a swindle than the woman being sawn in half."

"But the practice and method aren't so different from what you can find in primitive societies. The trance state is used by all kinds of religions for achieving enlightenment. Even Christian meditation works on something similar, not to mention the mystic religions of the East. If we could bring it into everyday life, think what a difference it would make to us."

"Are you talking about hypnotism," he asked, "or about imagination?"

"I think I'm talking about the development of new systems of thought. When I was studying mathematics, I sometimes used to see the answer to a thing, and that moment—you see, I have no words to express what happens. I can only say that those were the great moments of my life, entirely different from any other kind of thought. They were moments of discovery. I never came up with an important new scientific equation, but I know how it's done. It's just that there's no way of repeating the process at will. It's impossible to recreate any of it."

"Why?"

"It happens too fast, and nobody understands what the beginning stages are. I suppose you could have bits and pieces of thought lying around in your mind for years before you were struck by the idea that fitted them all together."

"But mesmerism is something quite different."

"I'm not so sure. It seems to me that it's all part of the mechanism."

"It's a circus trick. It's hypnotizing people who are strangers to you, and then—part of the business is pure fraud. Didn't you ever play those children's games where one person goes out of the room and comes back, and the other one makes him guess a number?"

"What I remember are the ones where I ended up hiding in a broom cupboard somewhere and kissing a friend in the dark. I spent years kissing other little girls until I realized that I could do it with boys, too."

"And now you want to mesmerize them."

"The principle interests me. What's the trick with the numbers?"

"As you go out the door, you put your hand on the frame and show the number of fingers that correspond to the right figure."

"Eighty-nine?"

"Five or less, or a combination of the numbers you can get by using both hands. The choice is limited. I expect you could do eighty-nine if you stood there talking for a while before you left."

"That's interesting, too," she said. "The tactic of distracting the eye. Frauds are always limited like that, but you don't notice it because your attention has been directed to something else."

"Exactly. Even in everyday life. The attention is attracted to the future, to the past. Romance."

"Romance?"

"The girls were talking about the book the other day. I asked them what sorts of books they liked to read, and they said: a book that was really romantic."

"That just means slushy bits about undying affection and proposals in the conservatory. And his manly chin and sensitive blue eyes."

"Is that all?"

"The sacrifice of a good woman, winning out against villainy—that kind of thing. Minute details about what they're all wearing and eating. I've seen the books they read. But I used to be almost as bad. There aren't many exciting stories for girls, so I was always poring over the books for boys. You probably grew up reading the same ones—I can't imagine they'd have changed much. They're a different brand of romance: heroism, danger, fighting and rescuing, capturing the lost princess, and so on. St. George and the dragon in various disguises."

"I suppose it's a kind of mythology we retain all our lives."

"But pure thought would be different."

"Pure thought would have no story attached."

"It's the way by which we discover new ideas."

"Don't the new ones grow out of the old ones?"

161

"Sometimes," she told him, "it looks as if there's no connection—that new ideas come like new genetic forms, in a jump away from everything that went before."

"If it's so different, where does it come from?"

"That's one of the questions I like: where do ideas come from?"

"Oh, from people. That wasn't what I meant. Maybe it's better to ask what it is that draws the ideas out of them." He kneaded his right hand with the left one.

"You can get something for that," she said. "A piece of india rubber to do exercises with. It helps to distribute the tensions."

"I thought it was improving, but it's still no better."

"They really work."

"It's from the writing," he said; "keeping it in a fixed position for too long."

"The book is nearly ready to be shown."

"Not for a while yet."

"We'll see," she said. "If you let me have your copy in two days, I'd like to take it into town."

.   .   .

The buds were still small on the trees, but the sun came out strongly. It didn't stay for long, though it promised the real spring. Everyone's spirits rose. The house was happy.

Erika came back from town to say that two magazines were interested in the book: one, a popular publication, the other a scientific journal.

"The scientific one," he said.

"I thought we might try both."

"I'd rather not."

"The scientists aren't so interested in the text."

"That's all right. It's the pictures that are important."

"And they don't have much space. I'll see what I can do."

She spoke to friends of hers and managed to divide the book and to share the sections between the two journals. The popular one was to come out first; the editors wanted a short, biographical introduction and photographs.

"Nothing about the expedition," he said. "Just the plants."

"But of course they're anxious to know all about the fever-ridden struggle, and so forth."

"Melodrama," he said shortly. "It was an expedition that failed. I want to forget it. Let them see the botanical drawings. They're as interesting as any Treasure of the Kings. You did a beautiful job with them." He flexed his hand again. He was getting stabbing pains over the back of it, across the knuckles.

"I'll bring you one of those things from town," she told him.

.   .   .

He listened to Ekdahl talk about the necessity of finding a really good tree man to go over the estate. And he wrote down the names and addresses of the people Ekdahl recommended. He spent a whole day looking through cupboards and spare rooms with Ingrid and Elsie. Elsie tried to convince him that the dining room trim should be blue and not the green Lina wanted.

He sent for samples of writing paper, letterheads, damask, lace and carpeting; he wrote away for information about restoring the foxed engravings in the upstairs hallway.

The scientific journal sent its proofs, which were in color and very handsome. His notes were printed at the side or beneath the pictures, his introduction had been kept to a minimum. Contrary to what Erika had been told, nearly all the drawings and paintings had been accepted and publication was brought forward. Several people, she suspected, had failed to hand in other articles on time, so there had suddenly been a whole issue to fill.

It came out within the week. He signed his free copies and distributed them among the family. Everyone was immensely proud of him, although at the special lunch, which was organized by Lina, he rose to his feet and gave a gallant testimonial in praise of Erika's work. She took his thanks without embarrassment and said something in her speech of acceptance that confounded him; she spoke of the perpetual need for a fresh discovery of the world; and of the importance of observation. Observation, she said, was discovery. The ability to look at familiar things in a new way was just as significant as the discovery of new things to look at for the first time.

163

She blew him a kiss and sat down, and the table became so intoxicated with talk, drink, merriment and its own good opinion of itself, that everyone ended up singing till halfway through the afternoon and all of them had to take long naps afterwards.

The next morning saw the arrival of the other offprint, the one from the popular magazine. As soon as Anders turned the first page, he thought that the fear he had sensed hanging over him for so long must have been a misinterpreted fore-knowledge of that moment. He stood up, rushed from the terrace doors without an overcoat and ran to the boathouse. He yanked at the latch and burst in.

Erika rose from behind her worktable, saying, "What's happened?"

He handed her the opened package.

"The new proofs? They seem to have cut down most of the pictures, don't they?"

"Read it," he said.

"They went through hell and lived like gods. The hungry tentacles of the jungle surrounded them on all sides, its menacing dangers lurking behind every tree—rather lurid style they've got."

"It's impossible."

"Weary with toil, maddened by fevers, they were forced to eat their precious specimens—that's inspired. Sounds almost indecent."

"They can't print it. I'll—it's got to be stopped. And the relatives of the ones who died—think of them coming across this trash."

"Of course. *Lusty men in exotic landscapes, from the taverns of Rio to remote tribes, where native women*—yes, I see. I had no idea it was going to be this bad. They seem to be pushing it for all it's worth. I guess this was another case of having to fill the issue. Well, don't worry about it, Anders. I'll make sure it doesn't get through."

"I mean it, Erika. It's very, very important. It isn't simply the sensationalistic style. I couldn't have my name associated with a publication that put out anything like this, ever."

"Right. It may actually have changed hands since I talked to the boys at the desk. One can never tell with magazines.

One good thing, anyway—they're always in financial trouble, so they don't pay up for months. You never signed anything—in fact, all the business was done through me, so you can withdraw and threaten to take legal action. Just leave it with me."

She was surprised to see how upset he was. It took her a long while to calm him down. At first she tried reading out more of the article, which amused her greatly, but it infuriated him. He couldn't bear to hear life described in that way, he told her. "The others—" he said. "The others—"

"Have some tea," she suggested. "I'll go up to town this morning. I can go with Louise."

She didn't come back till late in the evening and she had all the original papers with her, plus a signed statement by someone to the effect that nothing, not even his own version as first presented, would ever be used. And in addition, she assured him that she'd gone into the works and stood there while the men broke up the forms. "Just in case there was another mix-up," she said.

"One of those moments when they suddenly need to fill the empty spaces?"

"That's right. So, your worries are over. A successful day for both of us, me and Louise. Or maybe you didn't know."

"What's this?"

"If I tell you, you have to promise not to say anything to Lina before I give you permission."

He promised, and was told that Louise had fallen under the spell of a viola player in one of the musical groups that played for her ladies' music appreciation classes. The man's name was Oscar Kellner and Anders remembered hearing him play. He wasn't bad, although not a particularly interesting player, either, and certainly not good enough to be a soloist: a shabby, respectable widower, so Erika said, with two adolescent daughters each as plain as a post.

It wasn't long before Louise made the announcement herself. "We plan to marry," she said, "at the end of the summer, or perhaps the beginning of October."

He expressed his delight at her good fortune. Lina was the one who was horrified. "You'll think differently about it soon," he told her. "I've had nearly a week to get used to the idea. Erika made me swear not to let the secret out."

"I've been thinking so hard and so long about the girls: about sending them off to dances in their ballgowns, scheming to put them on the right lists, finding suitable young men, getting them married. I've been looking even farther ahead than that. It's been a long time now since there were small children in the house."

"All in good time."

"And here it's Louise who goes and springs this on us, with someone so entirely unsuitable. It's ridiculous. I can't bear it."

"Why not?"

"When I think of Ib—"

"Don't think of him. Remember what you told me about waiting and being faithful. She waited ten years. Ib is gone. You have to see things now as if we'd all lived through a war: everything has changed, all our fortunes were altered and reversed, our lives turned upside-down. But we've survived. Think of it that way. Let Louise find whatever happiness she can."

"You're right, of course. It's just that it's such a step down."

"Happiness is always a step up," he said. "And it's something for her to do with her life."

"That's a dreadful definition of marriage."

"Why? If that's what it amounts to? No worse than any other definition. And no worse than any other occupation."

"One always hopes for at least a glimpse of the deeper values, and for love. Now, honestly, who could love a poor, faded creature like that?"

"Louise, evidently."

"I used to think, before she got engaged to Ib, that she was a little in love with you."

"Oh, I've always been very fond of Louise," he said. And he had felt guilty about her ever since his return. He had felt worse about her wasted years than about his wife's. The guilt added to his hopes for her happiness and made him glad that she had discovered someone, even if the man she'd come up with appeared to be a rather uninteresting find.

166

A wedding, and before that an engagement, meant new clothes. The planned journey to Paris was therefore preceded by many trips into town, where the women of the household chose materials, were measured, fitted, and had to go back for more appointments at the dressmaker's. Sometimes they traveled in a group, sometimes in twos and threes. One day Anders took his two daughters out together; they had coffee, went for a walk in the park, looked in at the museum, had a long lunch and saw a silly comedy at the theater. The fittings took barely any time at all, the lunch was long and giggly. He saw to it that the girls had a good supply of champagne, and they were all in hysterics by the end of the meal. He thought how charming they were, and how lucky the men would be who married them. What fun it would be, he thought, to be in love with girls like that: as pretty as butterflies and apparently as carefree, but actually so soft-hearted that their eyes filled with tears when they thought about motherless children or mistreated animals, or the lot of the poor—though not the poor right there in town, who were dirty, insolent, foul-mouthed and work-shy.

The other diners looked curiously at the three of them laughing helplessly and enjoying themselves so much more loudly than was usual. Some people were obviously approving, others didn't seem to be sure, nor did the waiters. If they had been in another place, Anders suspected, a much larger city, people might assume that he was a rich man out with two fashionable girls he'd bought for the day, and that they'd go to a room somewhere afterwards. That was what they'd be thinking in Paris. Or Vienna. But no—anyone who really knew about those things could tell how innocent the girls were. His daughters were too fresh, too natural; they wore no paints or powders, no showy clothes or cheap jewelry.

They laughed inordinately at the play, a translation of an imported farce; the jokes depended on an initial mistake in identity, which occurred when army recruiting officers came to the door for a husband and found the wife having breakfast with her lover. The lover then had to pretend to be the husband and go in his place. Anders laughed so hard that his voice boomed over the rest of the audience. His daughters screamed with joy on either side of him. It was the first farce he had seen that didn't fill him with a sense of uneasiness and exasperation, and what he believed was probably a fear of madness—of a life that consisted in being constantly mistaken for other people.

. . .

The buds on the trees came out, at first black, then whitish, then suddenly, in two days of sunshine, green. All the land around the house, straight back to the dark boughs of the woods, was in bud. In the evening when the light dimmed and the outlines of objects grew indistinct, the trees seemed to form a series of delicate green veils. No one wanted to stay indoors now for very long.

Anders turned up at the boathouse one afternoon to find, for the first time, that Erika had a guest with her, a young man named Phillip Harding. While she was settling Anders in a chair, two more men arrived in company with an older woman dressed in gray; Erika called her Natalia and introduced her as Madame-Something—a French name: but as he drank his coffee and listened to the general conversation, one of the men with her addressed her as "Countess." Anders left as soon as he'd taken the last sip from his cup. He could see that Erika must have gathered the group for a meeting. He gave the excuse that if he didn't get to the gardeners soon, his wife and sister would start planting the coastline.

Erika didn't take her evening meal at the house. "She's off with her friends," Elsie said.

"Which friends are they?" he asked.

"Heaven knows. She's got so many."

"I met a boy named Harding."

"Phillip, yes. I'm afraid he's the one she likes best. As you can guess, he's not a very respectable young man. Hardly a boy, either—he must be close to thirty. Money enough in the family, but he's racketed around the continent doing nothing for years. I don't know what he calls himself—some sort of pamphleteer."

The next morning, he strolled by the boathouse but didn't go in. A few minutes later Erika came out and ran after him.

"I'm sorry about yesterday," she said. "They came at short notice."

"Has there been a revolution in Russia?"

"What?" She looked appalled, almost terrified.

"Countess Natalia looked to me like one of those types I've seen before. What are they—Anarchists?"

"They're just people, Anders."

"Ah. So are we all. But with political groups, you never know. They always want something for others. All they need for themselves is the central business of controlling the rest of the population. It's like the Church."

"It's exactly the opposite."

"Mr. Harding looked fairly well mesmerized. Your mother doesn't think much of him."

"He has qualities she doesn't know about."

"Oh, most men have those," he said, without particularly meaning anything by it. Erika blushed, so immediately and startlingly that it was as if she'd been hit in the face. He laughed. She took his arm and said, "I think you're beginning to know too much about me."

"Impossible. I just don't want you to get yourself into something you can't get out of. Something dangerous."

"There's nothing to worry about. And anyway, you should be the one in the family to understand politics. You believe that it's a good thing for people to want to change the world."

"Do I?"

"Of course. To seek out new knowledge, to explore one's thoughts, to change people's minds."

"Yes. I'm not so enthusiastic about throwing bombs into a café to gain a paragraph in the papers. That's what they're doing now."

"Have you ever thought of a post in the Cabinet?"

"Certainly not."

"I think you should. You have a good reputation; the family's an old, traditional family. You've got the means now. And the government always needs good men."

"I couldn't," he said flatly. "Never."

"Why not? Lina would love it, you know."

"Not even for her. And don't suggest it to her."

"You'd be good at it, Anders."

"It isn't a question of that. It's because my life wouldn't stand scrutiny. I haven't always been truthful."

"You don't have to worry about every single peccadillo in your life."

"The truth is often sordid, isn't it?"

"No, never," she said.

"And sometimes—much worse—it's simply unacceptable."

"No, no. It's the lies that are unacceptable."

"On the contrary. It's only through lying and prevarication that we're able to live with each other at all."

"You're talking about compromise?"

"That's one way of putting it, I suppose."

"Well, as long as you haven't committed gross crimes. The expedition would be a great help in capturing the public's imagination."

"That depends on how you look at it. The expedition was a failure. And the moment I stepped into the public light, Mr. Petersen would have a great deal to say about that. Can't you picture to yourself what it would be like? He'd be writing letters everywhere, asking if the country wanted a man in office who'd lead it to disaster just as he'd led his own ill-fated expedition."

"We'd fight it, Anders. We'd fight it."

"My dear Erika, I'm a tired man. I've had too many adventures already. Let the others fight. And you—be careful. High ideals can lead people into some very dirty business."

"It doesn't have to be like that."

"The danger of it is constant."

.   .   .

The ducks were back in the ponds and the swans on the lake. Long before the leaves were out, Louise announced that she and Oscar couldn't wait till the autumn, or even the summer. They wanted to get married now: immediately, as soon as possible. The house was thrown into pandemonium.

Elsie took charge. Louise did some supervising in the kitchens, but she seemed to feel that she had fulfilled most of her duties by deciding to get married in the first place.

Anders escorted Lina to town on a trip that was intended to be like the one to which he'd treated their daughters. But in the balmy air and new sunshine of the spring, it turned into a second honeymoon. They walked together hand in hand, arm in arm. They whispered secrets to each other, went back to their hotel in the afternoons, retired early at night. During the daytime, standing in front of famous paintings or incomprehensible new sculptures, they talked and talked, clinging together.

She wept at the wedding, which took place in a small, whitewashed church packed with family, friends, neighbors and people who had happened to see the procession heading towards the building. The weather was flawless. Louise looked happy and her bridegroom stood up to the test with a surprising degree of dignity.

The reception at the house was a great success; after the main crowd had been fed and dispersed, the celebrations went on for hours. There was music and dancing far into the night, and breakfast for the ones who were still awake as dawn approached.

They were two days clearing everything up again. Elsie said she was certain some items were missing from the house, though it was nearly always the same when you had to hire extra help, even in that part of the world, where everyone used to be so honest.

Over the weekend there was a rainstorm, a sudden flourishing of leafy growth hard upon it, and the countryside was reborn. Inside the house everything returned to normal. Anders sat at his desk with the french windows open on to the terrace. He started to flip through books he'd always meant to get to some day. As he read, he smiled. Every once in a while he'd look up to gaze out at the gardens and parkland. The whole world was lovely now.

He finished a novel and began a book of poetry, the pages of which had never been cut. It wasn't one of his own books, nor did it look like the kind of thing his father would have bought. Perhaps one of his father's cousins, or an uncle, had brought it into the house and found a space for it in the library.

171

The poems were odd, haunting and melancholy, with complicated rhyme schemes. He was intrigued by them.

When he'd taken his afternoon walk, slept a little, written off to ask about the horse sales and drunk tea with the family, he returned to his study. Soon, sometime in the next two weeks, he'd start to plan the coming year. He wanted to see about hiring an overseer or bailiff of some kind—someone who would really look after the woods. Perhaps he'd put that off till the summer. He knew that the preliminary stages of such a transaction would call for long evenings eating and drinking with men who knew other men who could recommend someone's friend or brother. It would mean submerging himself in the world of local gossip. So far, he had dealt only with the bankers and lawyers and city officials. Of course, he'd been invited by everyone. He'd even been asked, in a roundabout fashion, to become a member of a club that seemed similar to the Masons. But he had held back. "I'm still recovering," he'd say, or, sometimes, "My family comes first." Eventually there would be no way out of it: he'd have to join in everything. He'd be expected to.

He picked up the book of verse again and became immersed in a long poem about a girl who had been changed into a swan. When he looked up, the light was fading. A soft grayness had come into the air as if it had been falling slowly from the sky. The quiet gardens were like Paradise. But there, at the end of the terrace and apparently looking intently at him, was a strange figure: a stooped and wizened bald man of about sixty, or perhaps a great deal older; as Anders looked, he raised his hand in greeting and began to shuffle towards the open door.

Anders stood up. Long before he recognized the man, he felt that there was something repulsive about him. He didn't want his delightful study invaded by such a creature. He walked out of the door, on to the terrace.

The man came forward in a clumsy, crablike gait, although fairly fast and purposefully. If there had been a gardener or a groom nearby, Anders would have said, "See what that person wants."

They advanced towards each other until they stood barely

twelve feet apart. Anders stopped. The other man, using his stick, continued on, his head a little to one side, his body bent. He carried a knapsack or satchel of some sort slung over his left shoulder. He looked like a troll: his eyes bloodshot, and the color of the skull-face yellowish; it reminded Anders of the death's head that had been carved on the front of his father's favorite meerschaum pipe. The man didn't belong on his terrace, near his house, yet he kept coming forward. Anders suddenly had the impression that he wasn't quite sure what was happening.

"Good evening, Anders," the man said.

He knew the voice. He knew the voice very well. And all at once he knew the man. *If I shut my eyes for a moment*, he thought. *If I just shut my eyes. The earth might go backwards and it would never have happened.*

.   .   .

At the turn of the tide they moved. The crowd went mad. The ship glided forward, slow and dreamlike at first and then swiftly, racing away. The crowd was a toy, a speck, gone altogether. And the coastline went after it.

The weather held until well after Anders, Martin, Ib and Johann had decided that Gustav was impossible to deal with and that if he insisted on bringing his tame valet to the table, they could both eat down below with the crew.

"I shouldn't dream of subjecting Sten to such an experience," Gustav said.

"You gave us the impression that the boy could sew," Martin told him.

"I said he knew about clothes. That's an entirely different thing."

"Well, now he's here, he can bunk in with the sailmaker and help out there."

"Anders—" Gustav began.

"Absolutely," Anders decided. "I won't feed him if he doesn't work. It isn't fair to the other men. And if I tried to favor him, they wouldn't stand for it, you know that. What did you think you were doing, bringing a pet lapdog along on a voyage like this?"

173

"He's my friend," Gustav asserted.

"We don't doubt that," Martin said, "but he'll have to be a friend that knows how to work."

"I'll speak to him," Anders said. When he had a spare moment he took Sten aside and talked to him.

The boy's handsome, dark face grew tense. "I know nothing about this," he said.

"Gustav should have explained it to you. But there's nothing to be afraid of. The work is hard, but if you go at it with a good will, the men will respect you for it. We all have our work here and it's a fairly democratic life. No one simply stands back and twiddles his thumbs. Can't you see how much that would cause you to be disliked—and ridiculed?"

"But I'm not a sailor."

"You can learn. I've spoken to Olaf. He says he'll teach you. All right?"

"What will happen if Gustav wants me?"

"We'll come to that later," Anders said. "Gustav isn't running this ship. I am, and I can't afford to carry passengers."

Sten scowled. He looked resentful and unpleasant, but when Anders put a hand on his shoulder in a friendly way and smiled encouragingly, he said he'd try.

Gustav was the only one on board who was piqued by the change. "It takes me weeks of complaining and wheedling and presents," he said, "to get him to do anything at all, and there he is: working like a born deckhand just because you asked him. How did you do it?"

"I told him," Anders said. "And he saw the sense of it. He seems to be a naturally bright boy, despite your attempts to spoil him."

"Me? I was the innocent one, I can assure you. He looks so young, but the fellow must be nearly our age, if not older. Look at him carefully some day. He's got a light build, that's all. He's strong, too. Did I tell you he was an acrobat?"

"If he starts to cause trouble, he's going to need to be strong. That's a rough crew."

"Sten can take care of himself," Gustav said irritably. "You'll see. He always comes out laughing."

They zigzagged down the coastline and headed towards

the open sea. The weather broke, the wind rose, the waters thrashed themselves into a frenzy. Everyone on board was soaked to the skin for hours on end, day and night. The ship would rise to the top of a wave, stagger, and plunge into the trough below. Two men were washed overboard despite the safety lines.

They lost a mast, they shipped water, they were hit again and again. Pieces of planking flew across the decks. The ship stood on its beam ends, snapped back and started to roll. It could all have happened at any time—the special design need not necessarily have been to blame; there was no reason why the combination of techniques, and of the old and new, should not have ridden out many different seas and weather conditions. But Anders knew; Gustav had chosen the builders. On the outside everything looked perfect; that was almost Gustav's trademark. And Anders had not supervised every step of the construction: that hadn't been his job. He was the master.

He was too tired to be angry about the possibility of a defect in the fabric. Like everyone else on board, he needed sleep. They couldn't have slept, even if they had been able to spare men from the work; every particle of the ship was shaking and tossing from side to side as it reared and prepared to dive again. The boat heaved itself to the crests, hesitated, and lunged downward. After the third man went over the side, Anders began to wonder if they were ever going to get out of the storm.

He said nothing. The noise was so tremendous that no one could have heard anyway. Orders were signalled by hand or screamed into the ear. But when the sky lightened, everyone on board could see that the ocean was an immense, apparently endless battlefield of flailing, boisterous, mountainlike waves. And, from the distance, something they had never seen before but had heard about and always imagined to be a tall story made up by other seamen to impress the people back home: a freak wave, riding many hundreds of levels up above the others, was headed towards them.

"Think she'll hit?" Martin shouted up against his face. "Or go over the top?"

Anders shook his head. The craft struggled to the tip of the next wave and Johann threw an arm around him, screaming, "Look, another one!"

They turned to stare. A second wave, exactly and improbably as monstrous as the first but on a course perpendicular to it, was also driving towards them; one from the front, one from the left.

Anders yelled out the order to man the boats. *And get ready to go under*, he thought. It looked unavoidable. All the remedies he could think of were laughable against it. The wave ahead was bigger than they were; so was its double. This was going to be the end.

There was a scramble for places, but they had plenty of time. The wind rushed wildly around them, yet the sun seemed to be trying to break through from above. They could see the two waves clearly, like immeasurably high towers pushing forward towards them and towards each other. Anders knew that they would be hit: there was no question about it—they were right in the line of projection and had no means of moving away.

When the crash came, the impact knocked him out. It also split the ship in two, as he discovered later from the evidence of the driftwood.

He woke in the bottom of one of the boats, lying with his arms tightly holding on to Sten. The storm was over and they were being propelled across the sea on a long, rolling wave, as smoothly as if they were travelling on runners. They had food and water for two weeks, though they needed it for only six days.

They came ashore on a small island in the Cape Verde group. The bodies of all their shipmates came after them, almost untouched, like a huge catch of fresh fish, and, like fish, began to rot where they lay on the beach. They counted them, recorded them by name, tried to bury some of them and gave up. The tide took the corpses out again and washed away the lists written on the sand.

Anders went into a daze. He didn't know from one minute to the next where he was or what was happening. Later he was to wonder whether during the destruction of the ship he'd been hit on the head and had his skull fractured; on the other hand, his confused condition might have been the result of an inability to comprehend the extent of his loss. The jars and pots for transporting seeds and plants, the leatherbound books in which to draw pictures, were all gone in the waters, torn to pieces; and the fragments made smaller until they joined themselves to the element that embraced them, becoming water too. And now they would be mere thought, as they had been before the ship set sail. The men also: they had become memory and would never again be otherwise.

During that time he was cared for by Sten. Sten held the tin cup to his lips and pushed the ship's biscuits into his hand and mouth.

Anders couldn't speak. He'd lost his voice from the shock, although he didn't realize it until well into the second day. He hadn't spoken since before the actual wreck. His throat, his mind, his body had been stilled from the instant when he'd seen the two waves approaching, had known there was nothing that would help, and had called out the order to abandon ship.

As soon as he found that he couldn't talk, he panicked. He tried. He grabbed hold of Sten and mouthed at his face as he'd done to his friends in the storm. Now he was in a different kind of storm. He fell on the sand and scooped it up with his hands and beat the air too, as if trying to pull a voice out of the ground, or out of the sky. Sten comforted him; he said there was nothing to worry about: he'd seen it a couple of times before and the voice always came back, always, only it took longer if you kept thinking about it and let yourself get too frightened.

Sten explored their surroundings far enough to see that they stood a better chance of rescue at the other end of the island. He forced Anders on a march to the opposite side of the peninsula. Two days later they were picked up by a Spanish cargo vessel. Sten did the talking, and he lied. He said that they had been passengers on a luxury cruising yacht, that Anders and he were uncle and nephew and that they were of the nobility—the very top nobility.

Anders followed Sten and moved when he was pushed.

He was alive, that was one thing. He couldn't speak and he couldn't hang on to much more than isolated pictures and moments, but months later he knew that he must still have been thinking. Sten would come sit beside him, put his arm around him and stroke his head, face and shoulders, as if he'd been a dog or horse, or a child. "It's all right," he'd whisper. "Look what I've got for your dinner. Eat that up and get well." When he wrapped Anders in the blanket at night, he kissed him on the cheek as his mother had done long ago. Anders returned the kiss but still he couldn't speak, nor could he retain thoughts for long stretches; things came to him from moment to moment, without connecting links to past or future. Afterwards he was unable to recall what had been in his mind during that time. It was as if he hadn't been in the world.

He'd been rescued, he must have been thinking; and he had the rags he was still wearing. And there was one other survivor of the cataclysm. But what was going to happen next? How was he to explain the fantastic event—all those people killed at one blow? He could barely understand it himself. And how was he going to live with the failure of it? The crowd had cheered, the bands had played, and all for what? His family had laid out more money than they could afford on the outfitting of the boat and they were still back there— all the relatives and friends—waiting full of expectation and hope, to be told good news, to hear the results, to be given the reward they deserved. They expected success. It was their right.

He agreed that they had the right. Yet he was no longer able to supply the success. And so, he couldn't go back.

. . .

While his voice was lost, there were periods when the rest of the earth seemed silent too. He retained his consciousness through Sten, who guided his attention by touch and continued to hold on to him as if he were a large animal on a leash. The people around him were speaking a foreign language. They looked unfamiliar. He didn't know where he was.

Sten got a job in a circus. They lived in a gypsy caravan. There was very little in the caravan but the bed and some shelves on the wall and two cupboards. Anders was given the task of looking after the horses in the show. He was slow, but he did everything well and was thorough. They were in Spain. The other circus people thought he was a deaf-mute. Sometimes he would watch from inside the tent as Sten climbed high on to a ladder and walked across the wire or did dance-like exercises on a trapeze that swung in an arc all the way across the sandpits and back, from the ticket booth to the bandstand. Sten wore resplendent costumes scattered over with sequins, from which light and color flashed as he turned his body. The audience gasped and cooed as he tumbled above their heads. He looked like a bird that might have come out of the tropical forests on the other side of the world.

They moved from town to town and from country to country. One night there was a quarrel in the troupe and a big fight. Sten came for Anders, pulled him out of the caravan and pushed him towards the horses.

They galloped into the darkness, not stopping until they came to the bend beyond the train station, where the engine had to slow down on the track. Then they let the horses go and clmbed up on the train. Sten had stolen some money— a lot of money. And he had papers for both of them.

They stayed in cities, bought new clothes, ate in restaurants. Sten rented an apartment for them. Anders began to see everything as it was happening, rather than only remembering afterwards. He also heard that people were talking in German, a language he could speak himself. Eight weeks after the two waves had hit them, he turned to Sten and whispered, "Where are we?"

Sten smiled with delight. "Austria," he said.

"What are we doing here?"

"We're seeing the sights." He put his hand against Anders' cheek, touched the lobe of his ear. He asked, "Do you feel better?"

"I think so. Have I been ill?"

"Very ill."

"I couldn't talk."

"Don't concern yourself. It's all right. I told you, I've seen it before."

"I remember the wave. The two waves—double."

"Don't be upset. It's over."

"What can I do here?"

"Whatever you like. Enjoy yourself."

"Austria has no coastline. The empire is practically land-locked. You'd have to go all the way to the Dalmatian coast before you hit water."

"So?"

"I'm a ship's captain."

"You can do other things."

"Is there any money?" Anders asked.

"At the moment. For a while. We'll have a good time till it's gone, and then we'll think of something."

Anders looked around the room they were in, and up at the windows. He could see out for a long way, across rooftops and spires. Bells were ringing outdoors. He thought it must be Sunday. "All right," he said.

He remembered Spain and the journey, and that Sten must have done something so bad that they'd had to run away. He remembered the rotting corpses on the beach and the spangled dancers on the tightrope. Now that he was well enough to go back home or to write to his family and tell them where he was and what had happened, there were other reasons why he couldn't.

He remembered the wonderful yacht smashed to match-wood, the men before they were killed. He wondered if he too hadn't committed some offense for which the police might want him. And he was bound to Sten, who had cared for him during the weeks of his collapse. They were sleeping in the same bed; in fact, they appeared to be living together the way lovers would. Like all discoveries it seemed strange only beforehand, not afterwards. He had set out to explore a different world; and he had found Vienna.

.   .   .

180

They were in Vienna for three years, but at the end of the first month they were out of the comfortable apartment and moving downward through the city's architectural and social scales. They lived by their wits, doing anything that came to hand, taking jobs for a day or an afternoon. They began to look like people who lived that way. And their changes of luck, up or down, were extreme. When they had money they had large amounts and spent it as if throwing it away. Occasionally Anders would pay rent ahead, or invest in some object that could be sold when times grew hard again, but Sten never even bothered to pay their debts when the cash came in. Neither of them managed to save.

They worked with horses: as handlers and trainers, and as dealers. They unloaded fruit in the markets and set up a stall with the gypsies, where they told fortunes. They robbed men who were walking home alone or in pairs at night. They broke into empty houses when they knew the owners were going to be away, and they sold the carpets and paintings they took. Once Sten was interrupted by a porter who had been left to guard a place and Anders hit the man such a crashing blow on the head from behind that he was sure he'd killed him. He wanted to get out of town after that. Knocking down drunken burghers was one thing—this was worse: causing suffering to the innocent, crippling or injuring servants too poor and ignorant to have a choice about how they lived. Sten laughed at him. Anders was worrying himself about nothing, he said.

Through the fortune-telling sessions and the serving maids who came to them, they began to know a lot about the secrets of rich families. When his eyes had been shadowed with lampblack and he was dressed in his cap with stars and the blue-black silk robe set with magic symbols, women told Anders things he could hardly believe were in their minds. He'd had no idea that women had such wishes and hopes, such peculiar, intricate notions, or—in some cases—such actual knowledge.

He spoke with nursemaids and governesses, cooks, parlormaids, seamstresses, shopgirls, women who worked in the dairies. And they told him about the men they were in love with, the women they hated, the children they were afraid they might be carrying. They wanted herbs and charms for this and that—for conditions and emotions he hadn't known about before. Sometimes the girls and women were pretty. Sometimes he could tell that they were interested in him. Occasionally when he pulled the curtain and put the sign up, it was so that he could make love to the customer. The first time it happened, he had to be told; the girl leaned forward, placed her hand on top of the crystal ball he was carefully touching only at the sides, and said, "Let's have the present, instead of the future." When he still didn't understand, she lifted his right hand off the glass and pressed it to her breast. She had paid in advance, and when she went away, he forgot to say anything about giving back the money. Some of the others counted out extra notes when they left. He never thought of using the information and the women until Sten planned everything.

At the beginning, they were going to go right to the top: find some influential citizen, blackmail him, and set themselves up. Sten tried to do it alone. The man he lighted on wasn't the kind to stand for such tricks; he sent his two toughest and largest footmen to follow Sten from the marketplace and beat him up. Anders was at home when they came. He walked in from the other room, caught the men unawares and knocked them out. Sten was bruised and cut above the eye; he was furious when he checked his appearance in the mirror. It was always bad business to look as if you'd been in a fight.

"Leave this to me," he told Anders. "Help me tie them up and gag them, and then just wait here till I come back." He took one of his pistols and left. Anders waited as he'd been told. Sten didn't come back until it was dark. At midnight they carried the footmen down the stairs, loaded them on to a wagon Sten had brought into the courtyard, and hitched up the horse he had borrowed. They drove out to the suburbs, to the open fields.

Anders looked around and saw nothing but blackness. Sten reined in the horse. They climbed down and dragged the men across open ground. Anders kept stumbling. Sten seemed to know where they were going; he said, "Go back and wait for me."

Anders went. He could make out, very faintly, a shape he thought was the wagon. He fell against it before he expected it to be there in front of him. He climbed up. Sten followed soon after. Before they reached their street again, Anders asked, "Did you kill them?"

"Of course," Sten said. "And this afternoon I shot the man who paid them. I'm not going to have to leave this town just because one scheme goes wrong."

"They wouldn't have killed you."

"That was their mistake, wasn't it? We're in the clear now. You can forget about it."

"We should move house again."

"It won't be necessary."

"Maybe not, but we should."

They found better rooms with money that Sten produced. He hadn't had it before the murders. Anders didn't brood over the incident but he thought: *It could happen again; it came into his mind very easily. It could happen to me. It isn't that he's bad, but that circumstances goad him to action, and murder is something he doesn't have to deliberate about. Some people look at it that way—they'd just do it, like doing anything else.*

He told Sten that they should think about going separate ways. Sten cried; he said it wouldn't happen again, that Anders mustn't leave, that he'd never had any luck at all before they met, that he couldn't go on without his help and had he forgotten how much they'd been through together?

Anders stayed. They called themselves Hahn and Strohmeyer after two adjacent shop signs they saw in a street one day. They sold fake paintings and had a back room in a furniture storehouse where they made frames. They dealt in ribbons and perfumes and received regular payments from a prostitution ring Sten organized at the market. And they developed a passion for the opera. They sat up in the gallery with the students, though sometimes they made their entrance from the front: on a good night they could collect between ten and fifteen gold watches together with the fobs, to be put on the jeweler's scales in the morning. Once they got one with a sapphire on it. Sten kept that for himself.

Twice in three years they hit the bullseye, making a killing that they thought would set them up for life. They bought houses, gave parties, lived regally. And then somehow—gambling, drinking, wasting thousands on horses, cards, women, casino life—they lost everything again. And the moment you lost it all, Sten complained, it was very difficult to call on acquaintances from the good times. The very fact that you were asking became a warning.

They had one magnificent holiday in Budapest, when they gave entertainments out on the river and had music and dancing that lasted all night. It was a sentimental visit to the city Sten's family came from. He and Anders had their photographs taken together in their fine clothes and with their fine friends, but the picture Anders remembered best was of Sten throwing piles of banknotes up in the air and laughing, saying that this town had kicked his people out like vermin and now he could buy the whole damn place and screw anybody he liked.

He also remembered, from a later time, that they started to have quarrels, especially after they'd just made a bit of money, which was not quite so much as they thought they needed. They argued about nothing: one evening they sat and quarreled for two hours about where they were going to eat, and they ended up hitting each other. Anders stormed out of the house. He didn't go back for three days. As soon as he came through the door again, Sten screamed at him that if he wanted to fight—all right; but what the hell did he think he was doing just leaving, just walking out like that? And the quarrel went on.

One year they struck a particularly bad patch during cold weather. Sten was sick; Anders thought he was going to die. It was his turn to steal in the street and pick pockets. He began to hate doctors. Sten had always been drawn to medical men—he believed them all, and if he had fears about his health, he'd go to dozens; but he was usually only worried when he was all right. For Anders the facts were simple: there was no way of telling who the good doctors were except by trial and error—a system you couldn't risk. Even if you found one of the ones who knew what he was doing, if you didn't have the money, he couldn't afford to let you have the treatment. And if you didn't get the medicine, you died.

When Sten was better, he got up and looked at himself in the mirror, examining every inch carefully, like an actor preparing for the stage. He was very concerned that his appearance should be unchanged, both the body and the face. And it was, except for a small streak composed of three hairs which were growing out white at the roots and showed up against the other, dark hair. Anders had noticed them as he was putting the heel of his hand to Sten's forehead to see if the fever had broken. When he called attention to them, Sten pulled out the hairs in one quick tug.

"What's wrong?" Anders asked. "You look as if you'd seen a ghost."

"I never want it to happen."

"Everyone gets white hair. It's like rotten teeth and bad eyesight. We all come to it."

"I won't. And I'm probably not going to get that far, anyway. They told my mother I'd die young."

"Who told her?"

"The seers."

"A couple of other charlatans like us? You'll last another few years for sure."

"Who paid for the new things? How did you get it?"

"The usual ways," Anders said.

"You see? You're a real man now. Before you met me, you'd never worked, had you? Everything was handed to you. All that network of family and inheritance kept you afloat."

It wasn't completely true, of course. Anders had worked hard for years. He'd been a ship's captain and a good one, but he didn't say so. Arguments that didn't go Sten's way could make him frantic, so that he began to scream hysterically. And also, like so many things he said, there was at least some truth to the statement if you looked at it in a different light.

At the end of the second year they bought a ramshackle building and set up a brothel. All their serious collisions with the police dated from that time. If they had tried to run an honest establishment, everything would have been all right. But Sten hadn't wanted an ordinary house. He'd hoped to make more money through blackmail and the sale of information. He'd actually intended, from the start, to go against the law in several different ways. Anders knew almost immediately that they'd put themselves into a trap. And neither of them had realized that once you got into the business, it wasn't so easy to get out again. They were no longer on their own. Other people depended on them and other people could get them into trouble. The house itself, which made the trade more profitable, put them in danger. Anyone would know where to find them again.

There were fights in the house. Some of them began over money, although most of the time the cause was just drinking. Usually Anders managed to calm matters down before they got out of hand. Sometimes nothing worked and the police came in. They were paid to leave the place alone but if anyone outside called them in, they had to act on the complaint. Once there was a stabbing and the man, who turned out to be a respectable shop owner, sent squads of uniformed men in the next day. The girls were driven away and Sten was arrested. It took Anders a week to get him out of jail and it cost him all their spare cash. They had to walk home from the prison.

"Are you all right?" Anders asked.

"No."

"Did they treat you badly?"

"Of course. They always do."

"No friendly faces?"

"Anders, the police aren't interested in making friends. They like discipline and punishment, and they've got power over you as long as you're inside. They're also oafs, so they love taking it out on anybody that falls into their clutches."

"What's happened to the girls?"

"They're all right, naturally. In fact, they stood between me and some of the trouble. It could have been a lot more uncomfortable."

Anders said he thought they had to go into the profession

186

the way everyone else did, and make their accommodation with the law, or they'd better get out altogether, and try a different, less precarious line of work. They couldn't, he said, keep on worrying about being sent to jail. They shouldn't have their names—even their false names—on a police dossier, or have their faces known. "I'm still free," he said, "but you can be recognized by scores of policemen now. If they catch sight of you in a crowd, they'll remember: they'll think you're worth watching, maybe they'd follow you to see what you're up to. And then if anybody near you misses a coin or a button, yours is the shoulder they'd put their hands on."

Sten agreed, but he had no ideas about how to change their lives. Whenever they had any cash, he'd put it on a horse or a game of cards, and they'd lose. In the beginning they used to win half the time; now every stake went to other people. "It makes you think," Sten said one day, "that there might be something to the astrology business we used to peddle. It makes you wonder whether we're under some unfavorable aspect of something-or-other, like standing in the shadow all the time while the rest of them are playing in the sun."

"Nonsense," Anders told him. "That's what happens to mountebanks—they see the effect it has on the credulous, and then they're fooled by their own tricks. Most things will work for a little while. What we need to do is find a stable demand for something we can supply."

"We've got that already. The day people give up screwing is the day the world ends."

"I was thinking," Anders said, "more along the lines of chocolate biscuits or beer. Less money in them, but it would be steady, and a lot safer."

Sten said all right—as soon as they got some capital together, they'd see about it. For once Anders believed in his good intentions. He talked the scheme over with a few of the girls and discovered that some of them would be willing to work in a bakery or a brewery. He didn't ask all of them; some, he knew, were no good for anything else and liked the life for reasons that had nothing to do with the easy money or satisfying their own need; they would always revert to it because it was their method of wielding power over people they didn't like and who they believed to be enjoying an unfairly superior station.

They made plans to move at the end of the month. But before they could do anything, they were visited by something worse than the law: an epidemic went through the house. It appeared in many respects to be like the ordinary venereal infections they were used to dealing with all the time. But it also duplicated the characteristics of other diseases; it could go to the chest or break out as a skin rash, cause pain in the joints and glandular swelling. There were mild and severe cases. Most people ran a high fever for a short while at least. By the time Sten and Anders caught the infection, the girls—who had had it first and kept quiet about it—were too sick to work. Sten sold the house out from under them and rented another two-room apartment for himself and Anders.

They were in the hands of the doctors again. Anders recovered quickly. He'd had only a few days of swellings and fever and he followed the medical instructions to the letter. The measles he'd contracted in childhood had been, as he remembered, much worse. But Sten didn't do as he'd been told; he seemed to be cured, went out looking for trade, drugged himself periodically as the symptoms recurred, and then passed out drunk one night and couldn't get up in the morning. They were sleeping in separate beds now, drinking from marked cups, using their own forks and spoons.

Anders went to get the doctor—a young man, and a very good doctor—who never for a moment allowed Anders to think he considered him and his friend not worth saving; but he was extremely expensive and adamant about his fees, which were to be paid in advance. "I don't treat society ladies for the vapors," he explained. "I'm a working physician and if I don't have the money, I can't cure anyone. I didn't become a doctor to get rich. My family's got money. All I have to do is break even. But to do that, I've got to be paid."

He took one look at Sten and said that it was serious. After the examination he told Anders that the recuperation was going to take a long time and that there was a danger of pneumonia. The most important thing at the moment was that on top of gonorrhoea and what sounded like the beginnings of a lung ailment, Sten had picked up a virulent case of some other type of venereal infection, which might be a kind of syphilis, although it evinced several peculiar characteristics the doctor hadn't come across before.

"We've had a lot of that," Anders told him.

"This time it's more complicated," the doctor said. "And if he doesn't follow directions with this one, you know how it ends."

Anders nursed Sten for three weeks. He remained healthy while Sten coughed and choked, couldn't swallow solid food and broke out in red pustules.

"It's the smallpox, isn't it?" Sten asked, his eyes and voice full of terror. "I've seen it before."

"It's just another symptom," Anders told him.

"I'll be marked for life. And blinded."

"You'll get well again. At least, you'll be unscarred. I don't know about the rest. It might be one of those diseases that can turn around on you after twenty or thirty years and give you another lashing. So, you'd better do what he said. He sounded like a pretty good doctor. He's right, too—it isn't fair to ask for free treatment."

"What's fair? Being alive isn't fair. I've never understood that: how people can expect it."

"They hope for it. It's a wish—a dream. I had a dream the other night that I was in Paris at that restaurant with the glass ceiling. I was having dinner with my parents."

"I had a dream that I died," Sten said. "I died and you were there, standing by my coffin. And you didn't even cry."

"I had a dream," Anders told him, "that I walked out of this room and jumped on the first train leaving town, and left you to choke on your pills."

"Don't get angry," Sten said, "I'm not strong enough. It's going to kill me this time, I know it. I'm not worried about one more dose of the clap or whatever it is. It's this other thing. Not being able to breathe. And all these—just like the smallpox, Anders."

"If you just stay quiet, we'll get you over this stage of it, I promise."

Sten didn't believe it. When he wasn't throwing himself from side to side in the bed, he lay rigid and staring, waiting to be deformed by more sores and boils.

At last, just as the money ran out completely, he was well again. "I'll never forget this, Anders," he said. "You saved me."

"It isn't over yet. You've got to be careful."

"We'll find some other line of business for a while."

They tried to cheat a drunken farmer at cards. He was up from the country and was just as stupid as they had imagined. They had, however, underestimated his temperament. As soon as the man realized that he'd lost, he began to break up the room they were sitting in. Customers ran for the doors, chairs flew, the farmer bellowed for justice and the police were on the scene before Anders and Sten could move.

This time they were both arrested. They pretended not to know each other, so Anders had a cell to himself. He thought the squalor wasn't so bad, no worse than the decent poverty of much of the town outside, but when he was moved to the common cells, he changed his mind. And no matter how disheartening the physical conditions were, he was more profoundly shocked by the spiritual degradation among his fellow prisoners. He told himself that he had to get out of the city, of the kind of life he'd been leading, of everything; and that he'd never be able to do it with Sten in tow. In some way, without knowing it, Sten wanted to suffer, to keep losing his money and having to jostle and shove for it again, to have the drama of crisis and urgency always around him; he couldn't chart his own course—he sought complex or unlucky events that would prod him into plans he couldn't have thought of without them.

Anders was freed within hours. It took six days of bribery to get Sten out too, and they were broke again. They went looking for work.

As they were standing by a flower stall one day, waiting for an acquaintance who used to drive the beer barrels into a tavern on the other side of town, Sten caught the eye of an old woman dressed rather ludicrously in finery of the latest fashion for women half her age. She pulled out a lorgnette and smiled at him. He moved away. Anders saw what was happening and let him go. He himself stayed on, to meet the driver and get the job. In the evening he expected to hear all the news, but Sten didn't come back.

He heard nothing till the morning, when a letter arrived for him. A banknote was enclosed and the message simply said, "We're in clover." Anders went out to change the note, used half the money towards the back rent, and got something to eat. He didn't give up the job until the next day, after Sten had returned home.

The old woman was a baroness—an authentic one; and incredibly, sensationally, rich. She was also Hungarian, which always helped. And she'd taken such a fancy to Sten: she was going to leave him everything in her will; she'd bought him suits—you couldn't imagine; and found him a little house—a real house, not just rooms: and everything was going to be wonderful from now on.

"Do you make love to her?" Anders asked.

"A little. It's not bad. She's quite an interesting woman."

"But old. You're the one who thinks age is so ugly."

"Nothing is ugly if you're rich enough. And besides, you don't have to keep your eyes open all the time, you know."

"You could catch it all over again."

"Yes, and your tongue could drop off. Stop giving me the bad warnings. Everything's perfect now. Now's the time to celebrate."

"Could you do something for me? Get a large amount of cash out of her straight away: make some excuse. I just don't believe it's going to last."

"It wouldn't look right."

"I don't care how it looks," Anders said. "I've got a feeling. These May-and-December unions last the longest when there's no sex."

"Not this one. That's what she wants me for."

"You'd have done better to go for the sentiment and a tenth of the money. In fact, you'd be much better off with a man again. Old women can be capricious as well as demanding. Is she alone in the world?"

191

"She's got a family that doesn't appreciate her."

"Get the cash, Sten. If you have to, sell something she's given you and say it was stolen."

Sten handed him the money the following day. Anders rented a new set of rooms for himself, bought some clothes and shoes, and put most of what was left into a bank. For the next few days he enjoyed himself thoroughly. And as the time approached when he thought he ought to decide between the cake shop and the brewery, he wasn't surprised to hear that the baroness had sons and grandsons who—although not appreciating her—were determined that no one else should pretend to, and consequently appreciated Sten even less. Since the old woman was proof against all the stories they had raked up to discredit her lover, they were prepared to go to court.

"It's all right," Sten said. "She thinks they're maligning me, even though I told her a lot of what they found out was going to be true, because I'd been unfortunate and had such a hard life." He sat on Anders' new couch and hugged himself. There was no trace of his recent illness; he was only slightly underweight and in his new clothes looked as elegant and distinguished as one of the Eastern princes on holiday in the town that month.

"We're going to the races," he said, "and the opera, and —I'm late. I'll see you soon."

"Watch out, Sten. If this one backfires, we may have to get out of town fast. I think we should make arrangements now to meet somewhere. Paris, say. Or Rome."

"I wouldn't mind. It's been a long time since I've been to either of them. I remember a lot of competition. What about Berlin?"

"Not Germany. Too many people from home go there."

"But they'd never recognize you."

"I'm not taking the chance."

"St. Petersburg?"

"We wouldn't live through the winter. It's worse than home. Some other town in Italy?"

"Maybe. I had a good time in Naples till they caught up with me."

"Marseilles?"

"They know me too well there."

"This is what people mean when they say it's a small world."

Sten laughed. He said everything was going to be fine. "When I get my hands on what she's leaving me, we can really travel: Egypt, China, the Indies—America. We could buy land."

For the next five days Anders was so excited about the idea of them both emigrating to America as rich men that he almost considered it a possibility. But his first fears turned out to be right. In a scene that should have been tragic or horrible, but which according to all the accounts afterwards was a comic fiasco, the baroness's two sons, accompanied by lawyers, irrupted into her private apartments, where they discovered her and Sten entwined in the very act for which she had engaged him; and as from the silken recesses of the bed-curtains the old woman saw her boudoir invaded, she suffered a stroke, gave a single cry, and died. Sten was arrested, charged with murder.

Anders went to see him in jail. He'd hired lawyers himself, he said, and despite the money on the other side, he was sure the family wasn't going to want the scandal in open court.

Sten looked deranged. He said, "They killed her—not me. I'm never going to forget this, never. I'll get back at those two somehow, if it takes me the rest of my life."

"I'll get you out," Anders promised. He had long discussions with the lawyers. They seemed to be talking him in circles. He came to believe that the law would keep leafing through its books and copying out pages of notes until all his money ran out, and then Sten would be at the mercy of the two sons.

"I don't know what to do next," he told Sten.

"Anything. They'll hang me if it comes to a trial. I know it. They'll take one look and decide I offend their sense of propriety, the swine."

"The only solution I can think of is for you to break out."

"No. For you to grab me when they transfer me for the hearings."

193

"You really think that would work?"

"I'll tell you how to do it," Sten said.

The rescue was planned down to the split second. "And," Sten added, "make some provision for the thing going wrong. They could shoot me in the back and then they'd be after you."

"Or vice-versa. All right." They agreed on what to do if they were separated, wounded, or if either of them was killed. On the day, Anders' hired men stepped in front of the guard, swung their clubs in all directions, but forgot that Sten was manacled to the warder. While two of the men were breaking the chain, another contingent of bullies—presumably allied to the old woman's sons—converged on the growing crowd. Sten was knocked to the ground.

Anders waded in. The crowd became a mob. He lost his caution, pulled out his pistol and shot three of the ruffians from the other side. He picked Sten up and hauled him away, carried him around the corner into the alleyway, and managed to stuff him inside the cab he had waiting. They drove to Anders' rooms. He paid the driver and sent his landlady out for her doctor. He was already on good terms with her; she wouldn't give him away.

While he waited, he washed the blood off Sten's face and head. He kept trying to find a pulse, and couldn't. When the doctor got there, he couldn't, either. "This man is dead," he said.

Anders followed the plan. He slashed open the chair-covers, took out the money hidden there and left town. He kept going, across the border. He didn't stop until he reached Genoa. After that, he was drunk for fourteen months.

.   .   .

He took up with a woman who tried to reform him. He switched to another, who died giving birth to a child that was probably not his. Whenever he sobered up, all he could think of was that his life would go on in unhappiness, poverty and abasement, forever. He didn't even realize that he was engrossed in his own self-pity; he was too far down.

One day four people he knew by sight committed suicide:

two prostitutes from his neighborhood drowned themselves, a sailor he sometimes talked to in the taverns was found with his throat cut, and a woman he used to buy flowers from— an old woman—swallowed poison.

Not long after he'd been told the news, he sat down on the edge of a low wall skirting a small park. He thought about the four. It seemed to him that if they could do it, so could he. And then he thought: *Before I do that, I might as well try everything else.* He remembered, as if it had been a thing he'd heard about long ago, his plans to sail to South America and study the plants of the jungle.

He had been away from his country for nearly five years. He could stay away for another ten, twenty, thirty. On the other hand, he was still a ship's captain and he was in a port town now, and if he wanted to sail to South America, he could actually do it. There was only the matter of the papers to be attended to.

He sat for hours, turning over the prospects of death and of South America. It was like the time when the two waves came rushing at each other: he hadn't imagined such a thing before. Nor did he want to dream of another, future existence that lay beyond the park and the wall he was sitting on. He had reached a point where once again his life stood still, as it had when he had received all living action across the chasm of his speechlessness.

There was a choice. The thought astounded him. It kept him occupied for days. He stopped drinking. His heart pounded wildly and his hands shook. He had frightening dreams. But at the end of two months, he shipped out.

And during the next five years, when he was working as a riverboat captain on the Amazon, he did make many excursions into the jungle. He developed an affection for its plants and trees, and made drawings and paintings of them, even though he hadn't been trained for it. He caught the local fevers and fell victim to the prevailing crazes and superstitions, the most dangerous of which was the theory—the certainty—that a young man could make his fortune overnight in the gold mines. But he gave his belief shrewdly. He saw hundreds of the young men, poor and newly wealthy, riding up and down his river. He took their money at cards. Sometimes they paid in nuggets greatly more valuable than the sum of their debts. Anders began to amass a store of gold.

He saved. He put earnings in the bank. He used his real name, invested and bought stocks. When he made money from gold mines it was because he had shares in them.

Twice he was lost in the jungle. The second time it happened to him, he was sure he'd die there. He became delirious and was convinced that his old friend, Martin, was walking beside him, talking to him all the way, telling him how to get out. It really seemed that he was hearing the voice and aware, even though he didn't look, of another body keeping step beside him. He spoke back, glad to be using his own language.

When he reached the river again that second time, he began to long for his old home. He suddenly missed everything about it and everyone there. He thought of his children, especially his little daughter who had flung her arms around his neck and cried.

Would his family still be waiting for him? When he remembered them, he wanted to put his hands over his face. But he was unable to stop his thoughts; they turned more and more often to home. He had dreams about walking by the lake, hunting in the woods, sailing through the islands.

He made his decision. He worked out his story and he came back a rich man.

.   .   .

"It's been a long time, eh?" Sten said. "And what a big place you've got here. Enormous. Even your house: It's so big, I couldn't find the front door. But it's better this way, isn't it? I've found you instead." He leaned on the stick, which was of an elegant slimness: a thing designed for city walking. "And now," he said, "at last I meet the family."

"No," Anders told him.

Sten stepped forward. He opened his mouth, showing decayed brown and black teeth. As he laughed shortly, the stench of them reached Anders.

"Why not? One of your oldest friends. If you don't invite me in, my old friend, I'm going to begin to tell my story. I'll start by saying that all the time you were supposed to be having great adventures in South America, you were really just living with me in Vienna, where you earned your living as my pimp. That doesn't sound very nice, does it?"

"No, and it's only partly true."

"That's the part that counts, Anders."

"All right," Anders said. "Come in, but be quiet. If you make any noise, if you start demanding anything of me, believe me you won't get far. If you behave yourself, we'll see. I suppose you want money. You look as if you need it." He turned back to his study, entered and stood inside the glass door. He had grown to love the room so much that it pained him to allow the man in.

Sten dragged himself forward across the threshold, over the Chinese rug and up to a chair that Anders indicated. As he held out his hand towards the chair, Anders knew that he would never again want to sit there himself. Sten peered around the room. He dropped his knapsack on the floor and leaned the stick against the side of the chair. Perhaps his eyesight was beginning to break down, like the rest of his body; but he would still be too vain to wear spectacles. He took a good grip on the arms of the chair as he lowered himself into the seat and then stretched his right leg out in front of him.

Anders thumped down in his chair at the desk. "We're alone here in this part of the house," he said. "Just tell me first of all: where are you staying?"

"In the village."

"Where?"

"Some sort of rest home for sailors. It's like a hotel, but much more respectable. No liquor on the premises."

"Just as well. What name are you using?"

"Strohmeyer."

"Of course. When did you arrive?"

"Last night. I had to rest. I've changed a great deal, don't you think?"

"Naturally. So have I."

"But you—"

"Are you hungry?" Anders asked.

"Not for the moment. Later, perhaps."

197

Anders nodded. He was trying to plan ahead. They would talk; he could tell Ingrid that he had to discuss something with a man who'd come about the horses. And he'd ask for a cold supper and wine on a tray. There would be no need for anyone to see more than a glimpse of Sten. Ingrid's eyesight was pretty poor anyway. And when they'd settled the terms, he could drive Sten back in the trap. But—if he gave out too much money, Sten would be able to drink; if he drank enough, he might talk. It all depended on how strong Sten was and, of course, on what he really wanted. If he had come to blackmail, that was one thing. But if he had come back to try to destroy the family, that was something else. He might. That might be just what he would want.

"It's considerate of you to ask," Sten said hoarsely. His skinny hands rested in a knot at the top of the walking stick where there should have been an ornamental knob; the color of the wood showed that added decoration had once had a place there, perhaps made of silver or some other valuable metal that had been removed to raise cash.

"I eat very little nowadays. Everything seems to disagree with me. And you? It looks as if you're sitting just where all things in creation do agree with you. Yes, indeed. You were always the one who got away with everything."

Anders stared into the bookcase next to his head. He looked at the titles without reading them. He put his elbows on his desk, his face in his fists.

"I've had illnesses," Sten said, "some of which you know about. You got away without them too, didn't you? I never knew how you managed that, not when we were so close to each other."

Anders turned his head. He remembered every detail of how Sten had once looked and recalled how conscious and finicky he had been of his appearance, which had been his fortune long before they had met: the means by which he had—from the early days of his childhood—always obtained everything he wanted. It was nightmarish to hear Sten's voice coming out of this false front; it was as if the twisted, gnome-like old man had been the real person all along, and what

198

Anders had seen before had been the mask. But the mask was what he knew and remembered.

"Don't begin accusing me again," he said. "You loved prostituting yourself. You enjoyed corrupting people. It made you feel powerful. Whores usually have a rough time when their looks start to go. You were always complaining about every spot and pimple. And everything was my fault. You couldn't stand it that I wasn't like you."

"But you were seduced."

"Oh yes, for a time. As a matter of necessity."

"As a matter of choice, Anders."

"For a while. Does it make a difference any more?"

"It might make a difference to your respectable friends."

"And you could find out if you enjoy the jails over here as much as the ones in Vienna. I don't know what that would add to your health."

"Don't joke about it," Sten told him. "Once your health breaks down, there's nothing you can do." He looked suddenly fanatical. "It's like the bobsleds," he said; "you're on the downward run and there's no way to climb off. It goes down and down, and death is at the bottom."

"We all get there in time," Anders said.

Sten laughed again, uncovering the ravaged teeth. He said, "Well, well, that's how it is. I'm old and feeble now. And you look very sleek; hale and hearty—yes, a treat for the ladies, I'm sure. But I'm stronger than you, Anders. Do you know what my strength is? I've got nothing to lose: that's my strength."

"Everybody's got something to lose. Unless you've come here to try to force me into killing you."

"You'd like to, wouldn't you?"

Anders turned his head away again. He gazed at the volume of poetry on the desktop. There was a pistol in the top right-hand drawer and he knew that it was loaded. He looked up at the books on their shelf and at the long-breasted gold idol that seemed to be snarling at him. Of course the gods were like that. You couldn't believe otherwise for very long.

.   .   .

He could tell his family the truth. He was going to have to tell them; not everything, naturally, but the general outline. Who would mind the most? Or the least? Erika, he knew, was one of the few who wouldn't care. If it weren't for people like that, civilization would never move forward; their attitudes were ahead of the rest, towards the future, Of the others, his sister, Elsie, would be the first to understand, and next would come Lina. And even so, even if in the end they were to forgive him completely, they would regard the lie, the pretense, as a particularly reprehensible form of infidelity. And they would be right: he had deceived them.

There were some things Sten couldn't accuse him of without giving himself away; he'd have to keep silent about the whole of Vienna. But what really troubled Anders was before Vienna—the fact that the expedition hadn't gone anywhere, that there had never been travels and discoveries, that its very existence had been fabricated. All Sten had to do was point the finger at him.

If Anders told everyone, what could happen? Louise would be slow to forgive him, as she had been slow to forget the man she had loved. She hung on tightly both to injury and to sentiment. When he recalled the careful gentility of her new husband, Kellner, he doubted that either of them would be able to side with him against the weight of the gross, roistering scandal that would fall upon him and his name. That journalist, Petersen, would do his best to see that no one escaped the notoriety—one could depend on that.

He tried to imagine sitting them all down and telling them: *This is what really happened*. And, all at once, he knew what the worst would be—his children; the two daughters, who needed heroes and romance, and whose hopes of marriage to the kind of man they desired were going to depend on their father's ability to keep the truth hidden. Even money had its limits; if you were rich enough, you could get away with murder, but you couldn't expect your children to be invited out afterwards.

It was no good. He couldn't explain. If it weren't for the girls, he'd have the courage. It was too late now. He'd told the false story and then, to protect himself against the newspapers, he'd published. One error led to another; it was just like those French farces and there was the same confusion of identity, the same fatal ability to become mistaken.

"I thought you were dead," he said.

"And I knew you were somewhere, although I never suspected you'd come back here. But I keep up with one or two people in this part of the world. Friends of Gustav. Gustav was very good to me."

"Yes, I remember how you used to hold that over my head. How good he was to you, and how much he loved you."

"It's true."

"Oh, the truth."

"But that wasn't the way I found you. I was in jail, you know."

"Again?"

"A misunderstanding. And I was ill. I caught consumption. I thought it was the end. They took me out, and I finished the sentence in the hospital. I met a very interesting doctor there."

"I can picture it."

"The genuine article. A professor of medicine. A man of scholarship. He was the one who made the diagnosis. You know, they write papers about me now. Yes. I've got such an extraordinary liver, it's diseased in more ways than the doctors ever dreamed of. It seems to be quite a medical phenomenon. And my kidneys—they're hardly sure I've still got any: the poor things have just shrunken away. Yes, indeed. I've had everything in the encyclopedia. I'm a walking wreck. Only my head—my head is very hard. And my pulse was always erratic, you should have remembered that."

"One can't remember everything."

"No, but one should. I've got a good memory."

"Too good. It adds things."

"This professor: he thought my case was so interesting that he let me come to him as a private patient, for free."

"Yes?" Whatever else had gone wrong after they'd parted, Sten had retained the instinct for latching on to people who could give him the right information, or be helpful to him somehow.

"And while I was in his waiting room one day, I was looking through the medical journals there, and you'll never guess what I saw—what a piece of luck: your name, right there. And a story about the expedition you'd led to South America. The doomed, heroic attempt."

Anders rose from his chair, reached up and pulled the bell cord.

"What are you doing?" Sten snapped.

"If you're going to want anything to eat, I'll have to let them know in the kitchen."

"I would have found you anyway, in the end, no matter where you'd gone. I still know where people hide themselves."

Anders edged towards the door. When he thought he could hear Ingrid approaching, he said, "Stay right where you are."

"Don't excite yourself. It takes me a long time now to get up out of a chair. A legacy from my loving family. Broke my bones to make me limber. There was no shape I couldn't get into. As you know."

Anders opened the door and stood outside it. He gave Ingrid the order for two meals and said to tell the family that he was having a talk with a man about the horses; and that they were not to be disturbed.

He returned to his place at the desk. Sten said, "I did enjoy all your pretty little pictures of flowers."

If it weren't for Sten, he'd probably be safe. The only really uncertain time was the voyage from Genoa, but he'd made that under a different name. He hadn't resumed his own identity until he'd arrived in the New World. The men who had been on that ship might recognize him, though he didn't think so. They wouldn't be likely to visit his part of the globe. And he doubted that any of them could read. He wondered, while Sten talked, if there was another way in which the past might catch up with him.

"I've got a picture, too," Sten went on. "I've got a photograph of both of us together in Budapest. Remember?"

"In my experience, most photographs tend to make everyone look alike."

"Not this one."

"Let's see it."

"If you like," Sten said. "I've got lots of copies." He put a hand into his inside breast pocket, delved around, and pulled out a square of cardboard which he held up.

Anders crossed the room to see. He didn't want to touch the thing. He leaned over Sten, conscious of the reek of his teeth and what might have been the smell of his clothes and body too. He looked.

He remembered the picture, and when it had been taken. It was a good one. They both looked many years younger, well dressed, full of high spirits.

"Yes, very nice," he said "Could be anyone."

"It's unmistakable and you know it."

There was a knock at the door. Anders went to answer it Ingrid was outside with the trolley. "I'll take that," he told her. He wheeled the food into the room, shutting the door after him.

Sten wouldn't eat much. He drank a few sips of wine and started to ask if Anders remembered this and remembered that. Anders answered shortly: yes, yes.

"I remember, but what of it?"

"I think of those days as very happy times."

"And I think of them as dead."

"But I also remember that I never had the complete control over you that I wanted."

"Didn't you?"

"No. I always felt that your influence over me was greater than mine over you."

"I didn't. I thought we were equal."

"Would your wife want to know," Sten asked, "that you once loved me more than you could ever love her?"

"Not more than. That's not the truth, either."

"Pretty close to it."

"Is that what you've come for?"

"I thought you might be interested in reading something. Wait." He pushed the folding table a few inches away and leaned down towards the knapsack he'd left on the floor by his chair. "You'll have to get it for me," he said. "I can't reach."

Anders crossed to the chair. He picked up the bag by its strap.

"Go ahead and look," Sten told him. "There's a copy. And if there wasn't, I could just write another."

Anders shook out about a hundred and fifty pages of paper covered with writing. They were spattered with blots and cross-hatched by corrections and underlinings. He began to read the first page, then skipped, and skimmed through several more at random. The book purported to be a true account of the expedition to South America; Anders and his ship's officers had taken part in it, although Sten was the main figure: the pathfinder and hero.

"What's this for?" Anders asked.

"Publication, of course."

"No."

"Yes. It'll be a great success."

"It would contradict what I've already made public."

"And why not? It's my fiction against yours."

Anders re-read some of the lines. The style was worse than the paraphrases invented by Erika's magazine. It was quite possible that such a thing could become a success in the world. He would have to sue, but Sten would be made rich, could hold out for a long time while the lawyers on both sides ate up their money, and then bolt with what he had left, leaving Anders and his family to live with the publicity. The photograph would be very convincing, too. He'd seen how they could be faked and yet he too always believed in the veracity of pictures. Even when the methods of cutting and reduplicating had been pointed out, the joins revealed—they had the look of truth.

"Good, eh?" Sten said.

"You must have cooked this up in a hurry. It's a mess to read. And from what I can see, the story doesn't appear to hang together."

"As well as anybody else's. Anyway, the content may be negotiable. The style's the thing."

"You think I can give you more for it than the magazines or the newspapers?"

"Perhaps."

"I know all about blackmail, remember? And when you take a story like this to a publisher, the first thing they do is to check the facts, to see if it could get them into trouble."

"Oh, some of these outfits would print anything, especially if they saw the chance of money in it."

"You'd have to prove your identity. And if you did that, you might have to go back to jail. Or it could be worse, not being in jail; I expect there are a lot of people in Vienna out for your blood, maybe some from other places and from before my time. Or afterwards. I don't know what's really been happening to you in the past seven years, do I? Quite a lot, undoubtedly."

"I'm beyond all that now."

"You don't have children."

"Me?"

"Is there anyone in this world you'd want to think well of you?"

Sten grinned. He said, "Only you, Anders. And what's a good opinion worth? I'd rather have cash any day. Wouldn't you? It's just your vanity. I don't accuse you of anything bad."

"Only failure, stupidity, deception."

"There's something I've noticed about these famous explorers," Sten said, "and the stories about their discoveries. It's very interesting: there are always two. That's right. I've noticed that, haven't you? There's the official commentary and there's also the real story: the gentleman's version, and," he sneered, "the servant's."

"The original and the one somebody thought up for the purpose of getting rich quick."

"Even the famous ones—there's always the other story. I wouldn't be so quick to say which is more truthful. You aren't concerned with the truth—you never were. Your expedition after knowledge was a sham to begin with."

"Who's ever interested in truth for its own sake? Not many. I wanted to do something to make people admire me, and to live up to the expectations of my ancestors. Truth didn't enter into the scheme very much; if you could say what truth is, anyway."

"It's Vienna."

"That's only fact. There are a lot of facts in the world. The life here—that's a fact, too."

"The life here is hypocrisy."

"It's a good life for a lot of people."

Sten laughed. He looked at the food on his plate, pushed his fork at it, changed his mind and lifted his glass again.

Anders wondered how long the game was meant to go on, whether he could stop it in a few days, or if it would take weeks. He could leave, of course. But if he did that, Sten might become so infuriated that he'd take it out on the family.

"I may not need to use the book," Sten said. "We could write a new one together."

"How would I explain that? You're supposed to be dead. And I thought you were." He tapped the manuscript with the handle of his dinner knife. "Dead men tell no tales," he added.

"All you have to do is help. We can think up something. In the old days you were good at it."

"I don't know." His hand tightened around the knife and opened again. He leaned back in his chair. It was possible that Sten, entering prematurely into old age, had a wish for the respectability of having his name printed on the cover of a book that could be found in a medical scholar's office. It was also possible that, nearing death, he had become lonely, wanting the old times again, with both of them working together in some large city like Paris, Berlin or London, but being on top this time: that he wanted them to share a life again, perhaps even—as they had once planned—in America. Maybe he was crazy enough to hope for such a thing, and not to realize that it was too late for Anders to go back to the other life, just as at one time it had been too late to come back to this one.

And Sten really was dying, anyone could see that; he must know it himself. He wouldn't last any longer in America than in Europe. Perhaps he still never saw what he had no wish to see.

"Think about it," Sten suggested.

"I have my family."

"What do you care? You're the owner here. You can do anything you like. You could kick them all out, if you wanted to. Why not? Do they earn their keep?"

Anders smiled, but maybe with his damaged eyesight, Sten couldn't see.

"Think about it," Sten repeated. "I know a lot about South America. I've talked with people."

"There's a difference," Anders said. "I went there."

"In your dreams."

"No, I went."

"Not really."

"Yes, I can prove it." He picked up the gold statuette and took it across the room. He held it out, saying, "Look. Where do you think I got it?"

"I've seen such things in the salerooms."

"Oh? Like this one?"

"One meets a great many people who've traveled to distant places and have things to sell."

Anders returned to his desk. He put the idol back in its place.

"Ugly-looking thing," Sten said.

"I got it in South America, where I worked for nearly five years. I ran a boat up and down the river, taking the miners from place to place; and the ranchers and the traders and anybody else—everybody else, all on the move. I think it comes from farther north, but it's real, all right. How did you think I got my money? Where did you imagine I was for those years—back here?"

Sten looked hard at Anders. He frowned. Finally he said, "You lied about the expedition."

"I had to. It was too great a failure, and it was public. I lied because of my family."

"What a fine thing it is," Sten said bitterly, "to have a family."

Anders stood up. "I'll drive you back to the seamen's hostel myself," he said. "And we'll talk some more about this tomorrow. I have to think everything over carefully."

Sten nodded. He rocked from side to side, holding the arms of the chair as he prepared to lever himself upwards. Anders

207

moved the table away; he said, "You won't mind if I hang on to the manuscript?"

"Give it back, Anders."

"It'll be safe with me. Why would I want to get rid of it? I haven't even read the thing yet. I've got to read it before I make up my mind what to do."

"You can read it when I'm in the room with you. I don't feel right without it."

Anders put the strap of the empty knapsack into Sten's hand. He said, "If you're worried, just remember that you've still got the photograph. It isn't as though the book were evidence of anything It's only a story you made up."

"I want it back."

"I'll let you have it tomorrow afternoon. And now I'm taking you home." He held the terrace door open, pulled down the lantern from its bracket on the wall and lit it. He turned the light high so that Sten could see. Sten walked like an invalid—painfully and with many hesitations—and kept his head down. Anders was suddenly afflicted by a horror and remorse that continued to oppress him all night long, traveling down over his intestines like qualms of nausea. It wasn't fear. He didn't know what it could be. If it hadn't been associated with Sten, he might have thought it was compassion.

.   .   .

The family had, as usual, a great deal to discuss over breakfast. Among other topics, they touched on that of the horses. They asked about the last night's guest. They hoped that Anders was going to stand out for a really fine pair of chestnuts and, if they could afford it, a gray as well.

He followed Erika on to the terrace, where Elsie was talking to Ekdahl. "I need your advice," he said. "Would you have the time this morning—now?"

"I don't know," she said. "I made an appointment; nothing definite, but perhaps . . . ."

"If it's the Russians, all right. But if it's a beau, this is more important."

"Anders, is someone ill?"

"It's not so simple as an illness. Come for a walk. Half an hour."

She nodded. They set off towards the lake. The light streamed down over them. It was the first day of the year that had begun with a real heat in the sun—warm enough to row out on the lake and talk there. But he knew how well sound carried over water, as from parts of the forest, where some dips and trails were like echo chambers, throwing words and noises to people miles away. He knew all about the properties of water: the changeable element of which the human body was largely composed.

"Over on the path there," he said. "Where the bench is. And the hillside behind won't give back the sound. It absorbs everything."

"How do you know?"

"We found out about it when we were children. There's always been a bench there. I expect that's why: it's a good place for talking. And a good view. You can see the lake and the house."

They sat down. He thought how lovely the old building looked from that point, set in all its lands, and how pretty the sun was on Erika's hair and face.

"Well?" she asked.

He began to tell her most of the truth, beginning with the shipwreck, Spain and Vienna. From then on, he smudged the edges. He said that he and Sten had been friends and business associates. He didn't tell her that one of the businesses had been a brothel, but he admitted to having been poor, starving, sick, driven to living from hand to mouth, to cheating people, stealing, committing other petty offenses, and having been put in jail.

He could see that the disgrace of prison didn't alarm her. Prison, to her, carried the connotation of political acts. It was society's repository for anarchists as well as criminals. To the rest of his family, of course, the idea of jail was unthinkable, the shame indelible.

He told her everything that came after Vienna. And then he recounted the events of the previous evening.

209

"You've got the manuscript?" she asked.

"Yes. It's pathetic. And outrageous. It's just like him. I found myself laughing a lot. But—you see the quandary I'm in: it doesn't depend on me alone. I can't decide just for myself."

"The decision's easy, Anders. The man wants to ruin you."

"That's one of the things I've been wondering about. You may be right. I think he probably does. And I almost think I may be ready to let him do it."

"You can't. You have duties to others—you just said so yourself."

"If I could act on my own, and not think about everyone else; that was the trouble in the first place. And I kept doing it. I take everyone else into account. But one shouldn't."

"He hates you for your family and your house and lands, and your education and position of responsibility, and the work you've done. He's going to try to spoil the whole of that."

"Do you think the rest of the family could understand what I did? Do you think they'd forgive it?"

She shook her head. "I think you should keep quiet."

"But you understand."

"I approve of your motives. And I think it was actually more difficult to do what you did—to keep up a lie and not lose your nerve."

"Like you and your Russians?"

"Let's not talk about that. Do you think he'll bring the photograph with him, or leave it at the hostel?"

"He'll bring it with him. He doesn't trust landladies and chambermaids. But a photograph can be copied, easily. He's right about that."

"You see that tree down there?" Erika asked. "Near the lake, not far from my boathouse. Bring this Sten there at seven o'clock."

"What are you going to do?"

"I'm going to help. Don't think any more about it."

"How?"

"Perhaps we'll kidnap him. Put him in a hospital ward in

a white jacket. I know lots of medical students. Don't worry. If it doesn't turn out, there's tomorrow."

She stood up and began to walk back to the house. He didn't move. He still wasn't sure what to think. He wanted to stay with his family, not to be near Sten again, yet he couldn't quite rid himself of the feeling that had come over him late the night before. And after reading the manuscript, he no longer believed Sten was so dangerous as he had at first appeared. He didn't want to hurt Sten; for old times' sake, and also because it was so obvious that the man didn't have long to live.

"Anders," Erika called. He looked up. She was standing at the bend in the path, waiting for him. He got up and walked forward to her.

"There's something you have that I'd like you to give me," she said.

"Of course. Anything."

"That little gold statuette you showed me once."

"Ah. I'm very attached to that. We've been through a lot together. It's become like a mascot to me."

"I have an idea that it might bring me luck. And besides, if I do you a favor, who can tell—somebody might be able to ask me for a favor. You know how these things work."

"Not really," he said. He'd lost the sense of what she was hinting at. "But I'll give it to you. Come back to the house."

They walked through the lower gardens that were still half dug-up, climbed the stairs and went along the terrace. He opened the door to his study and took down the statue from the shelf above his desk. Without looking again at the face of the god, he put it into her hands. She thanked him and walked out of the door, heading away towards the boathouse.

·   ·   ·

Sten arrived early. He wouldn't speak, or go anywhere, until Anders had returned his manuscript. Then he agreed to walk down to the lake. Once again his progress was slow, but he appeared to be enjoying the exercise. He blinked into the hazy early evening sunlight and said softly, "It's a fine country.

211

I'd forgotten how beautiful it can be. They say it happens to us all as we grow old—we remember our early years more and more. Of course, my really early years weren't here, but it's strange how much it still affects me. Maybe it's partly because of you. This is a wonderful place, Anders. Did you spend your childhood here?"

"Most of it; yes. And my father grew up here, too. And my grandfather. It's not such an old house. My great-grand-parents had it built shortly after they married." As they skirted the sunken gardens, he held out his arm. Sten fastened on to it with a grip like a monkey. Anders thought: *He used to be such a good-looking man: his face and head, the eyes, his way of standing, all his postures; and with an easy, athletic walk.* Even if it was true that they'd broken Sten's bones, how was it possible that a body so well-proportioned had become this crabbed gremlin whom one could scarcely bear to be near? And what terrors he must have gone through as the change had begun; Sten had always hated every sign of age in himself, and looked for them all the time, fearfully, the way religious people watch themselves for spiritual failings. In seven years he had undergone a shrivelling change more profound than that which had overtaken Aunt Emmelina and Aunt Irminrude in the last thirty years of their lives.

"There's a good view over the lake from that point near the tree," he said.

"And some place to sit down?"

"Yes, quite near."

They reached the tree and stopped. Anders gestured towards the lake in the distance and the woods beyond. Sten propped himself against his stick.

"Do you want me to carry the book?" Anders said.

Sten withdrew his arm from the shoulderstrap. He handed the heavy leather bag to Anders and turned back to the lake. "To tell you the truth," he said, "my eyesight isn't all it used to be, but they can't do anything for it. There's a kind of skin that's growing over them. Horrible; I don't like to think about it. Still, I can see how beautiful it is here. We could have spent those years here, couldn't we?"

"Perhaps," Anders said. He meant no. Vienna had made

them equals. At home, Sten would always have been a servant.

"Do you remember," Sten said, "when I was so sick that time, and the doctor wouldn't look at me unless he got his money first?"

"None of them would."

"But we really had nothing. And you got so mad, you called him—"

"Yes, I remember. That was terrible."

"And he spun around and headed for the door without saying a word. And then I told you to shut up, and said. . . . At first I thought I'd complain that he wouldn't treat me because I was Hungarian; then I wondered whether it would be better to say it was because I was Jewish or homosexual. You can never tell what's going to touch people on the raw. You've got to have a natural feeling for it."

"You always were good at guessing."

"Yes. And I thought I was so clever that time. He turned around again and said, 'That's not true,' and I just sighed. Oh, I should have been an actor, Anders. I really thought I was dying, but I was enjoying it. I made myself sound completely beaten and victimized; and thank God, you didn't say anything."

"I'd said enough."

"So then he came over and put his bag on the chair and said, 'Well, just this once.' And afterwards, you told me I'd have to be dead to stop lying. Remember? That's what I always loved about Vienna: everybody there had mixed parentage and double allegiances. It made them so much fun, and so nasty to each other. It kept you on your toes. It stopped me from getting bored. Too bad it's the one place I can't go back to now. Do you remember working the crowds at the opera?"

"*Così Fan Tutte.*"

"That's the one. I was trying to think of it the other day. And telling the future?"

"Of course: I see a dark stranger, a letter, a knife, a long journey."

"Remember the banker's wife?"

"And her husband, the banker."

"And that little girl from Poland and the two cousins from Jamaica? What a life, eh? And I used to wear a sapphire on my watch chain."

"I remember," Anders said. He looked over his shoulder, away from the lake, towards the house.

"We had good times," Sten said. "Why are we standing here so long?"

"I like to see the light go."

"And remember the joke we used to have about Dr. Death? You said he was the best doctor in town because he was the one that cured all ills."

"Yes, I remember. He's still the best."

"You were the only friend I ever had," Sten said, "who—"

"Look," Anders told him. He took Sten by the shoulders and slowly turned him around. Coming towards them from the boathouse he could see Erika and her friend, Phillip Harding. Erika was almost running, as if she had some good news to tell him. She had obviously misjudged the timing. Phillip was striding beside her at a fast pace.

"What are you looking at, Anders?"

"At the house, how it catches the sun at this hour."

"I can't see it too clearly," Sten said, "but I know what it must look like. Gold in the windows, like the palaces in Vienna. I'll always remember that. Who are those people?"

"My niece," Anders told him. "And a friend of hers."

Erika stopped. She pointed ahead, up at the sky. Phillip too came to a halt. He appeared to look where she had pointed. He had a pistol in his hand. He steadied it with the other hand, then shifted sideways into the classic duelling position Anders himself had been taught. He raised the pistol, brought it down again and took aim.

Anders saw that he stood in the line of fire. He could have stepped to the left but he didn't move. He held Sten to him in a firm embrace that parodied the intimacy of friendship or love. They were attached side by side, like a portrait of parent and child or a representation of a married couple on the front of a tomb; or as the two of them had been posed, years before, by the photographer in Budapest.

"What are they doing?" Sten asked.

214

CAPTAIN HENDRIK'S STORY

Phillip fired. Sten went down on the ground in a heap, his walking stick out at an angle. The bullet had caught him smack in the center of the forehead. He'd slipped through Anders' hands like a bag of old clothes.

What an eye the boy had, Anders thought: like an eagle; he might have been spoiled and a dilettante, but as a marks-man he'd be hard to beat.

Erika began to run towards him. Phillip walked behind her. Anders knelt over Sten. He thought of him as he used to look in the days of his youth and health when they had huddled together in the cold: dirty, bug-bitten and starving. Tears gushed over his cheeks.

"Is he dead?" Erika said at his side. "God, Anders, why didn't you stand away? I was sure you'd get hit by mistake."

Phillip joined her. His shadow flared out behind him as he too knelt down. "A frightful accident," he said briskly. "I'll go get the cart and see that everything's taken care of. Go back to the house with your uncle, Erika." He stood up, turned, and marched away towards the stables.

Erika looked down at the body. She said, "You'll be glad of it later. He was trying to kill you."

"I suppose so." Anders rubbed his sleeve across his face.

"Let's go," she said.

"We can't leave him."

"Phillip wants us to. Come on. We shouldn't be seen here." She caught at his arm and began to pull him up.

"All right," he told her, "all right. Just let me close his eyes."

They walked to the house without talking. He had the leather bag over his shoulder. As they reached the terrace, Phillip and two of the stableboys ran down the slope of lawn that led to the boathouse. Erika put out her hand and pushed Anders towards the door to his study. He looked back once, to see the sun starting its descent into the line of trees beyond the lake.

ABOUT THE AUTHOR

Rachel Ingalls grew up in Cambridge, Massachusetts. At the age of seventeen she left high school and spent two years in Germany—one living with a family, the second auditing classes at the universities of Göttingen, Munich, Erlangen, and Cologne. After her return to the United States she entered Radcliffe College, where she majored in English. In 1964 she moved to England, where she has been living ever since.

Her novel *Mrs. Caliban*, published in 1982, was selected by the British Book Marketing Council as one of the twenty great postwar American novels. Simon and Schuster published *I See a Long Journey* in 1986.